A BROTHER'S SECRET

SACRED HEARTS MC
BOOK 12

A.J. DOWNEY

COPYRIGHT

~

Edited by Barbara J. Bailey

Book design by Maggie Kern

Cover art by Dar Albert at Wicked Smart Designs

DEDICATION

To Josh. You're an inspiration. Thanks for not giving up.

PROLOGUE

D ata...

The sunlight coming through the treetops dappled the field but I was fixated on her... She was my best friend and I loved her from the very bottom of my seventeen-year-old heart. She laughed and I was struck by how it lit her whole being up from the inside out. The high, crystal sound drifted over the wavering green grass we were hiding from our responsibilities in.

I smiled; I couldn't help it when she laughed like that. She rolled her head to look at me and her dark eyes sparkled where they were rimmed in kohl. The heavy eyeliner made them seem larger than life the way she did it, the smoky shadow and her black clothing out of sorts with the surrounding bright scenery.

"I can't believe you sometimes," she said, smiling. A wisp of her dark hair was stirred by the breeze and lashed her cheek. She reached up and chased it away with her fingertips, and I fought every screaming fiber of my being not to lean in and kiss her.

I was afraid.

Afraid things would change.

Afraid that if I gave in to my desire to make Amalia mine, that we would go on for a bit and then come crashing down. That our friendship would be ruined. That life would never be the same...

So I hadn't in real life. I'd just committed every curve, every highlight given by the sun, every dappled shadow across her smooth, café au lait skin, to memory.

Except this wasn't real life, this was a dream... and my dream-self gave into the urge, leaning forward, the moment drawn out, second by second, inch by excruciatingly-slow inch, like every movie you'd ever seen. The anticipation, holding your breath, wanting it to happen, the sweet, sweet ache of it as we each drew closer, eyes closing...

Just before our lips touched, the dream shattered as an alarm blared, but not the alarm I had set up to warn of danger to the club – no, this was a *different* alarm: *the* alarm. This alarm, I had been waiting to hear for seventeen years.

I sat bolt upright out of bed, the grating sound of a nuclear reactor in emergency meltdown painting the air with urgency even as the door to my room slammed open, crashing back against the wall as Trigger stood in the doorway yelling, "Data, what is it!? What's going on?"

"Something!" I yelled back over the noise, and then I lied to my brother and it left a metallic tang of bitterness across my tongue. "I don't know what, yet!"

That lie, that tiny white lie, was to protect my secret, a secret I'd held since before joining the club. I felt a hot rush of shame as I ducked past the big man and strode past Dragon, standing bleary-eyed outside his clubroom door. It was two in the morning by the digital display in my command room. I slid through the sliding glass door and flipped a switch and the noise cut out.

I dropped into my desk's chair, swiped the mouse's trackball and punched in the complicated sixteen letter, number, and symbol password to wake the banks of monitors up. There it was, larger than life on a subreddit forum. Buried in the deep web, where only my programs and proxies would find it...

LAYD33_B0NER:

Does anyone remember Amalia Rose?

I READ it over and over just to make sure I wasn't seeing things. I could feel Trigger and Dragon both at my back and anxiety seized my heart, which was slamming itself against the inside of my ribs.

"I do, baby... now, where are you? I'm coming to get you..." I whispered to myself as I let my fingers do the walking. I slammed my way through virtual back doors, tracked electronic signatures like a fucking bloodhound and felt a grim determination take over when I realized I wasn't back here looking for her alone.

"And who might you be?" I asked no one in particular.

It became a race, I couldn't shut the other seeker down and neither could he shut me out. It was a question of tracking the IP of that lone message faster than the other and shutting it the fuck down before the next guy got it. It was ugly, but I got it – the problem was I couldn't tell if the other guy had gotten it, too.

Still, there it was:

Lexi Duran
14820 SW 51st St
Unit A
Indigo City, MD 21601

"I HAVE TO GO," I said and turned around to look Dragon in the eye. "It's important."

"Slow down, now. What's going on?" he asked.

"Can I tell you while I pack?"

"Sure."

I nodded and got up, and started explaining while on the move. The guys didn't interrupt. They just listened, and I needed that. I really did.

My mouth moved, telling them what they needed to hear, filling them in about the situation all the while my brain kept repeating the solemn vow, *"I'm coming to get you, Mali. I've finally found you, and I'm coming to get you."*

1

A malia…

I knew what I'd done by posting that. I also knew that the message had been received when it disappeared. It was deleted from the thread almost as soon as I had posted it. Now, a day later, I was waiting for them.

I stared at my dad's shiny, nickel-plated revolver on my crappy 70's mint-green Formica table and wished he were still here. My heart ached. He'd passed last week from liver failure. He'd been pickling himself in alcohol since the night his seventeen-year-old daughter had turned into a killer to save him. The guilt of it was an overwhelming thing, even though it hadn't changed him one bit. He'd been a grifter and a cheat his whole life, even right up until the bitter end.

After that night, we'd gone into hiding immediately, leaving everyone and everything we'd ever held dear behind… well, that *I* had ever held dear. He didn't give a fuck about anybody but himself, as was evidenced by the fact that I still didn't know the *why* of any of it. Now my dad was gone, my old life was long gone, and I just didn't have the will to do any of it anymore. So I'd posted, and now I waited. The Colt .45 on the table was there because even though I'd given up, it didn't mean I was ready to go down without some kind of a fight.

It wasn't in the cards. That had *never* been in the cards.

I closed my eyes and tried to decide if I were *really* as in tune with dying as I thought I was. I mean, I knew I was leading them right here, but if I were so ready to die, why did I have a messenger bag slung across my back with my most prized possessions? All my sketchbooks, my tarot cards, and a few of my other favorite things. It was heavy, but not awfully so, but it seriously made me wonder… why sit here loaded for bear? What made me think me and six shots could stand a chance against the men coming for me?

The answer was, *I didn't*. The answer was that I knew I'd sealed my fate and that it was only a matter of time, but the answer also was that I was angry, and fuck them, and I would go down swinging because that was the daughter my father had raised me to be. It was probably the only good quality I'd picked up from him.

He'd fought hard his whole life, in his own way, and had died broken, and I couldn't say I would ever forgive him for that. Mostly because I was tired of the life and left with no one who knew or understood, and it just sucked so hard. This wasn't the first time I had been impulsive and changed the trajectory of my life so suddenly and so drastically, but it was a more than fifty-fifty shot that this would be the last time I would do it.

I watched the rain streak the kitchen window of the old brownstone and a shadow move past it. I swallowed hard, and put my hand on the Colt, thumbing back the hammer even though I didn't need to. My fingers curled around the grip, index slipping inside the trigger guard to caress the trigger itself as I slowly pushed back from the table.

The men that should be coming weren't exactly in the habit of knocking. Still, I couldn't tell if this was a ruse to lull me into a false sense of security or something else entirely. I got up and let my Doc

Martens carry me across the cracked and chipped linoleum floor that was probably older than the shitty table I'd been sitting at.

I yanked open the door and leveled the gun at the man's face. His hands went up along with his eyebrows and without any preamble, he said, "Mali, get your shit, we have to go."

I blinked, my jaw dropping open as I squeaked out in disbelief, *"Kyle?"*

"Mali, I mean it – we have to go," he said stepping past me into the kitchen. He went to the table and closed the lid on my laptop, yanking the cord from the wall and winding it around his fist.

I'd shut the door and went down the impressive line of locks flipping toggles and sliding chains demanding, "Where the fuck did *you* come from?"

"Home, which is right back where we're going, we can talk about all this later – we have three minutes. Turn around." I stared at him and he barked insistently, "Turn around!" which was quite the departure from the adorable nerd boy I knew in high school. So shocked, so startled by the fact that Kyle Cochran, my best friend from over seventeen years ago was really here, I swiftly turned around. He ripped open the sturdy Velcro holding my thick, vinyl messenger bag closed and shoved the laptop and cord into its gaping maw alongside the neatly stashed sketchbooks and graphite drawing pencils.

We both froze at the heavy footfalls on the wooden steps. My kitchen was at the back of the brownstone. A set of wooden steps leading to a small deck. Kyle and I exchanged a look. His liquid brown eyes which had once been so warm were cool and appraising as they whipped over my face. I could see the calculations going on behind his gaze and he produced a black gun from the back of his waistband, a long, slender finger from his opposite hand pressing to his lips. He ushered me behind him and told me, "Head for the basement."

"Are you serious?" I whispered harshly.

"Mali…" his voice was low, concentrated, and bordering on impatient. I scoffed and tugged on the hem of his black leather biker jacket, which worked for him as much now as it had when we were teens, by the way.

He stepped back, amazingly silent on his heavy black motorcycle boots. I opened up the door leading down to the divided basement and laundry room and he waved at me to go down before him. I heard the crash of glass and the hollow rattling roll of a can. A hissing filled my kitchen and he leaped onto the steps and slammed the door behind him.

"Down, down, down! Go, go, go!" His words were cried insistently but he still managed to keep his voice low. I went down the steps lightly in my knee-high laced Doc Marten's and he clattered down the rough wood risers right behind me as windows and doors crashed in above us. He pulled me over to a wall with an old bookcase against it and said, "Help me move this!"

"What?"

"Move it, Mali! Move it now!" I helped. The thing was massive, old, and the planks thick. We shoved and pulled and it moved grudgingly across the cracked cement floor.

"How did you know this was here?" I demanded at the sight of the door hidden behind it.

"Downloaded the place's blueprints and schematics from the city assessor's office. *Go.*"

I went, having to force myself through the narrow gap we'd made, my messenger bag sticking. I managed to unstick myself and push through and Kyle was right on my heels as the basement door from my brownstone's side of things exploded inward. Kyle shoved me aside and went straight across the basement to a grate in the floor.

"Come on!" It was already moved aside and I lifted my messenger bag over my head and dropped it in, leaping down after it. He fired off two shots above my head and I clapped my hands over my ears. He dropped down beside me and pulled the grate back over our heads, dropping it into place. He shoved me ahead of him and I went, lifting my bag back over my head.

"Should have packed lighter," he grunted and led me down a twist in the low tunnel.

"Yeah, well, you know I'm a girl – vag and all. How did you find this?"

"I have my ways. Figured you knew about it, that it was why you picked this place. Knew you were running, sorry it took so long for me to catch up."

"My dad picked this place and I think he took this secret to the grave like so many others, damn him."

"Shit. Sorry he's gone," he grunted and went for a ladder and climbed it. He threw open a trap door and stuck his head through and checked. Satisfied, he leaned down with a hand out and lifted my bag. I let him take it. He shoved it through.

"I'm not," I said, after snorting derisively. He looked at me with surprise so I added, "Suppose you want an explanation."

"Later, right now I want us alive and out of the city. We need to go to ground and find a place to regroup."

He heaved himself out of the trap door and reached down for me and lifted me cleanly through. Kyle wasn't the sixteen-year-old lean and wimpy kid I remembered. He'd filled out by quite a bit in the last seventeen years.

I helped him shut the trap door and to move several heavy crates of what looked like liquor over it to hold it down.

"What now?" I asked, taking my bag and lifting it back over my head, settling its weight on my shoulder and guiding the thick padded strap between my breasts. The adrenaline was still surging through my veins and I could feel every throb of my heartbeat in my head and the side of my neck. Kyle held his gun low against the side of his leg and thrust his chin at mine in my hand.

"First off, you can put that away."

"What? Why? You have one."

"Yeah, and I'm taking point and know how to shoot, do you?"

"Yeah, how do you think I got here?" I demanded harshly. "I killed somebody."

"Killing somebody doesn't mean you know how to shoot, Mali. You got any practice hours in at a range or anything?"

I swallowed hard, "No."

"Then do me a favor and put it away."

"You do?" I asked, shoving the gun into my waistband.

"Tell you later," he said and I scoffed. "Now is not the time to be stubborn, 'k?" he bit back.

"I guess not," I agreed, and it was totally bizarre. It was like there hadn't been any kind of gap in time, like we'd picked up right where we'd left off. It was both comforting and disquieting.

I stayed close on Kyle's tail as we surged across the basement floor, carefully working our way past shelving units and unused cookware to another set of steep stairs. Kyle went up to them, listened, and threw back a well-oiled hatch.

Diffuse light filtered down and he turned to motion me forward. He went up the steps and I followed him out, finding that we were up behind a gleaming bar in a restaurant that was closed for the day. He shut the trap and I watched him; the racking of a shotgun caused us both to whirl, hands up.

"What are you doing in my bar?" a man demanded.

"Just passing through, no harm meant, no harm done," Kyle answered quickly.

The man was in his fifties maybe, and fit through the arms and chest, but a bit soft in the middle. His iron gray hair and beard were kept neat and he was pretty much the epitome of a silver fox. Keen blue eyes moved over us, narrowed and calculating.

"No harm meant? Then why are you both armed?"

"Running," I squeezed out.

"Yeah, from who?"

"Don't know," Kyle said. "Mali, you got an answer for the man?" I shook my head and I heard Kyle behind me let out a sigh, "Seriously? Now would be a really good time to be honest." The man looked at Kyle and lowered his shotgun slightly.

"I seriously don't know!" I snapped defensively. "My dad got me into this mess then he fucking died, okay? I don't know who's after me. If I did, I probably wouldn't be running from them."

The man's shotgun had come back up at my outburst, and he looked at Kyle, then me, then back to Kyle again. Those gaping black barrels lowered again as he said, "Against my better judgment, I just want you the fuck out of here. I'll be calling the cops, though, so you better git."

"Appreciated," Kyle said and moved to go past me. I could feel him at my back and the man raised the shotgun and pointed it at us once more. A byproduct of Kyle's sudden movement. I didn't blame the guy, I would be as nervous as a long-tailed cat in a room full of rocking chairs.

"Keep your hands where I can see 'em and your finger off that trigger, son."

"Copy that, Mister. Mali, move – *slowly*." I moved forward, hands up and went past the end of the bar and the upraised section of counter. I slipped out into the dark dining room with its chairs overturned on the tops of the tables and Kyle followed me.

"Front door, you can unlock it, girly." I swallowed hard and moved to the front door, my back itching between my shoulder blades as I unlocked the deadbolt then bent slowly to lift the bolt out of the floor holding it closed.

"Up top too," the man said.

I reached up and slid the brass bolt down.

"I'm going to put my gun away before we go out on the street," Kyle said and the man raised the shotgun to his shoulder and took better aim. I turned, chest squeezed down tight, and swallowed hard. Kyle lowered his gun and tucked it into the back of his waistband.

"That your bike in my alley?" the man demanded.

"Sure is."

"You didn't trip any of the alarms earlier, just the one in the basement. I'm inclined to believe you when you say you're not looking for trouble but rather running from it. Still, I'm reporting this."

"Understood."

"You got a head start. Don't let me catch you 'round here no more."

"You won't," I breathed.

"Now get the fuck out," the man ordered.

I went out the door and glanced back at the gold leaf lettering on the glass, one-zero-one-three, just the address. I swallowed hard and Kyle let the door shut behind us. He grabbed me by the upper arm and towed me purposefully around the corner and into the alley.

"Put this on," he demanded, thrusting a helmet at me. I took it dumbly, and hands shaking put it on my head. He got onto the matte black Harley-Davidson like he knew exactly what he was doing, and started it up. I swallowed as he leaned it up off its kickstand and onto its wheels.

I was staring up the alley at the blank brick wall at the end, every single one of my runner's instincts on high alert. I could feel it without seeing, they were close. A wolf on the scent, the pack closing in. Kyle's voice shattered the illusion of calm, the resoluteness with which I had stared down my fate starting to crumble within his presence.

"Mali, keep it together, get on!" he demanded over the chug and thrum of the motorcycle. I got on behind him and put my arms around his waist. His presence here was a game changer. Resist, and he would die with me, and I didn't want that for him. Knowing he was out there, knowing he was safe, had kept me going on some of the darkest nights of my soul.

He twisted the handlebars and the throttle and pointed us down the mouth of the alley. He looked both ways and pulled out onto the street. I looked back at the bar we'd come out of. The hanging shingle above the door proclaiming it to be The Cormorant Bar and Grill. The man with the shotgun stood in the front window talking into his cell phone, shotgun at his side, keen blue eyes whipping over us and the bike and I swallowed hard.

"He's on the phone with the cops! He's reporting your plate!"

"Don't worry about it!" Kyle called back. "I got this, you're safe now!"

Safe. Me...

Yeah, right.

I cursed when the whoop of a siren went up, god, not even a block away. I would rather die than spend a night in a cage with real bars. The imaginary box and prison I'd been living in for so long was one thing, but there would be no way my gypsy heart would survive in a cage of concrete and steel.

"Kyle…" I said urgently and he turned at the next light, stealing down a different alley that branched into a 'T' and turning right down it, carefully walking the chugging beast between dumpsters and trash cans, through stinking puddles, even as the rain soaking us lessened and a fine mist started to fall.

"Tight, Mali. Hold on tight," he ordered and I settled up, fetching close to his back, arms wrapping around a waist that was far more solid than I'd ever remembered the boy being… *because he wasn't a boy anymore, no more than I was the girl he'd known.*

He nosed out of the alley, looked both ways, and turned left up the one-way street. He blended us back into city traffic, which was light this time of day, and headed for the freeway.

Probably eight blocks from freedom and the open road – our luck ran out.

"Shit!" he swore and I caught his worried gaze in the side view mirror. I glanced in the glass itself, diverting from the sliver of his face to the scene behind us and met the grill of a big, black, SUV; GMC spelled out backward in angry red letters.

"Not today, Satan… Not. To. Day." I muttered and gripped Kyle hard, jerking my chin down once. He swerved out between cars and twisted down on the throttle. The motorcycle wailed like a possessed beast, tires spinning on the wet pavement before lurching forward. The wind roared, my hair whipping out and streaming behind me. I heard a crash behind us, the scream of metal as the big black SUV bullied its way between cars, knocking them out of its path.

Oh, man, did they ever have a hard-on for me? Well, I had a lady boner right back, the adrenaline coursing through my veins, the helpless anger spiraling out of control, the barely suppressed rage blowing its lid… and I had a big, black, shiny fucking target for all of it right behind me.

I tore a page out of my favorite sci-fi series playbook, that if someone was trying to kill you, that you go on and try to kill them right back, and so I lifted the compact black handgun out of the back of Kyle's waistband.

I twisted fiercely, holding onto him with one arm, sitting up straight, letting the wind push my arm out and back, my hair whipping forward, lashing my cheek as I sighted down my arm and fixed my gaze on the giant black target. I tried to fix my aim on the indistinct images of the men in behind the windshield's glass, their features hidden by the glare of the sun through leaden gray clouds.

I pulled the trigger, the gun belching smoke and flame, fighting the kick as it reverberated down my arm. I hit, the bullet pinging, and I just kept firing, pulling back on the trigger over and over and over again. The SUV swerved, hitting the curb and rocking, tipping in slow motion onto its side before skidding and sending sparks out from beneath it, the image of it growing smaller and smaller the further we pulled away. I twisted back around and kept the gun out, clutching around Kyle, bracing my arm across him as he pulled us up onto the ramp across the damn bay bridge, leaving Indigo City in the dust.

2

D^{ata…}

 I had ridden all night to get to her. The GPS had declared the ride would be eight hours, but with traffic and other setbacks, it had been more like nine and a half. When I'd reached Indigo City, it'd taken me the better part of the morning setting up at an internet café to do the recon required to make such an exit strategy.

Now, four hours into the ride back the way I'd come, I could feel Mali flagging against my back. We'd made it two hours outside the city and I'd pulled off behind a strip mall. I'd swapped out the bike's plates with still-shaking hands and peeled off the artificial skin to reveal the real one underneath. I dug out my cut from the saddlebag, big ass safety pin along the side of it. That was to let any territories I was passing through know I meant no harm. I gave Mali one of my old jackets that I'd grown out of but had kept around and she'd tucked her hair into the collar.

Inside ten minutes worth of effort, it was presto change-o, and we were off of any law enforcement's radar. Not that they'd be looking too hard, especially once they realized that nothing had been stolen from the bar. I couldn't say if they'd be looking for us after the stunt Mali had pulled back near the on-ramp to the bridge. That'd been crazy. As for what had gone down before that at her place? I somehow doubted the guy I'd winged there wanted any kind of attention. I mean, what was he going to say? That he'd busted up her place trying to kill her and that I'd shot back?

Still, we needed to go to ground. The rocket fuel of adrenaline had worn off what already felt like an age ago, and combined with the utter lack of sleep that I'd had, and the fact that when I'd knocked on her door, she didn't look like she'd had any either? We weren't fit to ride much further. Especially not under the dangerous conditions of getting rained on while fuckin' doing it.

I pulled the bike into the driveway at one of the nicer hotels my phone had pulled up for me. It had a garage, which was a bonus. I parked on one of the lower tiers and we took the elevator up. Mali didn't speak. If anything, she stood probably as far as she could get from me inside the small box. Shivering, and silent, uncomfortable and... broken. It blew my mind, especially after what I'd seen her do. After what we had pulled off. That was one hell of a getaway.

Seeing her like this, it was like a punch to the gut. So far removed from the vibrant and carefree best friend I had grown up alongside since the third grade.

She wasn't a child anymore. Nor was she a teenaged girl. She had aged beautifully into the woman that stood beside me. Her long dark hair as long as it had ever been, the ends dipped neon pink. Her figure filled out and lush, her dark eyes still lined in black but something about it, the line of it too crisp to be makeup – that, and it hadn't run with the rain at all.

When she'd answered the door I'd seen the watercolor fantastic ink beneath her skin. Her arm sleeved out in vivid flowers. I wanted to see more of her, but I wasn't about to push my luck. As it was, I pulled out one of my more impressive, black credit cards from my wallet that was

17

under the name of one of the many shell corporations I had set up just for an emergency like this one.

I marched to the hotel's front desk and ordered a suite while Mali stood off to one side and a bit behind me. I could feel her like my shadow and I was grateful she hadn't cut and run on me. I didn't know the shit she'd been through, had no way of knowing, not until she told me.

There were more immediate needs to be met, though. While I was dying to know what had taken her from me for the last seventeen years, I was more interested in making sure she was warm, dry, rested, and fed, first. That she was *capable* of going back into what was likely to be a very dark place. My obsession for answers took to riding bitch in the face of all of that. I had her by my side. No one knew where we were, yet. We had time, for the first time in *forever*.

She stood apart from me again in the elevator up to our room, her gaze vacant and fixed on the buttons. I didn't try to make her talk. I didn't try to intrude on her thoughts. I simply stood by and watched her, my own gaze roving over her from head to toe. Her hair was windswept and tangled, the dark roots fading into a bright, neon pink where it trailed over the cracked black leather of my old jacket. She clutched at the broad strap of her messenger bag between her breasts, her knuckles mottled white with how hard she gripped it.

She was still on high alert, hours and hours later, and I wasn't sure how I was supposed to get her to relax or calm down. It had to be exhausting. I knew I was tired, I'd been here multiple times before, but only to visit. She lived in this state, all the time... I couldn't even begin to imagine what that was like.

The elevator dinged when it hit our floor and Mali nearly came out of her skin, she jumped so hard. I held out one hand, gesturing for her to go first; the other hovering over her back, but I didn't touch. Not yet. She looked both ways before stepping off and I had to use my arm to stop the elevator doors from closing on us.

"No one knows we're here, it's cool."

"Credit cards can be tracked," she said and I smiled.

"True, but they don't know who I am and the card isn't in my name. Cash for a place like this would be even more suspicious, as it is – we'll be lucky to have a night before we have to bounce. The only thing more likely to draw police scrutiny than paying cash for digs like this is a scruffy looking fuck like me dropping a black corporate card like I just did, even if it is legit mine."

I slid the key card the front desk had given me into the lock and pressed down on the handle. The door swung open and I gestured for Mali to go through ahead of me. She searched my face, looking me over with serious scrutiny before she took a deep, steadying breath and preceded me into the room.

I shut the door behind us and I could easily imagine the vibrating hiss of closing an airlock, shutting out the rest of the world, leaving us hermetically sealed in imaginary safety for just the time being. I latched the deadbolt and swung the arm of what passed for a chain over into a latched position.

Mali stood still by the king-sized bed staring at it, her hands still wrapped around the strap of her big vinyl messenger bag. I went over to her slowly, almost afraid if I moved too fast I might spook her. She lifted the bag over her head and let it drop to the bed and I pulled off my jacket and cut, hanging them on the back of the desk chair. She slipped out of my old coat that looked good on her and tossed it onto the bed behind her bag. Suddenly, we were just standing there within two feet of each other, her dark eyes roving over me, up and down, as if memorizing every etched line of my face.

"Hi," she said finally, and I smiled and held open my arms for a hug. The faint ghost of a smile graced her lips and she closed the gap and fit so perfectly into me, like my lock had suddenly found its key. I let my arms go around her and held her back, close.

She made to pull away but I wasn't ready to let go. We had a lot of missed hugs to make up for. She stood stiff and unsure and hugged back but again tried to pull away. Again, I just wasn't quite ready to let go. She stilled and let me hold her, her body still stiff and trembling against my own. I waited and waited for it, but finally, with a harsh sigh, she *relaxed* and really hugged me back.

"I missed you," I said, breathing in her slight scent of coconut and lime, whatever soap or shampoo she used. I didn't know, I didn't care, she just… she just even smelled the same and I felt the years pressing down on us. The pain welling up fresh. She had been my best friend and she'd just disappeared without a trace.

"I'm sorry," she said thickly, but aside from the slight change in her voice, there was no indication that she was any kind of upset, near tears, or anything else. There was nothing except that strange, maligned tone.

"Tell me what happened and I'll let you know if you have anything to apologize for," I said gently and let her go this time when she leaned back to look at me. Her eyes were glassy with unshed tears but she'd be damned if she would let them spill over. Instead, she looked pointedly at the gauzy curtains covering the suite's window.

"I still don't know exactly what he did; he took that secret to the grave, but the night that we disappeared, they came for him. I came downstairs and he was on the floor. A man was standing over him with a gun and… and I used my dad's gun and shot him, and I kept shooting until I was sure daddy was safe. He made me pack a bag and we were gone, just like that, and we've been ghosts ever since."

She lifted one shoulder in a shrug and I felt mine drop slightly. It didn't make sense. I had been past her house the day after and nothing was out of place. No blood, certainly no sign that anyone had died there… which made sense to my adult brain even if it'd gone over my teenaged head.

Whoever had died that night had likely had powerful backers that had had the mess cleaned up. No cops looking for Mali and her dad meant an increased shot at revenge. I rolled my lips together and nodded as pieces fell into place before finally asking, "Why didn't you try to let me know, or tell me?"

She shook her head and wouldn't look at me, wouldn't answer me, and for now, I let it go, applying a sort of triage to the situation. Deal with the immediate threat first, and then we would have all the time in the world for the rest.

"Look, get a hot shower, I'll get the clothes you're in washed up in the laundry here… for now…" I flipped open one of the packs I'd shoved into the saddlebags on my bike. My shit had been gone through but nothing was missing and I had a sneaking feeling that's why the older guy back at the exit point I'd chosen had let us go. I pulled out a pair of my boxers and one of my black wife-beater tanks and handed them over. "This is the best I've got."

"Yeah, thanks," she said quietly and whatever hint of vulnerability that'd been in her voice minutes before was firmly locked behind a new veneer of steely resolve.

"Bathroom's there, just throw your clothes out the open door. You're good."

She jolted like she hadn't realized she'd just been standing there staring at me and took the shiny, nickel plated revolver out of the back of her waistband and went with my wadded up offering of dry clothes in her other hand to the dark portal of the bathroom door. She reached in and flipped on the light, letting her eyes roam over every corner and then finally stepped in. I heard the shower curtain rattle then the click of the gun against the countertop. The door shut, leaving about a five-inch gap and after some rustling, a handful of clothing appeared.

I went over and took it, keeping my back turned, which was hard for me, and held out the arm that I had her shirt and bra over. I heard her kick off her boots and her jeans flopped over my elbow.

I think she snorted and she said, "Not exactly body shy as an adult."

"Yeah, well, maybe I am," I said with a rue grin.

"Huh," was her soft reply and the light from the bathroom dimmed as she swung the door an inch from closed and the water started up in the bath.

"Be back in a little bit," I promised.

"Bring food?" she called back.

"You got it."

I switched out my own wet gear for some dry drawstring pants and another one of my undershirt tank tops. Dry was only half the battle, though. I went in search of the laundry facility with a Ziploc sandwich bag full of quarters and got it going in one load with some of the shitty powdered soap that came from the dispenser. Someone had one of the dryers going in here and so I lingered, giving the wash enough time to finish washing while I soaked up the warmth and smell of clean clothes.

I was pretty sure Mail was going to kill every bit of hot water anyway, and I needed to think, which was tough with her right there. I was torn about that, too. Seventeen years I had been dreaming about that face and now that it was right in front of me, I needed a minute away from it to get my shit straight.

3

A malia…

I jolted awake, the lighting in the room soft from the bedside lamps which were both on but it was the way that light fell on Kyle's face that made my breath catch in my throat. There were these times, when we were kids, that we would lay under this huge oak tree in this field out by our neighborhood and the light would come through the leaves –

I quickly banished the thought. Those days were long gone; over with… and nothing about them would ever come back or be the same. Still, I didn't wake him right away, I traced lines that hadn't been there before with my gaze. Deep brackets to either side of his mouth, and I remembered that easy smile that always graced his lips. Light crow's feet fanned out from the corners of his eyes, too, but you had to be close, like we were now, to see them.

There was a decent expanse of empty bedspread between us. He kept himself a healthy and respectful distance away, but still, the warm weight of one of his hands rested familiarly against my side, just below where my ribs dipped, before the rise of my hip.

Reassurance that I wasn't going anywhere or insurance that I wouldn't without his waking? I couldn't tell, I didn't know, and it brought home just how much I didn't know about him. Not now, not anymore... seventeen years was a long, long, time without so much as a whisper.

I did know one thing for sure: not once in a million years did I *ever* picture nerdy, intelligent, and honest Kyle Cochran joining a notorious motorcycle gang. I mean, what was that all about? That was way more along the lines of something *I* would do.

His thumb smoothed back and forth over the light material of his borrowed undershirt and I jumped slightly. He opened his eyes and the grave expression in them made my breath catch for an entirely different reason. His features turned, lessening to something akin to sadness and he said, "Come to Jesus... time to talk."

I felt my heart sink in my chest and tried to stall because I didn't feel like breaking his heart all over again. It was clear my disappearance had hurt, and this conversation was only going to open up old wounds that had never fully healed... for both of us.

"Did you get food?" I asked, trying to deflect.

"You were out when I got back to the room, so no. I'll order up some room service but then I need to know."

"Why I left without saying goodbye?"

"No, you explained that part well enough, more of why you never reached out, not once, in all these years."

I swallowed hard, "That one's easy. It wasn't over, clearly, and I didn't want to drag you into my mess."

"Well I'm glad you finally called out to me, and I'm here now," he said, and dragged his hand from my side to plant it firmly against the mattress so he could push himself up.

That wasn't why I had posted what I did, but how to tell him that? How to tell him I had given up and made peace years ago that I would never see him again? Which clearly, he was the better man than I was on that front. I was still a little bit shell-shocked that I was even here, looking at him, looking at me... like that.

Heavy emotion played out in the air between us, thick and cloying, shimmering between us like something tangible, touchable, if only we would reach out and grasp it – *own it*, but I wasn't ready to. I couldn't. I was ridden by a deep sense of shame. I was my father's daughter and I was supposed to be tougher than all of that. Amalia Rose Junix wasn't supposed to be a woman who gave up or gave in but I had... I was tired. Tired of the game, of being alone, of living with what I'd done and with what I'd had to do since. Of stealing from good people, of grifting our way from one place to the next relying on people's good will while they were none the wiser as to who and what my father and I had been.

I swallowed hard and pushed my way up into a sitting position alongside Kyle, wondering at how he was here and at how the years may have changed him. How *I* may have changed him.

"Here." He handed me the room service menu and I didn't even look at it, setting it aside.

"Just get me a burger," I said and sniffed, not wanting to know or to look at how much this joint cost. The guilt of him footing the bill for a place like this was already starting to creep in. You see, Kyle had changed me, from the first day we'd met. He'd taught me honesty and core values that my father had clearly lacked, and I didn't know whether to kiss him or curse him for it because now, I was a screwed up mess on the inside over all of it.

"Burger it is," he said softly and picked up the phone to order two, charging it to our room.

Silence hung between us as he moved around the space. None of the ungainliness he'd had as a boy, none of the awkwardness of being a teen remained. He'd gained muscle in the intervening years, bulked up a bit in a way I hadn't expected. He was still slender but wasn't skinny anymore and those arms... How I would love to put needle to his smooth skin and decorate him with art and poetry. He had the arms for it, *holy god did he ever*, not that I would say anything about it. I mean, the awkward going on now was already awkward enough.

"What did you save?" he asked and at least that was somewhat of a safe topic of conversation. Too much adrenaline, maybe my hormones were raging, I don't know... but I'd never thought of Kyle as anything but my best friend and confidant before, certainly nothing especially romantic had crossed my radar from him. *For him is another matter entirely...* my rebellious brain whispered. I couldn't even tell you if what I was feeling between us was any kind of romantic now, I mean, I was still reeling.

That, and it felt like there was a chasm between love and sex that most people didn't realize existed and it was a tight-wire act to cross it. I didn't know if Kyle felt the same way about it that I did, though, and I wasn't about to friggin' ask. Instead, I got up, and complained "I feel like I got raped by a couple of horses." Which was both true and enough to put a damper on my jumbled thoughts and feelings for the moment. Bonus points, it made Kyle laugh and he shook his head.

"Not used to riding?"

"Not used to riding for like hours and hours at a shot like that," I said.

"I have something for that. After dinner, though."

"Fair enough, make me suffer."

Again with that laugh and it felt, for a moment, like there was really no time lost between us. I smiled some and hauled my messenger bag across the carpet, upending it onto the bed.

Mostly my art supplies fell out first. Black, hard bound sketch books, pencils both graphite drawing and Prisma colored, in their fancy hand sewn roll-up case that a fellow artist had made me. Two hard cases that looked like they should hold drill bits or a handgun or something, but really held my favorite tattoo guns, and a myriad of other sentimental crap that amounted to the most important parts of me.

"You didn't think to pack clothes?" he asked and I moved my laptop and cord aside to pick up the battered tarot deck that Kyle had bought me for my fifteenth birthday, wrapped in a silk scarf a girlfriend had bought me three years ago. She'd been fun, but I couldn't ever be anyone's serious sweetheart. Still, she'd known all the sweet spots and I could let her eat me out for hours. At the end of the day, though, there still wasn't anything like the 'D'.

"Clothes can be replaced," I said. "This stuff? No way."

"Fair enough," he said nodding and moved a sketch book or two aside, his long fingers plucking one in particular out of the bottom of the pile. I froze. "I remember this one," he murmured.

"First one you ever bought me…"

"My mom bought it, I begged her for like a week and she didn't want to get it for me. Knew I was shit at sketching, I mean, I was failing art. Didn't bat an eye when I rolled my eyes and said it was for you, though. Asked why I didn't tell her so in the first place."

I smiled a bit ruefully, "How is Mom?" I asked.

His face grew solemn and he opened the fragile, well-turned pages, "She and my dad died four years after you disappeared."

"Oh, shit…"

"Yeah," he cleared his throat. "Freak thing, actually. A storm caused a tree to fall on their car. Mom hung on for a few days longer than dad but succumbed to her head injuries."

"Shit, Kyle… I didn't know…"

"How could you?" he asked, "You were long gone by then."

Ouch… I sighed and didn't say anything. I mean, what the fuck was there *to* say?

"Look, I didn't mean it like that..." he started and I held up a hand and shook my head.

"No, it's all right, it came out exactly the way it was supposed to and you have every right to be pissed..."

"Mali..." he drew my name in that tone that had always meant to expect a lecture and I looked at him calmly. I kept the expression on my face as tranquil and as blank as I could make it. I didn't want him to see the truth, the hurt, the shame... His breath left him in a rush and he hung his head, scratching the back of his neck when a knock came at the door. He snapped my old sketch book, my first sketch book, shut, and laid it in the pile with the rest and went to get it.

"Yeah?" he called through the door.

"Room service?" a male voice, young, called back.

Still, Kyle checked and then opened the door carefully. He took a scrap of paper, filled it out and handed it back and said, "Thanks, man."

He brought the cart into the suite and I raised an eyebrow. He shut the door firmly and re-locked it.

"Dinner is served, I guess."

"Fan-fucking-tastic, I'm starved."

He set the table, and I didn't stop him. One of the things about being a kid in Kyle Cochran's existence that I had appreciated was that his family worked like a family was supposed to. You know, the whole Norman Rockwell painting? Dinner around the table every night... One of the things I missed the most, were all the times they made me feel like a part of their family.

My dad was a single dad, he worked and couldn't always be home to fix me dinner and so it was microwaved mac & cheese and Top Ramen a lot. Every time I could have a real meal at Kyle's place was a good night. Some of the best nights, but at his house, you *always* ate at the table, there just wasn't any other way of doing it. It was how they were. Some things, I guess, didn't change. The normalcy of it, the dependability, even while the world was on fire around us… well, it hit me right in the feels. All one of them that I had left.

"Come and eat," he said and pulled out one of the chairs for me, going around the table and pulling out the other in front of his own plate. He dropped into it and I went and sat across from him.

"So what happens now?" I asked and he arched an eyebrow at me as he put his first bite of food into his mouth.

He chewed slowly, swallowed deliberately and said, "Now, you eat your dinner, then I call up my President and we start to figure this shit out."

"Just like that, you ride in like some white knight to save the day?" I asked and I couldn't help the smirk that crossed my lips. I knew it was a cruel one, but he honestly couldn't be that naïve.

"Not our first rodeo," he said and took another bite, assessing me coolly. I returned the favor, chewing my own food thoughtfully as I assessed him right back.

"How the hell did you even get involved with a club like the Sacred Hearts in the first place?" I asked finally when the silence had stretched on far too long between us.

"I was in college, my folks had died, and I decided to build a motorcycle from parts. Found this classic frame that needed to be rebuilt from the ground up. I was blogging about it, reaching out over the internet on message boards and shit to help piece things together when I got stuck and I ran into this guy went by the name of *Unkind1* as a handle. We started a dialogue. He was a Sacred Heart. We became friends and when we figured out we were local he actually came over and helped me out a few times on some tricky shit. The bike was done, and the rest became history."

"Funny, the bike you picked me up on doesn't look like a classic."

"It's not, I sold the classic bike to buy that one and to start my business," he said.

"Which is?" I drew the words out carefully, half expecting him not to answer.

"I started in IT services with a focus on cyber-security and went into installing state-of-the-art security systems. The private investigative work was a side gig, but eventually, I integrated it into the rest of what I was doing and became a one-man show."

"A PI, huh?"

"Like I said, it was a side gig at first."

"How'd you get into that?" I asked, knowing the answer already by the way he looked at me alone.

"Don't be cute, Mali."

"I hate that word," I said and it was true. I would much rather be called a cunt than cute any day of the week. Kyle smiled at me and it was heart-stopping, always had been and probably always would be.

He nodded and said, "You. It's always been you. I looked high, low, and everywhere in between. Do you have any idea how aggravating it was being able to skip trace with the best of them, finding anyone and everyone under the fucking sun I put my mind to but the *one* person I *wanted* to find?"

My breath was stolen by how intently he looked at me, his eye contact level and sure, refusing to let me look away. I swallowed hard enough I felt my throat click and reached for my coke. I took a sip and swallowed and when I was sure that my voice wouldn't waver I said, "I call that success. I mean, I didn't want to be found, so I guess I was doing it right."

He barked a laugh and it was a bitter thing. He dropped his chin toward his chest and shook his head, letting out a harsh breath before returning his gaze to mine. I raised my eyebrows and dared him silently to argue with me but he knew he couldn't.

"Well," he said and scraped his top lip between his teeth, "I guess I can't argue with you there. You didn't want to be found..." he stood up abruptly and I realized that I'd hurt him, that my words cut deep.

"Where are you going?" I demanded and it came out surprised but could I really be?

"To make that call. Eat, I'll be back in a bit." He called the last back over his shoulder, moving swiftly past me, through the room. Before I could open my mouth to protest the door to the suite was clicking shut. I stared after him, my gob shut, teeth gritted grimly at his vacant seat, and I felt my eyes grow hot. I'd be damned if I would actually cry but I felt like a real asshole.

It wasn't that I hadn't wanted him to find me. I'd missed him with every fiber of my being at first. It'd been a sharp, aching hole in my heart and the absolute hardest thing about the night we'd fled – even above and beyond pulling the trigger. Kyle was and had always been, my best friend and a part of me and there hadn't been a day that'd gone by that I didn't think of him.

I stared down at my partially eaten plate, cheeks burning with a mixture of rage and shame with myself at making him feel like I didn't want him around which was a conundrum in and of itself. I desperately wanted him as far away from me as possible if only because I was afraid of what they might do to him if they found out about him or that he was helping me.

Fuck.

I was fan-fucking-tastic at just plain digging myself deep and deeper, wasn't I?

4

D^{ata…}

"Was wondering when you was gonna get around to callin' in," Dragon's gravelly smoker's voice came heavy over the airwaves.

"Yeah, well, we needed to sleep."

"Hm." I pictured him taking a long, slow, drag off of one of his cancer sticks. His slow sigh all but confirmed it and he sucked in a breath and said, "Boys and I been talkin' it over. It ain't our usual hospitality but we can't be havin' her anywhere near the clubhouse. Not with all the women and children. If this had been a couple a years ago it wouldn't be no thing, but now?"

"No, I feel you D. I just… shit. I just don't know where to go."

"Well that's easy, you go nowhere." I paused, brow furrowing and then I got it. The lightbulb went off and I nodded slowly.

"Right, off to points unknown," I said. It was a careful ploy, one that I knew Dragon would know. Going nowhere and responding with the word point just confirmed that we were on the same page. He wanted me to head straight for Point Nowhere. The club's back-up and last-resort safe house and body dump.

"Safe travels, brother," he ground into the phone and I pictured him stubbing out his cigarette at his favorite table in the club's common room.

"Thanks, P."

"Keep the dirty side down."

"You know it."

The line went dead, my phone giving the disconnect tone in my ear. I lowered it and wondered what the boys were going to put together out at Point Nowhere for us. The place wasn't exactly made for habitation for any kind of extended period of time.

I let out a pent-up breath and racked my neck back and forth. I was going to need to go back in there with Mali and throw on some real clothes. She needed more than what she had and there was a Ross down the road. I was planning on picking her up a few things but it would be better if I went myself. She needed to stay out of sight.

I went back in and she straightened up, staring at me plaintively from where she sat on the foot of the bed.

"What'd your buddies say?" she asked, but her voice was neutral, tone careful. I couldn't tell if she was trying to hide how she was feeling or what. Her eyes weren't exactly giving anything away, either.

"They're on it, setting up a place for us to crash-land," I answered.

"When do we leave?"

"Tomorrow. I need to go out and get you some things. You're going to need more than what you've got on."

"I hate shopping," she said.

"Yeah, well, you're off the hook on that score. Write down your sizes for me."

"You're going shopping for me?"

I hung my head and let out a harsh breath, "The less you're seen the better off we are until a time we can figure a few things out. Just write down your sizes, some of the shit you like to wear, and I'll do my best."

Her shoulders dropped and she put on a wry grin, "I was always a pain in your ass, why should now be any different?" she asked and I put my hands on my hips and shook my head.

"You were a lot of things, Amalia… a pain in my ass isn't even close to the top of my list."

Her self-deprecating smile dissolved into an expression of surprise and she dragged her messenger bag from the floor to the bed. She rifled through it, pulled out the newest looking sketchbook and opened it to the back.

"Need something to write with?" I asked gently and she shook her head and pulled out a roll of light purple paisley-printed material secured with darker purple ribbons. She untied it and rolled it out just enough to slip a drawing pencil out from the pocket sewn into it.

"It is so weird you buying me bras and underwear," she muttered and started writing.

"Better than tampons, but I'll buy you those too if you need 'em."

She snorted a laugh and it made me smile. She scratched out her sizes and measurements haphazardly across the thick white page and then started whipping out some quick sketches underneath. I didn't say anything, patiently waiting her out, and truthfully, actually pretty appreciative of the visual aids she was rendering. I didn't want to get her shit she wouldn't like.

She sighed finally, coming out of her little zone that she went into when she drew and carefully tore the page out of the book, holding it out to me.

"Thanks," I murmured and let my eyes graze the sizes and the little sketches she'd done, calculating how much room I had on the bike to store the extra shit. I had some leeway; I could strap a bag to the fender rack and sissy bar behind Mali. Should be able to get her straight for about a week's worth of clothes. I nodded and creased the paper into four quadrants and set it by the television.

"Right, I'll be back in a minute." I went into the bathroom and put on some real clothes and my riding gear. When I came out, she was still sitting on the end of the bed, feet up, crossed at the ankle, arms loose around her knees; folded up like a lotus blossom. She'd always sat that way when we were kids and it was as alluring now as I'd found it when we were teenagers. I just didn't know what it was about it that got me, but then again, some of the strangest things about her did.

"What am I supposed to do while you're gone?" she asked.

I shrugged and pulled the remote off of the dresser the television was on and handed to her. She rolled her eyes at me and made an 'ugh' noise; I smiled. I couldn't blame her, hotel TV pretty much sucked.

"You could draw," I suggested and she looked down wistfully at her sketch book, now missing a page.

"Don't think I'm in the frame of mind to pull off anything artistic at the moment."

"Don't say I can blame you," I answered, shoving her measurements into my back pocket.

She hesitated with whatever she was about to say next and I stilled, waiting her out. Finally, she spoke and what came out surprised me. She said, "Don't take too long, 'k?"

"Back in a flash," I said and tried to sound both nonchalant and reassuring at the same time. Mali had never been one to display any sort of weakness or vulnerability and her softer tone along with her hesitation was an unexpected crack in the hard exoskeleton of confidence she typically had on.

We still hadn't really talked about things. Bits and pieces that I was slowly putting together into a mosaic depicting a timeline, but I didn't want to push too hard. Not yet, not right now. There would be a time for that later when the buck would stop and she'd have to spill but in the interest of not piling on more frustration of her having to repeat herself ad nauseam, I let myself grow nauseous with dying to know everything in minute detail.

Mali gave me a nod and I returned it, scooping up my helmet and leaving the room, heading out to grab some items for her that would get her out of my underwear, because fuck, while I had self-control, it wasn't endless and I didn't want to push my luck by making a wrong move, you know? I didn't want to be 'that guy' and so she needed some extra things. Things that I could provide. I honestly needed to occupy my time during the hurry up and wait. I needed to be doing something so I didn't explode.

5

A malia…

I had no idea what to do with myself. I wasn't tired anymore, I'd slept hard and dreamless for the first time in forever but I didn't think it had too much to do with Kyle. No, it had everything to do with just being that fucking exhausted. Now, I felt restless and on edge; my body very nearly vibrating with the want to do something, *anything*, to fix this situation.

I stared at the silver surface of my closed laptop and felt as if it'd somehow betrayed me. I knew what I'd been asking for when I put my name on that forum but the universe had given me Kyle instead. I sighed and picked up my Tarot deck, scooting back against the headboard and shoving pillows behind my back. I shuffled the cards easily between my hands and took comfort in their worn surfaces and battered edges. The sudden silence, the absence of his presence, pressed in on me and I wrestled with the confused emotions that wrought.

I'd missed him, just been put back into his orbit, and even though I knew he'd be back, I felt his new absence keenly. We had a lot to talk about, he and I, and I had no idea where to begin. Now, more than ever, I wished I could divine the future absolute and not just the likeliest of a myriad of possibilities.

I decided to do a very basic three-card spread, each representing a cross section in time – past, present, and future. I closed my eyes and breathed deep and clear, focusing my energies on the simple task at hand, shuffling the deck between my hands until I reached an almost meditative state. When I felt calm, cool, and collected, I stopped and turned the first card, laying it in front of me.

My gaze skated over the image on its surface, a skeletal rider on a skeletal horse, bony hand outstretched, an hourglass with the sands trickling away perched in his palm. I couldn't agree with the meaning behind it more. Death traditionally represented change and not just simple change like moving from one location to another. It meant a deep, fundamental change to one's entire being. Something profound, life altering… looking at the card the night that changed the course of my life forever sprang immediately to mind. Like the monster under the bed, slithering out from the dark to loom menacingly above me. Although, as an adult, I knew that no amount of cowering under the blankets and wishing it away would make what'd happened disappear. It wasn't a figment of my imagination that could just be ignored.

I reminded myself that I was alone, that there was no one here to see me, no one I needed to impress, and I let the emotions wash over me and through me. I let myself drown in the despair I felt over taking that man's life, of altering my path and Kyle's so completely. Even if I hadn't had a choice, the guilt was still there. The horror at watching his eyes go wide, the dark blood spilling between his fingers as he fell, as if I'd cut him down with an ax as he'd fallen backwards, just as slowly as a felled tree. He was young. Probably no more than twenty, almost as fresh-faced as I had been at seventeen, and he hadn't even been the one I had been aiming for.

The one I had been trying to shoot was the one holding the gun on my father. I'd shot him too, but he hadn't died… I'd seen him again two years later when he'd caught up with me and my dad in Memphis and we'd run again. We'd had to bolt at least one more time since then and only the last ten years had our new identities stuck.

I let my mind drift, playing out vignettes from the past to present. Little bits of my life flickering past my mind's eye as if I stood like stone in the midst of a river or stream, letting it wash over and around me. When I reached the present, I opened my eyes and when I felt still and focused again, I turned the next card…

The Tower also represented life-altering change, however, unlike Death, it was a much easier card to swallow; at least this time. The Tower represented all of the things unnecessary to you falling away. They might be things that you didn't wish to lose, people and comforts and the like, but much like facing a car crash, or your house burning down you begin to realize that it doesn't matter. That it was all just *stuff*, not who you were, not who you are at your core. The Tower represented loss and change, but when it was all said and done what crumbled away left you back at your foundation. This was important and reassuring. Yes, everything was tumultuous, yes, everything was frightening and in a freefall right now, but my foundation was solid. It was *true*, and I could *always* rebuild.

I analyzed how I was currently feeling. So far the two cards drawn rang eerily true and were, in fact, indisputable when it came to my situation and their base meanings. I rolled my lips together and took a deep breath, holding it, as I cast my mind's eye to the future and turned the next card.

The Fool.

Interesting. Out of a deck of over seventy-eight cards I had managed, on a three-card draw, to pull, arguably, the three most powerful of the major arcana off the deck. Frustratingly, The Fool didn't tell me much, unless it served as a warning. I tilted my head and let my eyes roam the familiar image. The young man, entranced by the butterfly, about to step off a cliff. It spoke to me, saying *"Go forward with both eyes open...*" and I had every intention to but I still couldn't help but wish for something *more* to it. I turned over the next card as a sort of enhancement to The Fool, seeking clarification, something further to go on and felt my breath leave in a rush.

Here was a minor arcana, the Queen of Swords. I chewed my bottom lip. The suit of swords was an air symbol and typically meant power, rationality, and intellect. The Queen of Swords meant growth and clarity in an intellectual capacity. I took it to mean, in conjunction with The Fool, that there were many paths to take going into the future, and basically, not to be stupid about it. I needed to go forward with both eyes open and really *think* about what I was doing to avoid stepping off a cliff. The spread told me unequivocally that danger lay ahead and not to fuck up.

How quickly things can change. This time yesterday I was prepared to throw in the towel. Tired of running and tired of hiding – now here was Kyle, something totally unexpected and while I was still on the fence about some things, I still stood firm on my foundation, my truth, which was fuck whatever happens to *me* but I don't have any right to drag anyone else into it or cause collateral damage. I'd already caused some of that when we were teens. Already hurt him once, had hoped and prayed he would forget about me and move on with his life (as much as that killed me to wish it.)

So now what do I do? I asked myself, scrubbing my face with my hands. I let out a giant exhale, never thinking in a million years that Kyle Cochran would still be looking for me, let alone that he would find me.

I swept the cards leaving me with more questions than answers up into my hands and re-introduced them to the deck. I suppose I couldn't complain too mightily about what they'd told me. I mean, they certainly hadn't been *wrong*, but they hadn't exactly helped much, either. I wrapped them back up in their scrap of silk, my eyes falling to a battered old sketchbook covered in band stickers. I picked it up, older and more bruised than the rest, and let it fall open in my lap.

Most people had photo albums but I'd been too poor to have a camera. Instead, I stole art pencils from my art classrooms and drew the things that I wanted to commit to memory the most onto the pages of my birthday gift from my best friend. The book opened to the latter half of the middle, to the page I spent the most time on, the spine cracked there more than any other place from repetitive use.

There, in many varying shades of graphite, was my most beloved sketch. It was of Kyle, sitting perched on the back of a park bench in jeans and a black tee shirt, one of those black bomber jackets with the neon orange interior making him seem bigger than he actually was through the shoulders. On the opposite page, taped there, was the Polaroid I had been working from. One of our mutual friends had snapped the picture and I'd stolen it as soon as she'd set it down. She'd had a crush on Kyle hardcore and had been *pissed* the picture had disappeared.

I didn't care, though. I coveted my best friend back then, but he didn't know it and I didn't show it. I cherished the time we spent together and to this day had sketches of those times, the good times, in just about every book scattered across the end of the bed.

I heaved a sigh and pulled my laptop into my lap and opened it up. I called down to the front desk for the Wi-Fi password and plugged it into their network. I connected but it was slow as fuck connecting to the email of my alias and alter-ego, and when it took too long for the email from my job to open up I shuffled the computer off my lap and got up, taking my restless self into the bathroom.

I stared at myself in the mirror, hair a frizzing catastrophe around my face since I'd slept on it wet. There was no fixing it, short of another shower, a blow dry, and combing and since I didn't have anything better to do with myself, I did just that. I knew Kyle was bringing me some more clothes, but what I'd had on when he'd swooped in was clean now and would work just fine. I carefully dried and styled my hair and sighing in front of the mirror, hair smoothed and sleek, pinned down into a braid over one shoulder, went back out into the room to find a hairband or tie. I rifled one handed through the little pockets in my bag and found not only a hair tie but a small stash of my makeup.

I took my small haul back into the bathroom so that I could see what I was doing, and with time to kill, tied off the ends of my hair and set to work on my face. All I really had was some black eyeliner and some face powder but it was enough to take the shine off my oily skin and smooth out my already pretty smooth complexion. I'd lucked out with whoever my mother had been. Her genetics ruled the day when it came to me and as conceited and fucked up as it sounds? I could see why my dad got with her.

She'd left just after I was born, leaving my papa holding the proverbial bag. The diaper bag, I guess. It'd just been me and him ever since. Well, until it was me and Kyle for a good chunk of time. My dad just couldn't help himself and tended to fuck up a lot, and when he did, I always ended up at Kyle's place. It hurt my heart to know his parents were gone. They'd been my pseudo-parents for so long, you know?

I leaned heavily against the edge of the sink and stared wide eyed into the mirror. My eyes, rimmed in the dark kohl liner, seemingly much larger and taking up over half my face. I refused to cry, so I simply stared myself down until the choking sensation diminished and the hot prickling at the backs of my eyes receded.

I had no parents left at all, not even Mr. and Mrs. Cochran to go back to someday. I just had Kyle... *but do you?* I let out my breath slowly and closed my eyes, shutting out my shaken and crumbling visage.

It's been seventeen years, Mali... Everything is bound to be different now.

I hated the voice of reason. She was such a pragmatic bitch. I sighed and sniffed, racking my neck back and forth, working my shoulders loose and letting a deep breath rush out, then taking another one. I coughed lightly and got my shit back under control. Not a single errant tear snuck free. Small victory in a long line of lost battles.

The hotel room door opened and I watched Kyle pass the bathroom door into the rest of the suite, a shopping bag in each hand. I whipped my chap stick over my lips in the mirror and capped it, gathering up my few items to take back out to my bag.

"Mali?" Kyle called out, frozen at the foot of the bed, apprehension dripping from his tone. I smiled a little to myself.

"Right behind you," I said softly, and he jumped. I smiled a little bigger and stepped up to my bag, stashing my little bit of shit back in the pocket I found it in.

Kyle's eyes roved over the disaster on the bed, fixing on the laptop.

"Did you get on the internet?" he asked.

"Connection here is slow as shit, wasn't even able to really get into my email," I said, thrusting sketchbooks into my bag carefully, stashing my tarot cards back in the pocket they'd come from and just generally shifting things around to make room for whatever was in the bags he held, hoping I could make it fit.

"Shit, I should have said something. I didn't think about it. Keep packing up, we have to go."

"What?" I felt that familiar tingle of fear uncurling along the length of my spine.

"I brought it because I knew they could track it. It was supposed to be bait, I didn't think you'd try to use it. I didn't think —"

"Jesus, Kyle! *Why didn't you say something*? Am I supposed to know this shit through osmosis?" I demanded, thrusting things carefully away, my fear bringing out the saltiness in me. It always did. I got scared, I got attitude — it was just a given about me and I wouldn't apologize for it. Kyle didn't ask me to, and he didn't apologize either.

He just handed me the shopping bags and said, "We've got time, how long ago did you use it?"

"I don't know, maybe a half-an-hour? Forty-five minutes ago?"

"Okay, we still have time, we just have less of it than I thought. Keep packing."

I rolled my eyes thinking; *like I'd stop,* and stuffed clothes from his shopping excursion into whatever corners were left open in my damn bag. I rolled up the pair of jeans he handed me and stuffed them along the top, pulling the flap on the bag over and using the trident buckles, shoving them home with a satisfying click. All was secure. I hit the button in the center of the old-fashioned seatbelt buckle that served as a quick release on the strap of my bag and wordlessly shrugged into the leather jacket Kyle held out to me.

It suited me and I liked it. Although I have to admit, the reason I liked it probably had more to do with the fact that it was Kyle's than any sort of fashion sense. Though, it scored points in that department, too.

I stood with my back to the bed and hauled my bag by one strap up over my shoulder, the buckle digging into my hand, keeping the strap from sliding through. I groped down by my opposite side for the swinging other half of the strap, grabbed it and hauled the two ends together, clicking the buckle home, yanking on it a bit to make certain it was secure, before letting either strap go. Kyle was watching me and I arched an eyebrow at him and asked, "We going, or are you just going to stand there with your dick in your hand?"

He scowled at me but got back into motion, shoving his underwear that I'd been wearing into the top of his knapsack. He stalked around the corner into the bathroom and gave it a sweep, scooping up the toiletries and dumping them into the top of his bag before cinching it closed. I felt my mouth turn down and head nod, I could respect that. Never knew when that kind of shit would come in handy and waste not, want not.

"Cool," he said shrugging one strap of the bag onto a shoulder broader than I could ever remember. "Let's bounce."

I dragged my dad's gun off the bed and tucked it down the back of my pants under the jacket and he gave me a nod and held out his hand, gesturing for me to come up behind him. He opened the door to the room and looked up and down the hall both ways.

"Clear," he declared in a low husky voice and we went out, one after the other, the soles of my knee-high Doc Marten's hushed by the plush luxury hotel's thick hall carpeting. We smoothly made our way to the elevator and he pressed the button.

"Nothing's wrong, act natural when we hit the lobby, move for the parking garage elevators. Don't look around, just... talk to me," he said.

"About what?"

"Um," he smiled faintly and said, "Remember that time we were out in that spot in the woods and you were bossing us around and..."

I felt myself blush, hard... we'd probably been about eleven and these older kids had rolled up on their bikes and one had shot me with a BB from his slingshot right in the ass. It had *hurt* but I'd been determined to execute building the fort we'd been attempting and had just kept prattling on. It took me an embarrassing amount of time to realize why everyone else was so quiet behind me. It also took another agonizing shot to the back.

"Why you have to remind me of that?" I asked, scowling. We stepped onto the elevator down to the lobby. Kyle didn't immediately answer as I went back inside my own head to that day.

I'd cried, the BB had torn my favorite tee and had embedded itself in my back, next to my shoulder blade on the inside of it. It'd hurt so bad, and the other kids had followed the older teen's teasing and laughter. I'd fallen into the mud by the creek with that second shot, writhing. My jeans had protected me from the first shot, which he'd hit square in the back pocket. The double layer of denim too thick to penetrate but it had still stung like a son of a bitch.

45

"Yeah, I never forgot it either," Kyle said quietly and we stepped off the elevator into the lobby which wasn't too crowded. We moved over to the elevator down to the parking garage.

"So why you have to bring it up now?" I demanded.

"I don't know, I just thought of it for some reason…"

Kyle had stood up for me. He'd shouted at them and started throwing rocks. Had hit the kid who had hit me and the kid had gotten off his bike and come down the ravine. He'd popped Kyle a good one, knocked him on his ass in the mud beside me; gave him a bloody nose. I'd stabbed the little bastard in the leg with my pocket knife.

It'd been a big mess. Kyle and I had booked it, adrenaline pumping, through the woods that smelled of wet, green, and growing things all the way back to his house. His mom, a nurse, had me sit down at the dining table with my shirt off, a towel clutched to my chest while she spent the better part of a half an hour digging into the hole in my back with tweezers going after that damn BB. It hurt like you wouldn't believe.

The older kid and his parents showed up at my house; we hadn't told Kyle's parents I'd stabbed the kid. I thought for sure my dad was going to beat the shit out of me for stabbing the little prick. I hadn't told him at all what'd happened in the woods. The parents handed him the pocket knife he'd given me for my tenth birthday and he stared at it in his hand for a long time.

He'd surprised me. He stood up to them. Stared that kid's parent's right in the face and praised me for defending myself and told them to get off our front step. I'd been elated for all of five minutes. I'd finally done something right… until I hadn't. Once they were gone he'd taken a belt to my ass for leaving the knife behind. Drilled into me that you never, *ever*, left anything behind.

Then he'd hugged me, soothed away my tears and took a look at my back and asked me brokenly why I hadn't told him…

I was scared... I'd said and he'd looked startled and for a while, he quit drinking and things were better. For a while...

"Dad beat my ass after those people left," I said finally and Kyle looked over at me sharply.

"I thought you said you hadn't gotten in trouble for stabbing that fuckwit."

"I didn't," I confessed. "I got in trouble for leaving the knife, for leaving *evidence*, behind..."

"Shit," he said and I could tell he'd had no idea. His face contorting, warm brown eyes roving over my face as the doors slid open to the second elevator, spilling us out onto the level of the parking garage that held his bike.

Kyle hadn't gotten in trouble for anything. He'd told his parents everything, including me using my knife to defend us from the older boy who must have been fifteen or sixteen. They'd left it up to me to tell my father and I told them I had. My dad had never contradicted that.

"Why did you bring that up?" I demanded once again.

"Because I wanted you to remember that you were a badass from an early age. That, and I remember – get you fixated on something and you've got a one-track mind. You did great. Now get on and let's get out of here."

I scowled deeply at him and felt a sudden spurt of anger. "Don't manipulate me like that. I fucking hate being manipulated," I spat. He carefully considered my face.

"Duly noted," he said softly and the apology was carried in his tone.

I got on behind him but would be staying pissed for a while.

6

D ata...

She scowled, eyes unfocused and brooding behind the clear safety lenses I'd handed back to her. She was still pissed and I felt like a total shit. She stayed that way for over an hour into the ride, her expression smoothing out about a half an hour before hour two... I figured now would be a good time to pull off and eat. I'd texted Dragon what I could from the elevators on the way down to the garage and was pretty much itching to check out any responses by now. Freeway riding didn't exactly afford any stoplights to check messages, and unfortunately, traffic was clear; the road wide open in front of us, so there wasn't any stop and go to afford me a similar luxury.

I pulled off the freeway and I felt her perk up behind me, curious. It took an effort of will to keep my eyes on the road and off my mirrors to see what she was doing. It was drawing on towards evening, and we wouldn't be making it to Point Nowhere before dark. There wasn't any way.

"Why are we stopping?" she yelled when we reached the bottom of the off ramp.

"Food!" I called back.

"Good idea, I forgot about that!"

I laughed at that and shook my head, turning us out onto the surface streets in the direction of where the blue signs boasted food could be found. At the next stoplight, I called out, "What looks good?"

"Don't give a fuck, it's just something you eat so you don't die!"

I tilted my head and couldn't argue with her there, then again, Mali had never been picky out of necessity growing up. Food had been sometimes hard to come by for her and her pops, and he was one of those guys that were too proud to hit up the food bank. I turned into a Cracker Barrel Country Store's parking lot and let Mali off the bike. I backed it into a vacant parking stall and lowered the kickstand, shutting off the engine.

She stood not far from me, working loose the chinstrap on her borrowed helmet and I watched her for a minute.

She looked like she was born on the back of a bike, long legs covered in tight denim, flowy, loose black tank under my worn jacket that fit her better than it'd ever fit me. She was beautiful. She looked over at me and arched one brow.

"K, now I'm fucking starving," she said and I smiled and got up.

"Me, too. Let's eat, then we've probably got around four or so more hours to go."

She groaned and sighed out, "There had better be a hot bath or a shower at the end of this rainbow," she grumbled.

I took that into consideration and murmured, "I'll see what I can do." I don't think she heard me. She was up on the faux rustic front porch, opening up the door to the country store part of the building. I went in after her and we found the hostess.

"Two, please." Ever polite until someone gave her a reason not to be, I let her take the lead. No reason not to. She was a fierce, capable woman and there wasn't any doubt in my mind that she'd turn out to be anything else. We dropped into a two-person booth and Mali immediately lost herself behind a menu.

I pulled out my phone. Four missed text messages from D.

1/4: We'll get on it, get Point Nowhere setup in no time. Just get your asses here, carefully. Any idea who's doing it yet? Let me know what's up. I can't start working angles until I know.

2/4: Do you need your computer systems brought out to Nowhere?

3/4: That was a stupid question. Of course, you do.

4/4: We're almost set up here. If you stop, let me know where, for how long, all that happy horseshit.

Me: We're stopped, about four hours out at a Cracker Barrel. Food then we'll get right back on the road.

I set the phone aside and perused the menu myself. The waitress came by and asked for our drink orders. I looked over my menu at Mali who had a mischievous sparkle in her eyes matched by the ghost of a trouble-making smile on her lips.

"What can I get you to drink?" the girl asked and Mali ordered a sweet tea. I cocked my head and let my gaze rove her face and ordered the same.

Her smile grew a bit wider, despite the tiredness creeping in and she asked, "Do you know what you want to eat?"

I got back to the menu murmuring, "No, not yet," and decided that she was definitely up to something. I'd seen that playful look a thousand and more times and it always preceded some sort of shenanigans.

The waitress came back and asked us, "Do you know what you'll have?"

Without missing a beat, Mali said, "I'll have an explanation over why Brad's wife was fired."

I choked on my sip of tea and laughed, the girl blinked and blushed slightly, fighting not to roll her eyes. I couldn't help it, maybe it was the stress or the long, hard miles, but I laughed and laughed over her jibe over the viral internet sensation that had been some dude named Brad demanding to know why Cracker Barrel had fired his wife over their Facebook page.

"I wouldn't know, it didn't happen at this location..." the girl shifted, kind of uncomfortable, and Mali rested her chin on her hand.

She wrinkled her nose in the cute, impish way she'd always had and said, "Oh, well, in that case, I'll have the catfish."

I watched her as she placed the rest of her order and ordered what I would like, going through deciding on like the million different sides that they had. The girl took our menus and left hurriedly and I shook my head.

"Some things don't change," I said.

"I was just thinking that earlier..."

"Oh yeah? About what?"

"You set the table."

I paused and thought about it, nodding. "We always have dinner at the table."

"Yeah, that was a tradition that was lost after we had to bounce." She looked bitter and uncomfortable, shifting in her seat.

"Can you tell me anything?" I asked. She looked around the restaurant and shook her head slightly and I nodded saying, "Fair enough."

"I'm not trying to weasel out of it," she shot back defensively and I shook my head.

"I know you aren't. We have time."

She turned her head and stared out the slats of the wooden blinds, across a short expanse of blacktop parking lot and into a copse of trees across the way. I didn't say anything else. Something about what I'd just said had her retreating back inside her head… lost in thought. I let her stay there so I could study her profile.

Again, she was stunning. Her body coming into its own as a woman had none of the awkward angles or knobby points she had just been coming out of at the age of sixteen. Her neck was long and graceful to the point I just ached with wanting to put my lips against it, to feel her warm pulse against them, to breathe in her sweet and spicy scent that was just purely *her*.

All of the feelings I held when we were teenagers came raging out of nowhere as if they'd never left and it was devastating. It was as if a nuclear bomb blast went off in the center of my being and the blast was simply *this is real*… It was like it finally hit me, there, in the restaurant of all places that my quest was over. I'd found my princess… but then again, didn't I have to defeat some mega boss to make her mine?

I ran a hand over my face and shifted in my seat and she turned sharply. Her quick brown eyes roving over my face, quickly assessing, calculating, but whatever she was thinking she kept it to herself.

My phone buzzed at my elbow and I picked it up. Dragon had responded and I frowned slightly at the text.

D: Well bring it on home. We'll figure out what to do from there.

I was way ahead of him. I already knew what I was going to do, I just needed my systems and a place to lay low until it was done. I smiled faintly to myself and texted back,

Me: Stay in the cage, P. I got this.

He shot back with a quick: **We'll see about that**, and I chuckled.

Me: Mali wants a hot shower when we get there. Not sure what can be done about that.

D: YOU stay in the cage. If anything the rest of us got a better idea of dealing with females at this point.

Me: Mali's different.

D: That's what every single one of these assholes says about their girl.

Me: She's not my girl, D. She's just a friend.

D: Sure. That's why you dropped everything to ride to the rescue.

Me: Fuck you! lol

D: I'll leave that to her.

Me: Seriously, just a friend.

D: Uh huh. Get your asses back here.

Me: Sir, yes sir!

D: Fuck you.

"What's so funny?" Mali asked, expression slightly soured, tension radiating from around her exotic eyes.

"Just the guys," I answered and she frowned slightly, letting her eyes rove my cut. She opened her mouth to ask something but, as if on cue, our waitress returned with our plates. Mali shut her mouth and leaned back as the girl set hers in front of her.

"Thank you," she murmured quietly and I had to smile to myself. As caustic as Mali could be when she was scared or on uncertain ground, she was ever, unfailingly, polite. That said more about her than she realized. Now, did I imagine for one minute she would be so polite when it came to the guys and how bossy they could be? Nope. In fact, I figured this was going to be a somewhat rocky homecoming. Not just because Mali was... well... Mali, but also because I'd kept her a secret all of these years.

The guys didn't know, and I don't know why I'd kept it that way. Maybe because I was afraid I really would never find her. Probably because I didn't want them to see me as a failure, not about this... I couldn't stand to fail when it came to this, to her.

"Kyle, why are you staring?" she demanded, shoving some collard greens into her mouth and chewing thoughtfully, staring at me right back.

"Guess it's finally sort of sinking in that this is real, that I finally found you."

"Well I'm not a mirage and this sure as fuck isn't a dream. A nightmare, maybe, but certainly not a dream." She looked down at her food and speared another bite with maybe a little more force than was absolutely necessary. I watched her for a minute and deliberated on asking the question on the tip of my tongue.

If there was one thing the MC life had taught me, and hell – even life on the internet – it was that you didn't ask questions that you weren't absolutely sure you wanted the answer to. I bit the bullet and asked for this one anyway, though; just without phrasing it like a question.

"Sounds like you maybe aren't all that happy I found you."

She dropped her fork with a clatter and gave me a look that could peel paint. I couldn't help but smile, reading her loud and clear. I ducked my head over my own food, pleased that yes, she was indeed happy to see me, she just was having a tough time, like me, with processing all that entailed.

"Don't be a dumbass," she grated quietly under her breath and picked up her silverware.

"I'll try not to be," I answered and she startled again like she hadn't realized she'd just said that out loud.

"Good, we don't have time for it."

I smiled again and told her, "You ain't gotta worry about a thing, now. I've got this, I promise."

She snorted and shook her head like she didn't believe me but didn't contradict me much beyond that. It was a role reversal, for sure. All growing up she'd had all the street-smarts while I'd been the book-smart one. I just think that she, like me, was still struggling to reconcile the adult in front of her versus how we'd each been when we'd last seen each other.

I knew one thing for sure, I would give anything to be back under our tree, gazing at her sun-dappled hair, laughing about the movie we'd just seen rather than trying to stitch together the ragged ends of our childhood with who we were as people now.

7

A malia...

Dinner was good, but I was definitely feeling it and ready for a nap. Still, Kyle seemed determined to make it to wherever we were going before we stopped for any kind of real rest. I was fighting a food coma for a good portion of the ride but finally, after what seemed like forever, we were well inside the Kentucky state border and headed through hill country; the familiar smell of the state's famous bluegrass more than just a memory. I missed that smell, bright, green, and growing. I wished it wasn't so damn dark, I would have liked to see it.

The turns he took once he was off the freeway and onto country highways told me that we were close to our destination. Everything felt deliberate, and like he knew where he was going. I was comfortable with the ride and with his capability steering and controlling the beastly Harley-Davidson so I no longer felt the need to hold onto him for dear life. I sat back slightly, hands on top of my thighs, just trying desperately to find a comfortable position to sit in. My lower back was tense and screaming from the long hours of unfamiliar riding and I knew my body; if I thought it was bad now, I just had to wait until tomorrow morning.

All I wanted was a hot shower, some pain killers, and a decent bed by the time Kyle took the final turn off the paved road and through a rusting livestock gate to head up a dirt track. I grabbed onto him, wrapping my arms around his hard waist as he crept over the loose dirt and gravel up over a rise onto a plateau. I blinked at the side of the rusting corrugated building. A long and tall, barn or garage – I couldn't tell in the dark that well. It had power, a shop light with a fluorescent bulb shining a harsh blue light down over a man-sized door and flooding the dirt lot next to it with cold illumination.

Motorcycles were parked in a line off to one side, and the rusting, weed-choked hulks of cars were lined up at a right angle to the building and bikes, in front of thick woods traveling further up a hillside.

What the fuck is this place? I wondered inside my head as he pulled up to the line of bikes out front and tapped my knee to get off. I swung my leg over the bike with a deep groan as muscles protested loudly at their mistreatment. I stood aside as he backed his bike into the line of them and cut the engine. Immediately, I could hear the cricket- and frog-song and the question I was going to ask died on my lips. I closed my eyes and let the music of the country night wash over me, tilting my head to listen.

A nameless tension I hadn't known I'd carried loosened and slid away and I only opened my eyes when I heard the rattle and click of buckles against the side of the bike's glossy painted skin. Kyle shouldered the pack that he'd liberated from one of his saddlebags and I realized a rectangle of warmer yellow light had opened up beside me.

I turned and eyed the tall, broad-shouldered man standing in the doorway as Kyle grabbed the rest of his shit that he wanted to bring in.

The dude in the door was a fine example of the male half of our species. Aside from the height and those shoulders, which by the way, *those arms!* He had long blond hair in a loose ponytail over his cut. The white tee shirt he had on under the vest was struggling to keep up with his physique, which again, I could totally appreciate. His light, silvery blue eyes traveled over me just as surely as I was checking him out but whatever he thought, he was good at hiding it.

I turned back to Kyle and held out a hand to take some of what he was pulling out of the bike but he waved me off saying, "I've got it."

I let him go first, past the Nordic god in the doorway and went to slip past him myself muttering, "There is such a thing called 'personal space' there, Thor."

He chuckled, a deep, almost dark, sound that rang sinister to my ears and said in a low smoker's voice, "It's Trigger, not Thor, and I'm kind of up against a wall here."

It wasn't precisely a wall, but he was backed up flush against some kind of a work bench along the outer wall that was snug up by the door that he was leaning on to keep it open for us. Between his sheer size and the fact that I was nearly double my width with the heavy ass messenger bag strapped to my back, it made for awkward passing through no actual fault of his own. I felt myself blush with embarrassment but wasn't about to lose face any more than I already had with some sort of lengthy apology.

Still, I gave him a quiet, "My bad," so I could feel like less of a dick. When I got past him and into the large space, my discomfort, unfortunately, only grew.

There were quite a few pairs of eyes on me, and I fucking *hated* being the center of attention. I didn't even realize I'd stopped short, the mountain of a man at my back until Kyle held out his hand to me and waved me forward.

I took enough steps across the cracked and unfinished concrete floor to let the big man behind me move into the room and close the door behind us, keeping the night-time bugs attracted to the light outside. He, thankfully, stepped around and in front of me to join the rest of the men present.

"So you're her, huh?" A Mexican guy, old enough to be sporting some gray in his beard and long ponytail was the one to speak. His big arms crossed over his chest almost awkwardly due to their size. Veins traveled under his skin, like a roadmap, his tattoos stretched and indiscernible from this distance.

"Lexi," I introduced automatically, using my cover name I'd been living under for the last seventeen years. "Lexi Duran."

"That's not who you are." My gaze snapped to a man bouncing in his old-school Adidas sneakers. He had brown hair and icy blue eyes, a teardrop tattooed at the corner of one of them. *How cliché*. I raised an eyebrow and planted my feet, expecting trouble when he lurched towards me. He walked around me and I twisted to keep him in front of me, in my sight, at all times.

"Reaver..." Kyle said and I gave my best bitch grin.

"Somehow I doubt that's who you are, either..." I said and the man, Reaver, grinned.

"You'd be wrong."

"Yeah?"

He kept going around me and it was quick, too. Trying to dizzy me, or disorient me if I had to guess. I didn't like where this was going, so I hit the button on the seatbelt catch on my messenger bag and let it drop.

"Oooooh, we gonna fight?" he asked, his smile charming but with an edge of madness.

"If you'd like," I answered and felt my adrenaline spike, my heart throbbed painfully in my chest as fear swirled through me and my blood rushed, pummeling through my veins.

"Mali, don't," Kyle said and I shook my head and kept Reaver in my sight.

"I'm not doing anything, Kyle – tell your new friend here to back off." I felt my hands go up into my trained fighter's stance and Reaver's eyes lit up. His hand flashed out and I acted rather than reacted, swinging forward with my opposite hand even as he caught the wrist he was going for with his hand.

I clocked him but good, his head snapping to the side and I heard a couple of the guys cry "Oh!" One of them laughed and said, "Woo hoo!"

I almost heard Kyle facepalm and heard him say, "Fuck, Reaver. Just don't hurt her."

Reaver pulled me into him, right up against him, and ran his nose against the inside of my wrist, breathing me in like I was wearing some kind of perfume or something. I scowled and brought a knee up but he deflected. He shoved me back and I frowned again – he put space between us, and I didn't get that.

I circled, putting my forgotten bag between us as a stumbling block for him and like magic, a knife appeared in his hand. I blinked, and the blade snapped open with a soft and terrifying little snick. I swallowed hard and stilled and his grin grew wide.

"There it is!" he crowed triumphantly and I shook my head. He lunged, keeping the knife back and I dodged, going for my gun. I pulled it free and aimed, thumbing back the hammer. Everyone went still.

"Didn't anyone ever tell you? You never bring a knife to a gun fight." I swallowed hard and his grin went rictus.

"I like her!" he declared and I glanced at Kyle. It was a mistake. Reaver lunged impossibly fast, he ripped the gun out of my hand and hooked a leg behind mine. We were both falling and there wasn't shit I could do to stop it but he was a crafty son of a bitch. I hit hard, the wind almost, but not quite, knocked out of me. My head cushioned from the pavement by my messenger bag. Icy blue eyes were staring into mine and I could feel the pulse in my neck bouncing wildly against the tip of his knife blade.

"You need to make better choices, Amalia Rose," he said, his breath fanning my lips. I tried not to hurl from fear even as his words snapped me back to the Queen of Swords I'd held in my hand just hours ago. I blinked and swallowed hard, thankful for the reminder and *damn*! He got up off of me and held a hand down to me, the knife just suddenly gone. I swallowed hard and took it and he heaved me to my feet.

Kyle looked equal parts embarrassed and pissed, the rest of the guys looked amused, and I felt flushed. I held out my hand for my gun but Reaver took it over to the Mexican, who was still looking me over, dark eyes stormy.

"Just what've you brought home with you, Data?" he asked, and even though he was staring at me he was clearly talking to Kyle.

"Dragon, Amalia… Mali, this is Dragon, our president."

"Charmed," I spat out and saw Kyle's shoulders drop out of the corner of my eye. Reaver grinned from his place next to the man, Dragon, who was going over the big old revolver with a practiced eye.

"Yer daddy's gun?" he asked.

"Mine now, but yeah, what was your first clue?"

"Way too big for a little girl like you," a dude off to my right said.

"Ghost," Trigger intoned.

"Guys, please – I get it if you want to be pissed at me, but Mali didn't do anything," Kyle said and the frustration in his voice had everyone turning in his direction.

"Sweetheart, can you give us a minute?" Dragon asked me and his tone was decidedly less irritated with me. I blinked and threw up my hands, turning.

"Rev, Reaver, go with her."

"No thanks," I snapped. "I'm fine." But nothing about this was fine, I turned to Kyle – "You good with me leaving you alone with these fucking lunatics?"

He smiled at me and it was tired, "These 'lunatics' are my family now, my brothers, and they have been for a long time. Let them go with you and watch your back, please?"

I scoffed. "Seriously, Kyle?"

"Mali…" his voice was strained but tinged with pleading. I sighed.

"All right, fine…"

I went to the door we'd come in through, Reaver and the one they called Rev at my back. It was a decidedly uncomfortable sensation.

8

D ata...

Mali threw open the door and it slammed into the workbench beside it, causing the whole damn side of the building to shudder. Dray scowled and Dragon smirked and I just hung my head.

"Always like that, brother?" Trig asked gently.

"I think she's gotten a little more fire, maybe it's the stress."

"She tell you much?" Dray demanded and I shook my head.

"Not a lot, not yet."

Trigger sighed and Ghost stared at the big man, asking the question, "Who we gotta kill?"

"Nobody, if I have anything to say about it," I answered.

"Eh?" Dragon asked.

"I'm not bringing them here, not with all of you and your families. This one I can handle," I said, wandering over to a chair and dropping into it. I looked around and my shoulders dropped again. "Thanks, you guys... this is going to be a long operation."

"What do you have in mind?" Dray asked and I never expected to see him shift nervously.

"Whoever is after Mali, I have the feeling is some kind of criminal organization."

"Yeah, that's pretty much a given," Trigger said.

"So, I do my thing. I figure out who, piddle around on the dark web, pick them apart and make the pigs do my dirty work for me."

"I don't even want to know how you plan on accomplishing that, do I?" Dray asked with a sardonic smile.

"You wouldn't understand it even if I explained it to you," I confessed.

"Did you just call me stupid?" he demanded, his brow crushing down into a frown.

"Compared to the lot of us he's a goddamned genius, boy. He's not being disrespectful, he's just telling the fuckin' truth," Dragon grumbled and I put up my hands and nodded. He was right. I wasn't trying to be an asshole, I just seriously doubted I could explain what I had planned in layman terms well enough to not generate more questions than answers.

"As long as he keeps Em and our boy out of it, we're good," he said shoving off the edge of the workbench he was leaning against.

"Where you going?" Dragon demanded.

"Home to my woman and my kid, since I'm too stupid to know what the fuck he's talking about, anyway."

"Dude, Dray, don't be like that," I said.

"Relax, homeboy. I didn't mean that the way it came out. My boy isn't sleeping through the night yet, and I'm fuckin' tired."

"Oh, gotcha."

"We'll talk another day about why you never told us about her."

I shook my head and answered him now, "I couldn't. Not being able to find her has been my biggest failure…"

He looked me up and down and nodded, "Can't be good at *everything*, you know." He smiled and turned around and walked out the door. I caught a glimpse of Mali whirling and looking through the portal, concern mixed with the anger on her face and I felt an echoing smile in my heart, even if it didn't quite make it to my face.

"He's going to make a good Pres someday," I heard myself say but then I had to sigh. "Never thought I would ever hear myself say that."

"Just needed a good woman was all." Dragon said, but I could hear the shine of pride in his voice. I turned back, tearing my eyes from the battered metal door and the woman I knew lay beyond it to essentially face the music.

"Look, guys, I'm *sorry*… but there wasn't anything any of you could do about it. I mean –"

Dragon waved me off, "Hell if you couldn't find her, there wasn't no way we were gonna. The problem is what do we fuckin' do now?"

"Can't neutralize the threat without a fuckin' target," Trigger stated. Ghost grunted in agreement.

"I need to go fish. Pick Mali's brain, gather the information and find the proverbial man behind the curtain," I said. "Then I *should*, in theory, be able to neutralize the threat before it gets inside a hundred miles from here."

"It'd be nice," Ghost said and I nodded, the worry plain in his eyes.

"Let me do this my way, we'll stay here until it's in the bag, I'll keep you updated every step of the way."

"You're fuckin' right you will," Dragon grunted.

"How deep am I in with the rest of the guys?" I asked.

"Not as deep as you'd think," Trig answered.

"Every man's got his secrets," Dragon agreed. "We just never figured yours was this big."

"Go big or go home, right?"

He chuckled and nodded, "What're you gonna need out here?" he asked.

I sighed, "Hot water would be a good start."

Trigger grinned, "Ain't pretty but we got you covered."

"I appreciate it, more than you guys can know..." I bowed my head and pressed fingers into the base of my skull in a shitty bid to relieve a tension headache that was brewing.

"What're brothers for?" Dragon asked.

The silence stretched between the three of us for a long moment, a silence that was finally broken by Trig when he said: "You know it's not going to be easy, right?"

"What part of any of this has been easy up to this point?" I asked, knowing, likely, where he was headed.

"True enough, she was gone, but now she's here but everything is different... She's going to be different."

I nodded, "You don't have to be gentle about it, man. I know."

"I don't know that you quite get what he's driving at," Ghost said uneasily, and I nodded.

"I do, I may have been born at night but I wasn't born *last* night... she's high-strung, been looking over her shoulder for seventeen *years*. It will probably take seventeen more and she still might not come back from habits that deeply ingrained. You don't have to tiptoe around the subject, brothers... I know PTSD when I see it."

Trigger, Ghost, and even Dragon looked relieved and I sighed. "And before you even ask, *no*, I don't know how I am going to handle it except a step at a time. Mali is stronger than you think, though, so it'll be tough and take some doing but I have to believe that ultimately she's gonna be fine."

"First things first, gotta know what's doggin' her steps and put a stop to it before she can put any kind of healin' on her."

"True, that… some sleep and I'll work on that but we only just got here and I know I'm tired and I'm used to rides like that. She isn't."

"Rest up tonight, find out what you can about who's after her ass and why, and we'll get on it."

"I know the 'why': she killed somebody to save her dad. The problem is the *who*… No idea on that front, but he must have been some kind of important to someone somewhere in the underground."

"Well, we'll figure it out in the mornin'," Dragon said and bowed his head, scraping a boot against the cement in front of him; I nodded.

"Thanks for that, P."

"Hell, you've helped us bury enough bodies, I figure turnabout is fair play." I nodded again and we all let out closely timed big sighs.

"Should probably go save her from Reaver," Ghost said with a grin and I smiled.

"Screw Mali once, shame on you. Fuck her twice and you'll be the saddest motherfucker on the block. She doesn't like to lose."

"Good thing I took her shiny cap gun away," Dragon muttered.

I shook my head, "When it comes to Amalia Rose, that doesn't mean a thing."

I told them about our escape from Indigo City and it was met with a mixture of dubious and impressed expressions.

"Well, she ain't getting this back until we get her some range time," Trigger said, going over and taking the revolver from Dragon.

"She's not going to like that," I said flatly and Dragon huffed a laugh.

"No, I don't suppose she is," he said and I could tell, he didn't give a fuck. I smiled, stuck in the middle was a place I was used to being when it came to Mali. Seems times hadn't changed all that much after all.

9

A malia…

I sat up on one of the rusting car hulks and kept my mind and body ready for either of these two assclowns to pull something, but they didn't. They just stood chatting amicably a few feet away. I was tired, I was irritated, and I *really* didn't like Kyle's new friends. A short time after they'd shut me out, President Junior came outside.

"Yo, Dray, what's the verdict?" the one named Rev called out. He was short and stocky with arms like a slab of beef and fists that looked like they had crashed more than a few motherfucker's parties.

"Fucked if I know! I'm going home. They'll sort it out eventually," Dray said and sat astride his bike. He pulled on a helmet and stared across the short expanse of dirt and gravel lot in my direction. I raised an eyebrow and met his smoldering gaze, giving no quarter. He smirked and shook his head and I scowled.

"Something funny?" I demanded.

"I'll see you boys, later," he called, not even looking in my direction anymore, ignoring me, and I *hated* that. It harkened back to how life was for me growing up around this shit town until I met Kyle.

"You got a chip on your shoulder something fierce, ain't you, baby?" Reaver asked and I turned my tempestuous gaze on him.

"The fuck did you call me?" I demanded, putting on a braver front than I actually felt. He'd taken my father's gun from me like it'd been easy. He grinned at me, eyes gone feral and cold. I swallowed hard, which only made his grin grow into something almost rictus. He looked crazy, and you didn't fuck with crazy.

"Reaver, knock it off!" Rev said, scowling and Reaver shook like a dog coming out of a bath.

"I can't help it," he whined, "It's been a while, and Doll isn't scared of me anymore, not like she used to be."

Rev shook his head and looked at his dusty, red Chuck Taylor high tops. He glanced up at Reaver and said, "Sounds to me like you need to up your game then, buddy."

Reaver stuck out his bottom lip in a pout and sighed. I blinked and looked from one to the other.

"Did this seriously just turn into relationship counseling for the resident psychopath?" I demanded.

Reaver frowned at me, "I'm not a complete psycho, I mean, not anymore. I just have some sociopathic tendencies." He almost sounded defensive, which given the actual words coming out of his mouth was utterly fucking ridiculous.

I rolled my eyes and leaned back, scoffing, "What are they even talking about?" I demanded of no one in particular. Seriously, I just wanted to get out of this stupid-assed episode of Dr. Phil.

"That ain't for us to know," Rev said, but not rudely. He twisted back and forth, raising first one knee then the other in the opposite direction that he twisted his upper body, in an effort to pop his lower back. I took the time to study what I could see of his ink as he twisted into the light from the building's exterior but it was no good. Just quick glimpses, flashes with no detail. He had on a sleeveless tee, so his arms were bared, so I still tried to decipher what was there, but it was hard to tell in the dark what he had going on. The only thing I could tell was that one arm was fiery and the other was in cool gray scale. I didn't ask for a closer look. I wasn't *that* bored, but I was getting pretty anxious.

I was worried what they were doing to Kyle, who had obviously piqued their ire over me, and my old friend guilt settled over my shoulders like a scratchy stole. I couldn't tell you how many times Kyle'd been busted for one of my dumb ideas. How many restrictions, how many times he'd taken the heat for me with his parents just to spare me the beating from my dad when we were growing up. Seventeen years apart and that apparently hadn't changed either.

I was frustrated, growing agitated by the minute, the heel of my Doc tapping out an irritated staccato on the cracked black vinyl bumper that I rested my feet on. The nervous energy mounting until I thrust my legs up beneath me and leaped lightly down from the car. Reaver jerked slightly, going on guard, and I shook my head. I knew when I was outmatched and between Reaver's speed and Rev's obvious strength… well, I had no interest in becoming hamburger tonight.

I paced with nervous energy. I couldn't hold still even if I wanted to. I felt caged and I hated that feeling, but at the same time, I'd probably hate being dead more, now that Kyle was back in the picture. Another wave of guilt crashed over me, raising gooseflesh along my skin and bile in the back of my throat. I was turning into a nervous wreck but, other than the angry stalking back and forth over the dirt and gravel drive, I wasn't about to show any other signs of agitation or weakness.

It seemed like an iron age dragged on before the door opened, interrupting the eerie blue light from the fluorescent fixture above it with a swath of golden electric from inside. The big man, Trigger, stood in the doorway and called out, "Hey Reave, Rev, come on in here. Dragon wants to talk to her alone."

"Okay, Queenie; up against the car. I gotta frisk you," Rev said and he didn't exactly look happy about it, to which I could attribute him a few brownie points.

"Why?" I demanded, suspicious.

"Because ain't no way we're letting our revered leader out here with you alone until we know you aren't packing more than your daddy's pistol," Reaver said and gave me a grin. He tilted his head *just so*, and I didn't know what disturbed me more: The maniacal look he was giving me or the fact that he knew just how the light would fall to give it its full effect. Dude had being scary down to a science. He said, "If you don't want Rev to do it, I could," and I grinned back.

"Fuck you," I said and his smile softened, a little boy dimple appearing on one side of his mouth, the side lit by the shop light on the outside of the building.

"I didn't think so," he said, and Rev stepped up and pointed at the ground twirling his thick finger in a bid for me to turn around and assume the position.

I did as I was told and sniffed like I was bored saying, "You get handsy and we'll put my speed against your brawn. I'll emasculate you."

"My wife likes my dick right where it is, Queenie and I like my ol' lady right where *she* is, which is in my life. You ain't got nothin' to worry about."

It was food for thought. I just didn't know how to digest what he was saying just yet. The vibe was still a cautionary one, but these guys had backed way off. We were almost circling in this battle of wits and it was interesting. My sixth sense about people, developed over seventeen years of living a life on the run, was telling me I could be a little more optimistic about the situation but I wasn't about to run with that. I always remained cautious far longer than was warranted. It was a good thing, too; it had saved my ass more than a couple of times.

Rev kicked my feet apart gently and I leaned my hands against the front end of one of the old cars. He whisked his hands over me quickly and efficiently, earning a few extra brownie points when he apologized about getting near sensitive areas but didn't skimp on the search. He took my pocket knife, and that left me feeling fairly dejected. I was completely out of weapons at that point except for my wits and whatever around here was handy.

"'K, you can get up," he said and I turned a harsh eye in his direction.

"I'm going to want that back," I said and I caught Reaver grinning nearby like I'd done something to get after his own heart.

"You'll get it back, Queenie. Don't you worry," Rev said and he jerked his head at Reave. They trudged across the lot, gravel and dirt scraping and crunching under their shoes. They slipped into the building around the big man and the door closed. A second later it opened back up spilling the man of the hour out into the dark with me. Although, between his coloring, and how he moved, it was like he was a piece of the dark coming home. I didn't know if that was some kind of an omen or not.

I stood, hands loose at my sides, and waited on him to come to me. I wasn't about to defer to him. I mean, he may be their leader, and Kyle may choose to follow him, but I had sworn no fealty and didn't have the same compunctions. I didn't follow anybody, leastways not blindly, and in my world respect wasn't something that was always freely given… it had to be earned.

He stopped a healthy distance away from me and brought his cupped hands up, lighting the end of his cigarette. He took a decent drag off of it and held it, smoke curling from his nose, well, like a dragon, as his dark eyes raked me from head to toe. He kept one hand raised, cigarette between his index and middle finger while the other mirrored mine, kept loose and at the ready at his side.

A slight breeze ruffled past us, dragging a loose lock of my hair from my braid across my cheek, but I didn't move to brush it away. I waited to see what he would say or do.

He'd exhaled a few heartbeats back, and rather than speak, he cocked his head and took another thoughtful drag off his cancer stick. He let that breath out much quicker and said on the trailing end of it, "Y'know, we're a pretty peaceful lot nowadays. Doin' our best to leave that other world bullshit in our rearview mirrors. A lot of these guys have wives and children, and up to a couple a nights ago, we didn't even know you existed."

"You're pissed," I said with a shrug and he echoed the movement, shrugging back.

"Not especially, just curious."

"Ask whatever you wanna ask. Not like I can stop you." He huffed a laugh and shook his head, but his coal dark eyes never left mine.

"Got a chip on your shoulder, ain't you, sweetheart?"

"Maybe."

He nodded slowly, "Fair enough, we ain't especially welcome you with open arms – part of that bein' because we don't know you, or what kind of trouble you're bringin'."

I shrugged and felt bad. I honestly did. I didn't want there to be any collateral damage as much as these guys didn't want to *be* collateral damage. I kept to myself for a reason, that primarily, being it.

"Look, I don't want to cause any trouble. Never dreamt in a million years I would ever even see Kyle again…"

He pointed at me with his two fingers, the coal of his cigarette glowing an angry red, but his voice wasn't unkind, just genuine when he said, "Now that I believe."

He dropped his thumb over his two fingers and I felt my chest seize up with anxiety until I realized that it wasn't some kind of threat, but rather an unconscious motion by him that he'd finally confirmed something he'd suspected since meeting me.

"So now what?" I asked, swallowing hard.

He sighed, "Well, now you tell me what you want to have happen." I opened my mouth and closed it, brow crushing down into a confused frown. "Humor me," he said, adding, "And for once you can be honest. Don't be tellin' me what you *think* I wanna hear. I know bullshit when I smell it."

"Huh," I relented eventually, leaning my ass back against the hulk of the old beater that Rev had frisked me against. "Guess we have something in common after all." I sucked in a harsh breath and let it out just as quickly. I needed to make a decision and the Queen of Swords haunted me, Reaver's words echoing... *Make good choices...* This, trusting someone other than Kyle, was a blind corner for me. Hell, trusting Kyle after such a long separation was a blind corner but I have to confess, all the same, old feelings were there and strong as the day I'd left. The vibe I got off of Kyle was a good one and he trusted these people... I swallowed hard and prayed this was the right choice.

"I want to know who's following me and I want them to stop following me. I didn't do anything wrong," I said and Dragon searched my face, nodding slowly.

"I understand why Data – sorry... *Kyle* kept you from his brothers. It'd been a long time before he got himself hooked up with the club." His gaze roved over me again and he changed tack. "Lemme ask you something."

I raised an eyebrow when he didn't immediately come out with it and I realized he was waiting for me to give him permission, a big departure from our reception so I nodded and said, "Go ahead."

"What do you think would lead a man to follow some girl who dropped off his radar without so much as a goodbye seventeen years ago?"

I shrugged and shook my head, an uneasy feeling creeping over me. It was a legit question, but I didn't know where he was going with it. He nodded, apparently satisfied with what he was seeing out of me and chuckled darkly. He didn't provide an answer, instead, he said to me, "Well, when you have an answer to that question you go on and promise to let me know what it is."

I nodded mutely, caught off guard by the strange request. He took another drag off his cigarette, his dark eyebrows rising into his hairline. He jerked his head in the direction of the building and I felt a breath I hadn't realized I'd been holding creep out of my lungs. He turned for the corrugated steel structure but didn't lead, instead, he waited for me to fall into step beside him and I felt a quiver of anxiety that was my usual paranoia but it quickly fizzled out.

I still hoped like hell I was making the right choice, my fingers damn near itched to hold my cards and ask for insight into the mysterious figure that Dragon cut.

10

D**ata...**

Dragon opened the door and came in, Mali behind him, her dark eyes curious, her expression as guarded as I'd ever seen it. I could see the wheels and gears turning and clicking along behind her eyes and had to hand it to D. Whatever he'd said was making her think, but also, she was a little more relaxed, less stand-offish. She moved like a cat, gliding rather than walking with that feline grace and I had to smile.

I'd carried a torch for her since about forever and it looked like neither time nor distance had changed that much. I let my gaze wander over her, checking her out, making sure she was okay, even as she did the same to me. Questions floated up behind her eyes and I gave her a slight chin lift. I'd answer what I could, but there were some things that were strictly club business and I'd already set my brothers on edge with this. I wasn't about to betray them, or her, but asking for trust from either side at this point was probably going to be asking a lot.

"All right, decision made... Data, you find out what's what and if'n you can't, well, then, time for plan B as much as we don't like it."

"I like plan B, can we just skip to plan B?" Reaver asked, and he was bouncing on the balls of his feet again.

Dragon shook his head, "We don't have any idea what it is we're playin' at. Plan A first; I'll let you fill yer lady friend in. You two get some sleep and gimme a call tomorrow on the burner."

"Will do," I said and Dragon nodded.

"Come on, boys."

The men made to follow him out and Trigger turned, "Text me when you wake up, I'll bring some of Sunshine's cookin'," he declared and I smiled.

"Thanks, I really appreciate that, man."

"No problem," he said and the door swung shut behind them. I turned to Mali as the bikes roared down the drive and up the country road back to the highway. She was standing there, staring back at me, a fine tremble in her hands the only clue that she wasn't any kind of calm. Her eyes were frantically bouncing over me and I felt my shoulders drop. I went over to her and pulled her into a hug. She hugged me back, her long, elegant fingers digging into the shoulders of my leather jacket, kneading like a nervous cat; feeling for any hurts or damage.

"I'm okay," I whispered into her hair and she shook her head.

"Kyle, they're the *Sacred Hearts,*" she said voice strained and I curved my arms around her body, my hand finding the back of her head, kneading the tension at the base of her skull, playing along either side of the back of her neck.

"They aren't the club they used to be when we were kids, Mali."

...but we still hold onto the reputation. I thought to myself. I could understand her fear. Just because we weren't bad, didn't mean we weren't bad-asses. She rested her forehead against my shoulder and took some deep and even breaths.

"So what happens now?" she asked.

"Thought you wanted that hot bath and I believe I owe you my miracle cure for a hard ride."

"Look around, the place isn't exactly equipped for luxury… or indoor plumbing."

"Ehhh, you'd be surprised."

I took her hand and led her to the third of the shop curtained off, over by the back door leading out. The guys had strung up curtains from the track in the ceiling. The thick canvas they'd used was probably painter's drop cloth once upon a time, given the amount of spatter and staining on it. I whisked it down the rail, revealing the setup behind it, which granted, wasn't pretty by any means, but it *was* functional.

"Is that what I think it is?" she asked and I laughed to myself.

"Ah, if you're thinking it's a horse trough, you'd be right. One of the brothers works out on a thoroughbred ranch that his ol' lady owns. My guess is they donated to the cause."

"It's fucking huge," she said and she wasn't wrong. It was more like half the size of one of those above-ground outdoor swimming pools than it was bath tub sized. Pill-shaped, it could easily fit three adults comfortably, but then again, I had a suspicion that was my brothers' goal… insightful bastards.

"They jerry-rigged the water supply, so hot water here," I turned the one tap and the water rushed forth, loud against the aluminum bottom of the trough, "and cold over here." I twisted a completely separate tap, cold water pouring from a different spigot.

"Who cares?" she asked, a little dumbfounded, "It's hot and we can be *clean*… maybe your new friends aren't as big a dicks as I thought."

I smiled to myself and chuckled. *Mali, always had a way with words and was twice the guy of most guys we hung around growing up.*

Although, with a daddy like hers, she'd had to be tough. I sighed and turned back to her from leaning over the trough.

She had a weird look on her face I couldn't place, staring at the water filling the tub and finally she broke her gaze away from the flowing tap and rising steam to look at me, her expression guarded.

"So what's this miracle cure?" she asked.

I held up a finger, "Ah, be right back."

I went over to my packs, her eyes following me curiously, and dug around until I found the citrus/mint, muscle-relaxing bath bomb that I didn't know about anyone else, but I swore by it. I also dug out a package of Epsom salts pausing to look at the trough, thought better of it, and pulled out two of each.

"Seriously?" she asked as I upended the first package of Epsom salts.

"Shut up and try it before you start with your snark," I said grinning to take any bite out of it. I handed her a bath bomb and she peeled the sticker and started unwrapping the orange foil around it.

I finished with the salt and peeled mine out of the foil and dropped it in along with hers, the water much less loud now that the trough had filled by about a foot. She shook her head eyes a little wide as she watched them bob and fizz, the water turning milky and opaque.

"I'll give you some privacy," I said wiping my hand off on my jeans after testing the temp. Dragon had warned me that the hot water had been turned up *hot* so it wouldn't take forever and to use more cold to balance it out.

"Get in with me," she said and I blinked.

"What?"

"What?" she echoed, "The thing is big enough to fit six of me," she exaggerated, "and it's not like you haven't seen it all before. You've seen one you've seen 'em all, and besides…"

I waved her off and tried not to fucking blush. It'd been a long time ago and we weren't rowdy teens anymore.

"Fine," I said because I would be lying if I tried to play coy. I was hot, tired, and dirty and weary from the road, so if it got us into the bed across the shop faster, I was all for it. I was fucking tired.

Mali, as fearless as ever, deftly stripped down and I followed suit. It wasn't like I had anything to be ashamed of. I'd been working on my body quite a bit the last few years, deciding after our club had been raided by a rival outfit that I couldn't hide behind anyone. I needed to be as fit and ready as the next guy.

She got into the water and sank into it and I followed, opposite her. The trough was so big that we had to extend our legs all the way and point our feet just so that our toes would brush... which, like the dorks we are, we did. When they successfully touched we laughed and the oppressive atmosphere that had always accompanied any dealings at Point Nowhere lifted.

I didn't think the trough had filled as much as it had but when we got in, the displacement caused the water to rise by quite a bit. It wasn't all that high on me, but it was enough to just barely brush the underside of Mali's breasts. She'd filled out there, too and the fact that each one of her dusky nipples was graced with a silver barbell went straight to my prick. I was glad as hell that the water was murky, clouded with salts and the baking soda fizz of the bath bombs we'd dropped in.

She smiled at me and it was wan with remembrance. As a small mercy, she drew her knees to her chest, covering those tantalizing drops of silver to either side of each pert nipple and I felt like my brain could maybe function again to concentrate on what she was saying.

"Remember all those times we went skinny dipping at the quarry?" she asked. I laughed. It had become our new favorite pastime the summer she'd disappeared. Mostly because of how hot and miserably humid it had been. Anytime you'd stepped outside it was like you were trying to breathe someone's bathwater. Speaking of which... I reached over and twisted the taps on the spigots providing *our* bathwater shut. The cold water first, so that the heat would stay a little longer.

I spoke honestly when I said, "To be honest, what I remember the most about the quarry was how hard I had to hide my erection from you."

She laughed and it was a good sound. I leaned back against the side of the aluminum trough and stretched out, putting my arms up to lay along the sides, lounging and finally trying to relax. After the row with the Suicide Kings, I learned how fleeting the chances to relax could be. You had to take them when you could get them between fires you were running to put out. Then again, that was also the nature of my business in security and private investigative work, too.

"What about now?" she asked, and it wasn't coy. Mali didn't do coy, she did frank. Mixed with her curiosity, it was something else. Of course, me being me, I said the first thing that came to mind. I was always really good about misplacing my filter when I was around her. She was the kind of person that you just didn't need it, and if you tried to tiptoe or beat around the bush with her, all you were likely to do was put her off or make her suspicious.

"You're probably twice as beautiful now as you were then, so yeah…" I cleared my throat and shifted slightly uncomfortable with the turn in the conversation. "I'm hard."

She put her arms down and scooted closer. I blinked and froze as she moved through the water, crawling towards me, and *oh, shit…* that was hot. I felt my mouth go dry, my pulse leaping in the side of my neck, the shock of her dark, almond eyes raking over me *that way* left me reeling.

She settled on my lap and my hands traitorously drifted to her hips beneath the murky, citrus scented water. The softness of her skin under my hands, her warmth, and her heat so close… it was like a shock to the system. I felt like my heart was slamming against the inside of the center of my chest, trying to escape, to go to her, which was only fitting as it didn't matter time or distance, it had always been hers.

"Why did you come for me?" she asked, breath soft against my lips, eyes locked on mine, her intensity somewhere out of left field. I swallowed, and a strangled sound escaped my lips but I couldn't make words. Not with her this close, the heat of her sex mere inches from my own. She settled in my lap completely and I sucked in a sharp breath as the lips of her pussy wrapped around my cock. Not penetrating, not yet... but not exactly dry humping either. No, she was much too wet for that, even with the water rinsing vital natural lubricant away.

"Loyalty?" she asked lips against my ear, her hips grinding her sex against mine, sliding her body tantalizingly along my shaft.

"Oh it's an 'l' word, all right, but that's not it," I growled back. I kneaded her hips, fingers flexing, pressing her back and forth to cause more of that delicious friction that I was now suddenly craving like a starved man.

She chuckled darkly by my ear and nipped it lightly, drawing back to look at me. Her eyes were intense, roving over my face as if committing every line to memory, as if she would never see it again. Not happening, not on my watch. We swore when we were kids we were going to grow old together, and I aimed to make that a reality.

I brought my hands up from the water and cupped her face, drawing her down to me, her lips to mine. She opened to me, her breath rushing out in a shuddering sigh and I felt mine echo in relief. Our tongues twisted and dance, carefully, slowly, each of us savoring this moment, this first kiss, over twenty years in the making.

She drew back enough to look at me and demanded gently, "Why didn't you stop looking? Why did you come for me?"

I smiled and said, "Because, I love you."

She closed her eyes, soaking in the words and slid my cock inside her, taking me in one long, damning stroke.

There wasn't any way I was letting her go now.

11

A malia...

I had to know. I had to know if what the old man had hinted at was true, and I knew it was a dangerous game, but it was one I thought I could control... Ha. This was a Pandora 's Box. Something, that once opened, would release things into the world that I could never put back. As much as I feared change, I feared things always staying the same more. Enough opportunities had been missed and I *needed to know*...

"Oh it's an 'l' word, all right, but that's not it." His voice was low, as intense as I'd only heard it a scant handful of times and it nearly broke me. The implications were beautifully devastating.

Just like that, Kyle had taken control of my little game, as if I had been standing solidly on the shore one minute and he, a rogue wave, had swept all the sand out from beneath my feet, sending me tumbling into the sea.

I drew back and searched his face and it was there, every single dangerous implication that Dragon had hinted at outside laid bare. There was only one reason a man, especially a man like Kyle, would drop everything and ride to the rescue after seventeen years apart… but I needed to hear him say it. I was desperate to hear him say it first.

He brought his hands up from the water and cupped my face, drawing me carefully, sweetly to him. He kissed me and I felt a wicked throb of relief. As if my soul had finally been given that sweet shot of morphine after a long, painful, wasting illness. I wanted to let him sweep me under. I wanted to give up and drown in him but I had to know, no, I *needed* to hear him say it, like it was my air to breathe and I had none, like I was suffocating without it. So, I pulled back; even though it almost physically hurt for me to do it, and I asked…

"Why didn't you stop looking? Why did you come for me?" *No more games, not between us…*

He smiled at me then and I could swear, if angels were real, I was looking right at one and then he said, "Because, I love you."

I let myself go, sliding down over the top of him, taking him inside of me, and pressing my mouth to his, even as his arms went around me and he pressed me to his chest. I wasn't a weak person, I had never been, but in that moment I melted, let myself be vulnerable, because it was *Kyle*, and I loved him, too. I always had, *I always will.*

I moaned into his mouth and his thumbs skated through the slick tears I hadn't noticed escaping down my cheeks. I rolled my hips, grinding against him, his body in mine doing amazing things; the water, swirling around us, warm and soothing in its base element, matched on the outside the pleasure coming from within. I'd done a lot of kinky shit over the years, and the way Kyle touched me told me he was certainly no virgin either. Still, I did with him what I'd never done with anyone before… I let down my walls and became intimate with him. Let him into my being on a base sub-level, deeper than I had ever let anyone, man or woman.

I had never let anyone into my soul before. I probably never would again, but it was Kyle, and he loved me, and it was the first time that I could ever remember anyone loving me without condition... hell, at all...

His hands smoothed up my body to cup my breasts. He thrust his hips up gently to meet my descent and I gripped the edge of the tub to either side of his shoulders, just concentrating on the feel of him. He took one of my nipples into his mouth and I gasped, tipping my head back, my braid trailing in the water.

He gripped the barbell in his teeth and growled, the vibration through the sensitive flesh surrounding it causing my pussy to clench tighter around him. He grunted and moved to the other side to give the other breast the same consideration and it drove me wild.

I was used to fierce, hot, and most of the time, punishing fucks, but this wasn't that. Not even close. This was a carefully choreographed dance between the two of us. Kyle's every movement careful and deliberate. He was so controlled and it half drove me nuts and half made me melt.

"Gonna have to stop," he whispered against my skin, planting a kiss in the center of my chest.

"Why?" I gasped.

"I want out of this damn bath and to take you to bed," he murmured.

That sounded nice, even to my euphoria-soaked mind. I liked that idea, but not enough to give up the feel of him inside me. Not yet.

I cupped his face with my hands and pressed my forehead to his, rolling my hips insistently and he half chuckled half groaned.

"*Fuck*, Mali..." he rasped and it was a far cry from the boy who wouldn't swear, even as a teen, for fear of disappointing his mamma.

"Just a little longer," I begged breathlessly.

He gripped my upper arms firmly but carefully and I stilled, groaning. He leaned up and kissed me and that soothed my irritation some. I knew he was right, that once we were out of the bath and in the bed we could go as long as we'd like… I just… it'd been so long since I'd been in his presence and never like this before. I was reluctant to stop. Scared I would wake up at any moment, back in the hotel room, or worse, back in my brownstone to discover that it was all nothing but a beautiful, tragic dream.

I got up, and he followed suit less than a half second behind me. He got out of the tub first and held out hands to me to help me over the side without slipping. The cement was cool, and faintly gritty beneath my feet. Before I could look up I was enveloped in a large, fluffy gray towel, Kyle's hands rubbing my body briskly through the absorbent material.

"Bed," he ordered with a crooked grin, and then he swatted me on the ass. My mouth dropped open and he laughed, toweling himself off briskly. I whisked off my own towel, wound it up and he dodged running, twisting his body away and just barely missed the snap. I took my time laying my towel back over the wooden rack it'd come from and followed him over to the bed.

He pulled aside the mosquito netting for me and I got up onto the thick mattress, walking across the cloud-like comforter on my knees. This was yet another clue his friends weren't nearly the assholes I'd initially thought them to be. It was a real bed, like from somebody's house. The mattress was thick and comfortable, the head and footboards real and beautifully carved wood. They'd also taken the time to hang mosquito netting from the ceiling of this place in copious enough amounts to really protect us from the biting insects.

Kyle got up onto the bed with me and turned to make sure the netting overlapped properly and to keep the little bloodsuckers out. I couldn't resist, I knelt up behind him and curled my arms around his body, kissing his shoulders and back. He let out a sigh, shuddering under my touch, body loosening and relaxing, bowing his head and letting me have my way, which was nice. I mean really nice. One of the things I had always appreciated about Kyle was that he let me do things and didn't veto much, so when he did, I could usually tell that no matter how good of an idea it sounded to me, it really wasn't. He'd always been my compass growing up; as teens... my true north.

The more things changed, the more they stayed the same, I guess... however, none of this was ever something I had imagined happening. I mean, the whole sleeping together. I had wished for it, for Kyle to do what I had always been afraid to do. To close the gap between us and put his mouth on mine, god, more times than I could count. Especially after we'd reached that age of hormones and desire... but he never had. Always the careful one, always the good twin.

"I want to ride you, like before..." I murmured against his warm skin and he put his hands over mine and pulled them away from his body, twisting and laying down for me to do just that. I swung a leg over his narrow hips and he reached between us to raise his cock from his stomach so that I could slide over the top of him.

The desire in his eyes was raw and powerful, stealing my breath with a single look. His hands slid up my body to cup my breasts, teasing my erect nipples with his thumbs. It was perfect, and I closed my eyes and concentrated on the feel of him deep inside me, touching the most intimate parts of me, evoking pleasures that were simply marvelous without my having to do anything. It was like he touched every wanting, aching, nerve just right, and I was almost scared to get moving because if it felt this good sitting still, I was almost afraid of how good it was going to feel when I started to ride him.

His hands glided to my hips, his strong fingers digging into my flesh *just so* and I got with the program, biting my lower lip, hands on his rippling stomach, I rolled my hips. Sparks swept out from my core, flitting along fibers and nerves, lighting me up in a way I'd never felt with any of the encounters, casual and not, that I'd had before. That was just it, though. *Nothing* about this, about Kyle, was casual and none of my other meaningful relationships ever were... How could they be when the other person didn't even know my real name?

I swallowed hard and closed my eyes, head tipping back as I did it again. The feel of him, deep and fitting my body like a key, twisting in my locked heart until all my secrets came spilling out. God, the connection with this man was *unreal*. Our bodies were poetry in motion, breath spilling, world narrowing, hands gliding over damp flesh, smoothing over one another to make sure we were both whole and unharmed by the years and experiences that were lost to one another by the cruel twist of fate that had pulled us apart.

He thrust up gently to meet me when I came down on him the next time and a sweet cry of surrender escaped my throat. I was perilously close to orgasm, just by benefit of him inside me alone. I could never remember that happening with anyone else before, not that I thought much about it beyond that. All I knew was that this was what it must feel like when you found your other half and finally became one whole.

I mean, there were second chances, and then there was *this*, which I didn't even have a name for. All I knew was that I was incredibly wet. Wetter than I had ever been in my life, turned on to the nth degree, and it was both wonderful and terrifying, the euphoria of being astride the only man I think I'd ever loved almost too much, and I think he sensed that. His hands smoothing over my skin as we rocked into each other until finally, his arms went around me, and faster than I could blink, Kyle Cochran crashed over me and swept me under, both figuratively and literally.

12

D ata...

I'd never, in all our years together before she'd disappeared, seen Mali let go. I watched her come apart above me and while she wasn't orgasming, not yet, she was close. Her body trembling finely above me and around me, her muscles lax, eyes closed in perfect love and perfect trust as she met me halfway and she felt *incredible*.

Her metaphysical walls were down, the hardness went from her expression and it was an intimate glimpse of her. I had only seen it a scant handful of times on her face, usually under our old oak tree confiding our deepest and darkest hopes and dreams. I knew I was her number-one confidant back then, and she was my greatest secret, my one heart's desire that I coveted above all else.

...and now she was really here, really mine, and I was never letting go.

She was finally in a place where she was ceding her hard-won control and I would be a fool not to take advantage. I smoothed my hands over her silky soft skin and sat up, rolling her off to the side and under me. She gasped, holding onto my shoulders but I didn't give her time to react, I didn't want to lose her to the dark fear that plagued her. The one that was always there threatening to pull her back from me, so I stroked deep, deeper than our position of a moment before would allow. She gasped, her pussy flaring around the head of my cock, clamping down around my shaft and I knew she was almost there, so close, so damn epically *close* and I wanted so bad to take her there.

I cradled her body against mine, lifting one leg up over my shoulder and pressing her into the cloud of a mattress. She shuddered beneath me, her cry sweet and beautifully real and true. I smiled to myself and covered her mouth with my own. She was as passionate as I imagined she would be, holding me to her tightly, kissing me fervently, her body tight, squeezing down around me until it was almost hard to thrust. She was a coiled spring, and I wound her tight and tighter until she tore her mouth from mine and with a piercing, passion-filled scream she sprang apart beneath me.

Her body jerked and she stiffened, and the way her pussy milked my cock there was no way I could hold out anymore either. I drove deep and felt myself spill inside her and it was probably the most satisfying experience of my fucking life.

Of course, then reality set in. We'd just done it without a condom, although, to be fair, she'd definitely started it and while Mali wasn't reckless, she was definitely the more reckless of the two of us. Thus, it bore talking about. Just not right this second. Right this second I was getting us both under the blankets, gathering her close in the dimly lit interior of the shop building of Point Nowhere.

I don't think this place had ever witnessed anything beautiful before and the vibe of the whole building rang like a tuning fork that'd been struck against a stone. The life-changing reverberations of what we shared echoed back at us from the very walls. Mali and I panted, concentrating on regaining our breaths to a steadier cadence before either of us tried to talk.

She immediately pressed herself to my side, laying her head on my shoulder and one of her legs across both of mine. Her body pressing as tightly as she could make it to my side, and I loved that. I held her close with one arm along her back, my other hand atop her thigh, smoothing up and down her leg to reassure myself that yes, this was really happening and it wasn't just another one of my fanciful dreams.

"Say it again," she breathed against my chest and I looked down at the crown of her head, her expression hidden from me.

"What?" I asked, drawing a blank.

She looked up at me, and the keen sharp look she gave me led to my 'oh duh' moment of the night. I smiled and said, "That I love you?"

"Yes." Her voice sounded relieved, her body relaxing against mine; eyes fluttering shut as if tasting my words and savoring their flavor.

"I've loved you since the third grade Amalia Rose Junix. Nothing about that ever changed and I never thought for a minute you left by any means other than foul play." I sighed and she laid her head back down, cuddling close. I could feel the tension returning to her muscles and I wished I hadn't said anything now. I could feel her going back on the defensive and she was *always* on the defensive. She may have loved her daddy, but I don't think her daddy really knew how to love her back, at least not by traditional standards. Not with all the shit he put her through.

She came from the epitome of a fucked-up broken home and the scars from that ran deep. They were deeper than skin, deeper than blood and bone. These scars weren't something that could probably ever be fixed, but I didn't care. I loved her for who she was, damage and all, difficult as that sometimes made her.

At least, with Mali, I would never, ever, be bored.

"No more secrets, no more games," she murmured. "Not between us."

"No games, no secrets," I agreed immediately.

"I missed there even being an 'us' so much," she said and she shivered against me, the same sort of shudder she gave when we were kids and she was fending off tears. The same sort of shudder that always led someone to ask *'are you all right?'* which of course led to Mali blowing up in their face in over-compensation to prove that she was just fine.

I didn't fall for the trap, I just held her a little closer and smoothed my hand up and down her sexy, toned thigh and said, "Yeah, me too. You have no idea how much."

She huffed a bit of an incredulous laugh and I smiled, too. If there were anyone on the planet who knew or had any idea, yeah, it would be her. I didn't know exactly where to go from here. What to say, or if I should ask, and I didn't want to ruin this carefully cultivated calm. Seriously. We were safe here, even though we couldn't stay here forever, for obvious reasons. We had time, though. Time before we had to make a move.

"Sleep, for now, baby. We'll deal with it tomorrow."

"Pretty sure it *is* tomorrow, and I like that."

"Like what?"

"That you call me 'baby' so easy, like you've always said it."

I chuckled and kissed the crown of her head. If she only knew how many times I struggled *not* to say it in the weeks and months leading up to her sudden disappearance. Or how many hours I searched internet back alleys, how much time I spent immersed in the dark web muttering over and over, 'Where are you, baby?' into the dark.

Amalia had been mine for a long, long, time. She just didn't know it then, and I'd had no way to tell her.

"You really like it?" I asked, a little worried by her sudden silence. "You're not just saying that?"

She pushed herself up, twisting to look down at me. Her lips echoing the movement by twisting into a wry smile that warmed her eyes to a deep caramel.

"I love it," she whispered and brought her mouth down to mine for a lingering, decadent, sweet kiss that had my dick stirring beneath the sheets all over again. She didn't hesitate to go exploring, wrapping sure but gentle fingers around me; stroking me to life the rest of the way.

"Do I need to get you the morning-after pill?" I asked against her mouth. She smiled back against mine.

"Implant," she said, "but I wouldn't say no to condoms if you decide you want this to be an open kind of deal…"

I froze and pulled back from her scowling, demanding… "Is that what you want?"

"No, but I know how MC's work. Club girls aren't always out of bounds whether you're in a relationship or not. I'm telling you right now though, I find out about her, I'm cuttin' the bitch."

I felt a lazy smile cross my face, she was fishing. I shook my head and told her, "Not how I operate."

"I didn't think so, but I wanted to be sure."

"I thought no more games…" I murmured, and pressed my mouth to hers, kissing her breathless even as she stole mine with her careful, nimble fingers.

"Wasn't playing," she said straddling me and looking down from her perch across my hips. She was sliding her pussy up and down my length, teasingly… not penetrating, just driving me wild. I laughed and put myself in her. She sucked in a sharp breath and settled into a slow, rocking rhythm.

"I ain't playing either," I said, "You're mine now and you disappear again? I'll hunt your sweet ass down all over again and spank it." I swatted her on the ass to make my point and she yipped and laughed before letting out this sultry moan.

"Mm, I'm good with that."

"You sure?"

"You give *fantastic* dick. I'm sure." I laughed and she grinned and once again I marveled at the fact that it was like we'd picked right back up where we'd left off. Like nothing had ever happened.

13

Amalia…

I woke slowly to the sound of masculine voices and lay still for a minute, just listening, trying to decide on who was here. I heard Kyle's voice, the low, steady cadence a comforting thing. He was still here, and comfortable with whoever he was talking to, so there was no danger… not yet.

One of the cardinal rules of living on the run was that you were *never* safe. You could never take the illusion of safety for granted, either. The minute you did, shit would go sideways and you would find yourself running again at a severe disadvantage and when you weren't seven steps ahead of the hunter, that's how you became very dead prey.

The low, gravelly tone that responded to Kyle mismatched the dude that it came out of. I mean, the big guy couldn't have been more than forty on the outside and yet he sounded like a regular grandpa. It bespoke way too many cigarettes in too short a time. I knew a couple of other guys like that. Some people, it damaged the voice after a couple of months sucking down a pack a day or more. Made you sound two to three times your actual age. By the time this dude was seventy, if he even made it that far, he might not have any kind of voice at all.

The smell hit me like two seconds after that gravelly smoker's voice spoke, and my stomach clenched and was like, *yes! Feed me bitch!* I pushed myself up and stretched and Trigger said, "Whoa, hey, sorry! Uh…"

"Would you look at that?" I mused aloud, "I make the big biker blush." I swatted aside the mosquito netting and hopped out of bed. Kyle was struggling not to laugh. I'd never been body-shy in my life, and I didn't particularly care for modesty on a physical front. I kind of viewed my skin the same way I viewed clothes. Just something to wear to hold your soul. You know what I mean?

Still, it was totally worth it to watch the big guy curse, twisting this way and that in the big, pretty much empty building, looking for something to duck behind to give me privacy. I was going to go straight for the bath, but the chance to get a little lighthearted revenge for my discomfort last night made me divert passing the desk full of computer equipment in the center of the large space in favor of going to it.

Kyle leaned back in his desk chair and I leaned a hip against it, draping my arm across his shoulders. He was sitting in just jeans and boots, shirtless save for his motorcycle vest over his bare chest. The look suited him, my pussy giving a bit of an aching throb at the sight that I couldn't honestly tell if it was in excitement or protest. It'd been a while, and we'd gone at it more than a few times last night. I was sore enough that I couldn't quite classify it as the good kind anymore, but I wanted to anyway. I also couldn't deny the deep sense of soothing satisfaction it gave me when his hand went to my waist, around my body, his arm against my ass and the tops of my thighs.

"Grab a bath and get dressed, baby. Rest of the guys will be here soon." He smacked me on the ass and laughed.

"Oh, you're going to pay for that one," I remarked and he smiled and winked at me.

"I don't doubt it, but all the same…"

"Yeah, yeah, I got it." I waved over my shoulder and started up the water carefully. He'd drained the horse trough last night and this morning I went to my knees in it and didn't even wait for it to fill. I used the pitcher hanging over the side from an 's' shaped hook to dump over my hair and made quick work of it and the rest of me with the stolen hotel shampoos and conditioners and a sliver of a bar of soap.

I didn't much care for the cheap shit; my skin felt tight and dry with a layer of soap scum on it, but it was better than sweat, the leavings of our sexcapades, and the barely-rinsed road grime of the day before. I got up, wringing out my hair, and shutting off the tap just as Reaver and Dray walked through the door.

"Shit, put some fuckin' clothes on," Dray grated and averted his eyes. I rolled mine while Reaver stared openly, grinning like a happy dog who'd just spotted his favorite tennis ball.

"Eh, I give you a solid seven, but my Doll is a ten in my book."

"Fuck you," I said, "I'm at least an eight."

"Nine," Kyle called, "be a solid ten if you had more of an ass." He wasn't looking at me, though. He was clicking through screens in front of him and I smiled to myself, drying off and wrapping one of the large towels around me. Just another reason I loved him. He didn't bullshit me, and yet, even when he was saying something that might have been taken as a dis or derogatory, he still had a way of being fresh, honest, and complimentary. He knew I hated how skinny I was as a teen and that my biggest pet peeve back then had been my decided lack of a chest. That hadn't changed too much. I went from a late blooming solid A cup to no more than an overflowing B… but he liked my tits. That gave me the warm fuzzies, right there.

I went back across the place and pulled on clean panties and some black yoga pants. The door opened up and admitted more men, these ones I didn't know, just as I pulled a loose dark gray tank top with some pithy saying in shiny silver on its front over my head. I fished through my bag for a comb, pulled the netting against the four bed posts and secured it, before dropping onto the bed and curling my legs across each other to start working on the snarl of my hair.

I picked through endless knots in the dyed ends. Three guys had come in, one with long brown hair, one with short dark hair, and one with hair the color of dirty straw. All three were imposing in their own way. The first and third were both built like a brick shithouse, the second was wiry whipcord over bone in a way that still managed to be imposing. They eyed me just as much as I eyed them, each of us taking the other's measure.

"Archer, Rush, and Nox, meet Amalia. Mali, this is Archer, his brother Rush and that's Rush's twin, Nox," Trigger made the introductions, Kyle was lost in his mass of computer screens and networks.

"Hi," I said and looked them over one at a time.

"Don't look like much, does she?" Rush asked.

"Guess we'll be fast friends, then," I said sarcastically. "Right back at you." Archer and Nox laughed, and I smiled. "And *she* is sitting right here, so don't fuckin' talk about me like I'm not," I added.

"You were right, Reave," Nox said and turned back to me, "You're a firecracker."

"More like a mortar, you haven't seen the whole show, yet," Reaver chimed in finally.

"Was that a compliment?" I asked. "Or are you being a dick?"

He grinned from ear to ear and I raised my eyebrows and turned down the corners of my mouth in an attempt to look impressed as I was saying, "About time you got with the fucking program… speaking of…" I turned to Kyle and sighed, "What *is* the program?"

"Save it," Dray ordered. "No sense in having to repeat yourself, we're not all here."

"Fair enough," I conceded, even though it pissed me off slightly to do it. I didn't like being cut off like that, and I sure as fuck didn't take orders, but it wasn't worth putting up a racket right now. Playing nice was the rule of the day, even if it did suck monkey balls.

The rest of the guys finally ended up getting here, starting with Dragon and Ghost with some New Zealand tribal motherfucker named Zeb, traditional tribal face tattoos that I could seriously appreciate and all. Additionally, there was a guy named Blue, but with how nervous he looked about being here instead of wherever he'd come from, I immediately labeled him 'Little Boy Blue' in my head as well as a liability.

The final man in Dragon's retinue was a rough-looking sort with a blue denim motorcycle cut instead of black leather. I wondered if that was a preference thing but didn't ask. He had long, shoulder-length brown hair shot through with gray and a beard getting on the long side that was much the same. His blue eyes sparkled and he had an air of crazy around him but it was crazier like a fox if that made sense. He was introduced as Lucky and I didn't think it had anything to do with a rabbit's foot.

Finally an older guy, bald, with a handlebar mustache came in with Revelator. A tall, skinny young guy, covered neck to fingertips in wild ink walking through the door behind them. Everyone was introduced as I wound my hair into a tight knot at the base of my skull and waited to see who would be coming next.

"Looks like we're all here," Dragon declared as a last and final bike had just shut off outside.

"Fuck you, man!" A ginger guy, sweeping a hand through his hair which was getting long on top said, coming through the door.

"Well, then hurry your fuckin' ass up, Thirteen," Dray commanded.

Ginger Thirteen grinned savagely and let fly two one-fingered salutes in Dray's direction and it was out of my mouth before I could stop it, "Can't argue with you there."

The guys all laughed and I took a deep breath letting it out slowly. I was definitely out classed, outmatched, and for once in my fucking life, should probably watch my mouth.

"Go ahead, Data… let us know what you've found."

Trigger pushed off the edge of Kyle's setup and walked over, shoving a Styrofoam clamshell of food at me with a plastic fork with a wink and I gave him a wry smile. Good man, definitely not a dick. If I were shoving food in my face I couldn't talk and I was fucking starving.

I opened the lid to soggy French toast soaked in syrup and several sausage patties, likewise drowned in same and didn't bitch. It was food and last night's dinner was a long time ago. He leaned his jeans-clad ass, which was framed really nicely in black leather chaps, against the footboard of the bed, back to me, and all eyes were on Kyle as he took a deep breath and let it out slowly.

"I got nothin'," he said, and without missing a beat added, "and I hate to say it, I really do, but it's not like Mali is in the 'know' and she ghosted off the grid so efficiently…"

I swallowed the bite of food in my mouth and swear it went down sideways, sticking in my throat that was suddenly tight.

"You were good at this computer shit even back then," I said honestly. "I didn't need you finding me. I couldn't stand the thought of you, of all people, becoming yet more collateral damage in whatever my dad got us involved in."

"I know, babe, but it's made it a royal pain in the fucking ass to figure out who or what is behind all of this." I sighed and straightened up, doing a second's worth of battle with the food that was suddenly trying to fight back on me.

"Forget what we don't know," Dragon said and rubbed a giant paw over his beard. "What *have* we got?"

"Well, what we *have* got is one grade-a fucking shining beacon," he said holding up my laptop. "Only problem is, that will bring them here."

"Yeah, but if it's organized crime like you suspect…" Trigger said and I cut him off.

"It is. I don't know who, there are a lot of flavors to choose from, but these guys are tactical ready. They showed up at my brownstone with fucking tear gas and shit. Followed us in a black SUV… White guys, but beyond that, I don't know. My dad was great at keeping me out of it right until I shot one of them to protect him."

"Well, shit. There you have it right there," Dragon said.

"What?" Kyle asked, frowning.

"Only way someone like her gets hunted to the ends of the earth, even seventeen years after the fact is if she killed someone *important*." Looked like Revelator had some brains to go with that brawn.

"Yeah, I thought of that," Kyle said unhappily. "I have algorithms running through old news reports looking for any crime-related anything… but do you know how long that could take? This *is* the criminal underworld we're talking about here, and while I *can* go hacking into the NSA, FBI, and whatever other alphabet law enforcement soup you want to come up with, it's really inadvisable unless I have something specific to go diving their web servers for, you know?"

"You got anything for us, girly? Anything at all?" Archer asked and I felt my shoulders drop as I searched through all my memories begging and pleading with it to just come up with that *one* thing that would make everything fall into place and any one of these guys go 'ah-ha.'

I let out an explosive breath and said, "I got nothin'. I legitimately have no fucking idea *what* my dad was into and I was honestly just a kid. Even when he was drunk, that made him even more of a closed-mouthed bastard with a side of violent. He didn't get to talking about anything more. He was gypsy, even if he was outcast, and fuck... our lineage knows how to keep a secret."

"Not helpful," Reaver said with a pout.

"Thank you, Captain fucking Obvious," I rolled my eyes and shoved the forgotten food aside. I suddenly wasn't all that hungry anymore, my stomach churning with nerves.

I mean, it was pretty obvious these guys weren't terribly interested in getting involved and I totally got why. Most of them, according to Kyle, had just found their true loves in life. Most of them also had children, some of those children only months old. All of them had recently lost one of their brothers to a nasty accident, and he'd told me the story of Little Boy Blue and his woman, Hayley and their son that was on the way who might not even be genetically his, but possibly the only remaining, living, breathing, relic of his partner and best friend. I guess they'd been working on being some kind of triumvirate before he'd died so unexpectedly.

I sighed, I didn't want to be the cause of such a great strife with these people. I was falling, spiraling down, I knew the feeling and I was so frustrated... By making love to Kyle last night, had I made a right choice? I mean, I knew it'd been a *good* choice, but had it been the *right* choice? There was sometimes a difference.

I scrubbed my face with my hands, frustrated. I'd worked so hard and been so alone these last few years to protect the other people around me, and now I was here among all of these people Kyle clearly cared about with a stigma attached to me like no other. I was a regular Typhoid Mary in their midst and I could destroy so many lives simply by being here…

Panic spun my thoughts around and they started to fall from their neat, orderly shelves, jumbling one on top of the other. I was going to get someone hurt, someone killed and I *really* didn't want to do that. I really didn't want to destroy the life that Kyle had built for himself. I looked around and saw clearly that these fools were the family that Kyle no longer had in his parents. Did I really want to be the destruction of that? He would hate me forever and worse… he could die and knowing my luck? I would live. And if I didn't die, and he didn't die, but one of these men did? One of their family did? Fuck, the implications were horrible. The mercy would be that *they* would kill me. Quickly would be nice but men like these? Like Reaver, over there? Quickly was so not their style… Worse yet, Kyle could possibly resent me forever and there were some things that were indeed a fate worse than death. That one certainly topped the list.

"Mali… *Mali,* look at me." I shuddered hard and looked over to Kyle who was staring at me intently.

"What?" I demanded and it came out harsher than I intended. It always did when I was scared, but Kyle saw right through me. He always did.

"It's going to be fine, sugar. This ain't any of us our first rodeo…" Dragon said and I shook my head letting out an explosive breath. I got down from where I sat and paced, stalking back and forth.

"Even if that's the case," I said bitterly, "The stakes have never been higher for all of you, *any* of you, have they?"

"Hmm, that's the God-given truth," Trigger agreed.

"That's what makes it more fun," Reaver said grinning and it was a grin that was echoed on a few faces, Thirteen's and Revelator's among them.

"Seriously not the time to get cocky," I derided. "These people mean business... seventeen years, one post on the internet and they were there inside twenty-four hours loaded for bear. What does that tell you?"

"Tells me neutral location with plenty of high ground," Ghost said and exchanged a look with Trigger who nodded.

"Controlled explosions," Thirteen said, and someone laughed.

"That leaves me out, you'd need Duracell for the controlled part." I looked over to Lucky who was grinning but shaking his head a bit ruefully. That wasn't disconcerting at all, the guy named Lucky playing with explosives that *weren't* controlled.

"Eh, I'm sure your homemade brand of firepower has its uses; I bet I could help tweak them so they'd color inside the lines," Thirteen, said.

"Where, though?" Lucky said.

"The lodge?" Archer asked.

"Too far and it's tourist season through there," Dray said. "Plus, we really try not to shit where we eat."

"Got my fishing cabin, but there are neighbors up that way," Thirteen mused.

"Here?" I asked.

"Could make it defensible and it's pretty much off the grid," Dragon said.

"I could be bait. I'd like my gun back, though..." I said.

"Won't need you for bait, baby," Kyle said, and he sounded disapproving.

"Well, you sure as fuck aren't going to be here for the big show and not have *me* here. Fuck that!"

"Uh oh, trouble in paradise," Revelator mocked, and Kyle and I turned at the same time.

"Shut up!"

"Stay out of this please, Rev…" we both barked in unison. I'll give you one guess as to who was nicer.

"Look," I said, "I am a *big* fucking problem for y'all, and I would *really* like to be part of the solution. So if you don't mind, this self-saving princess would really like to be a part of the action up to find out who the fuck I killed and why he's so goddamned important. It's not like *that* hasn't been haunting me for the last seventeen years."

"All right, all right, calm your tits…" Dray said pushing his hand down at me in front of him twice, the classic sign to slow down and pump the brakes.

"She has a point, son." Dragon sighed and met my eyes, the dark, burning coal to his gaze considerably cooled. "Much as I hate to say it, they come lookin' they're apt to scout this place and they're gonna want to see she's here…"

"Great," Kyle muttered and hung his head sharply. He pulled on the back of his neck and I drifted to him, digging my thumbs into his shoulders at the base of his neck, doing my best to smooth out the tension there.

"We need to come up with some kind of a plan, figure out who is gonna be involved, who is going to look after things back at the proverbial ranch… Shit." Archer hung his head and I felt my breath still in my lungs, my chest tighten up.

"Mali, it's fine, they're going to help, ease up." I startled and let go of Kyle and he turned in his desk chair and pulled me down into his lap to make eye contact with me.

"Trust me…" he said and I nodded because whenever had I not? He was my compass, and he'd absolutely *never* steered me wrong.

"Right… I think we can all make an exception on a kind of she's here and we're stuck with her for now?" Dragon winked and I frowned at him. The rest of the guys grumbled their assent. He nodded and said, "Okay, we'll put it to a vote."

14

D ata...

It wasn't as simple as just putting it to a vote and me plugging Mali's laptop in and sending out a signal, hoping they'd bite. No, we had shit to do and it all started with a division of labor.

We had two snipers in Trigger and Ghost, more effective together but in this case, it was a luxury we couldn't afford. Not with so many wives and kids' lives on the line. Trigger had no kids, so he would be staying here to pick a few of the bastards off that would more than likely be coming. No one here would be wearing cuts, either, to give any that might get away any ideas.

Still, as a precaution, Ghost would be stationed up on the roof of the club, which was going into lockdown until further notice. He would have Revelator, Blue, and Nox on the ground and Disney manning my club control center, watching the cameras and tripping and sounding the alarm if anything came near the fenceline. Dray would remain at the club and be in charge of operations there while Dragon was out here with us.

Speaking of out here, we had the majority of our firepower. Trigger would be out there, likely on some high ground inside a half mile radius, so he would be safe no matter what. Mali and I would be in here, eyes on the cameras and running central. Archer was out there with some of his more impressive bows, a silent killer from a distance. Reaver would be prowling around out there in the same capacity.

Red-Thirteen and Lucky were working up some explosives. Thirteen had struck up a pretty solid buddy system with Cell in the year before Cell had died and had been learning from him. Sort of a natural evolution of things seeing as his ol' lady, Dani, was fast and solid friends with Cell's partner, Blue. I digress, though.

Dragon, of course, would be in here. Our general, giving orders; and Zeb would be our first line of defense along with Rush. Of course, if the bad guys got that far, we were in serious trouble. Still, we wanted at least one, maybe two survivors.

It was a busy day after church which, it was both weird and fantastic having Mali by my side for it, to see how the guys really were. Not just the jaded and guarded fronts they put up. She'd sat in my lap, toes pressed against the cement beneath us, idly and nervously pushing us back and forth as she listened. Her expression was both guarded and full of open curiosity. She was street-wise enough to know she didn't belong here and that what she was witnessing was rare. It was a mark of how much my brothers trusted me that none of them blinked or raised any concerns about plotting this much illegal activity in front of her.

I trusted her implicitly and that was good enough for them, even after me keeping her a secret for as long as I had been. I think that was saying something.

"Right, you all know yer jobs. Go to it. Data, I'm afraid yer gonna have to go to the club and check things over, run Disney through his paces and make sure he's got it. Anything pertaining to this little pow-wow we've had here needs to go over burner not yer regular lines."

Mali got up off my lap slowly saying, "I'll just stay here then."

"Yeah, you will, but not by yer self."

"I'll stay," Trigger said. "Need to make sure you aren't gonna accidentally blow somebody's balls off with this."

He brought out Mali's father's gun and she nearly jumped, stopping herself at the last second from lunging for it. She tried to be cool but I could tell it was the last thing she had of her dad's and she wanted it back, *badly*.

"Go on and put your boots on, baby. I'm probably going to be a while," I murmured.

She looked back at me and I could tell that she didn't want me to go, but I could also tell that she was going to be brave and let me do what needed doing, too. It was the way Mali was, never showing weakness, never showing any kind of vulnerability in front of *anyone...* except me.

I don't know what had made me her chosen one, way, way, back... but it was a duty that I took seriously. I took it just as seriously today as I did the first moment I realized that she looked up to me, despite being almost a year older. God, we must have been what? Eight or nine? Just kids who didn't know a fucking thing about how the real world worked. I couldn't take care of her then, even though I tried. I couldn't take care of her as a teen, even though I wanted to be her everything... but now we were neither of those things . I was a man and as the old line goes, *it was time to put away childish things.*

I'd never killed a man directly. I doubt that I would, even now... but I would start the game and then, if I had to, I would finish it. I had to. I just had to do it the best way I knew how and right now, that was this way. That was by entrusting her care to my brothers while I went to the club and got things set up to protect their families, their loved ones so that they could focus on protecting what was mine.

That was what this brotherhood was about. Give and take, protecting our own and knowing without a shadow of a doubt that the man next to you had your back; had your best interests at heart. That you could put your life, the life of everything you loved and held dear, into his hands and know that it was *safe.*

"You guys mind if I have a word with my girl before we hit the road?" I asked and a bunch of the guys shook their heads, some even started moving for the exit. Dragon gave me a look that told me not to take too long and I gave him a nod.

When they were all outside, and Mali and I had the illusion of privacy, I pulled her to me and covered her mouth with mine. Her arms twined around my neck unbidden and she leaned into me, holding her body in a tight press against me.

"I won't take too long, I promise," I murmured.

She chuckled a little darkly and said, "Afraid I'll sully your big friend's virtue?"

It was my turn to chuckle and grin as I said, "Something like that." I let my tone become more serious and asked her, "You sure you're going to be okay?"

She rolled her eyes and let out a bit of a scoff, "Sure, I get to have Thor out there mansplain my daddy's gun to me. What could possibly go wrong?"

I chuckled again and sighed, "He's a Marine Corps sniper, he might surprise you and you might actually learn a thing or two."

"I have a feeling I might surprise *him*..."

"Now of *that*, I have no doubt." I pecked her on the nose and reluctantly let my hands slide off her waist. She sighed and went over, grabbing her boots.

"How long you think you'll be?" she asked.

"If I say a couple of hours it'll end up being like four. Truth is, I don't have a clue, so don't wait up."

She scoffed, "Good luck getting me to follow *that* order."

"Hey, if I had to pick, that would be the one to ditch."

"Be careful," she said softly and she had that still and quiet way about her even as she tied off the lace on one of her high boots. She pulled the other one on with purpose and I indulged in just watching her for a few seconds. Leaving her here with Trig wasn't my first choice. Not because I didn't trust him, but totally because I'd only just found her again and didn't think I would ever be ready to let her out of my sight.

"I love you," I whispered, never taking for granted my ability to tell her again. After not having her close to hear it for so long, I would never deny it a chance to pass my lips.

"I love you, too." She finished tying off her other boot and stood. She came for me and we shared one last kiss before someone, likely Rush, banged on the outside of the metal sheeting, causing us to jump apart.

"C'mon let's go! We're burning daylight!"

"On it!" I called back.

"I mean it, be careful," she said.

"You know I will."

15

A malia...

"You ready for this?" he asked in that gravelly smoker's voice. I fought not to roll my eyes and lost.

"Why do you think because I've never been to a shooting range that I don't know how to shoot this thing?" I demanded.

"It's like any skill, practice makes perfect, right?" he asked. I held out my hand and he turned my father's gun over to me. He let out a gusty sigh and said to me, "All right, let's see what you can do, first. Then I might have some pointers for you after that."

We were behind the rusting out building and the sun was beating down pretty mercilessly. I wanted to go back into the shade. I wasn't cut out for dealing with the daystar. I was pretty much a night dweller both by choice and by trade and would much prefer keeping it that way.

Reaver sat on yet another rusting-out hulk of a car and was grinning at me. I didn't get the impression that either one of them had faith in my shooting ability, and truth be told, while I *knew* I was good with a gun owing to natural talent, I'd always popped off under extreme pressure owing to a life-or-death situation. I let out a breath, took aim at the dirty mason jars and bottles they'd set up on a fence post and squeezed the trigger on my exhale.

A chunk flew off the fence post down and to the right. Reaver laughed and I glanced in his direction, a surge of anger and a little adrenaline swirling through my veins. I *hated* being discounted for being a chick. Like somehow their cocks were a magic wand between their fucking legs. I popped my neck and letting my irritation fuel me, fired off the rest of the shots my dad's gun held. I hit all of the remaining targets and cleared my throat.

"Heh, not bad," Trigger relented.

"Beginner's luck," Reaver called.

"Shut it, Reaver!"

"Yeah, shut it, psycho!" I called over.

"You say that like it's a bad thing," he said and almost sounded affronted. I couldn't help it, I laughed.

"So if I'm seein' this right, you gotta be a little pissed to hit the target?" Trigger asked.

"I guess so," I muttered, emptying out the shell casings onto the ground and accepting bullets from him, loading the old gun a round at a time.

"Try this one," he said and brought out a matte black, more modern handgun. "More rounds for one, plus, I think it'll fit your hands better. I do get the sentiment, though."

I traded weapons with him and let out my breath slowly, firing on my exhale. The kick wasn't as bad as the old Colt, but at the same time, it was unfamiliar. I made my shot but didn't try firing in succession.

"Feels weird," I said a little self-consciously.

"I bet, but go on, you're doing good."

Bolstered by the lack of ridicule, I took out the rest of the glass that'd been lined up and turned to find the big man nodding and Reaver grinning with a shine of what looked like pride in his icy blue eyes.

"Confident I won't be blowing any of your balls off now?" I asked.

"Eh, I wouldn't go that far," he said and I looked up at him sharply. "Confident you won't be doing it on accident, though."

I blinked and asked, "Was that a joke?"

"He has been known to make them. You know, from time to time," Reaver remarked from his perch. He was scratching out dirt from under a fingernail with one of his switchblades.

"No. No intentions of blowing your balls off," I said handing over his gun. "At least not right now."

Trigger laughed and shook his head, "Never figured Data the kind to go for a firecracker like you," he said.

"Are you kidding me? I did," Reaver said getting up and jumping down from the car's trunk.

"Dude!" Trigger cried.

"And if I wasn't curious before, I am now…" I muttered.

"Let me guess, bro. Me and my big mouth?"

"Yeah, and I am taking myself and these guns away from this conversation…" he said and trudged through the tall, dry grass back towards the building.

I rolled my eyes. "Please, it's not like I expect that Kyle was celibate for seventeen years." He couldn't be and fuck like we did last night.

"Eh, let's just say it was his regular choice in club girl before she got snatched up…" Reaver said, and dare I say, actually looked pretty embarrassed.

I crossed my arms and debated on whether to sweat him or not, finally deciding to, but just a little.

"Just tell me," I said.

"Ahhhhh…" he bounced in place looking from left to right but Trig was gone and wasn't going to save him. Not from this one.

"Seriously, I promise not to be mad, but I'm curious."

He let out an explosive breath and said, "My cousin Shelly."

I raised an eyebrow, and asked, "You let your cousin whore around with your guy-pals?"

"Uh, no, Shelly does whatever the fuck Shelly wants to do. Leastways when it came to it, I knew who she was doin' it with and if any of 'em laid a hand on her…"

I nodded slowly, "all right, fair enough, I can see it."

"Anyways, it's been a couple of years. Shelly is Ghost's ol' lady now and off limits."

I stopped my head from its slow and steady bouncing and looked at him, "I get it," I told him. "And I am probably the last person to throw stones, living in a glass house." Still, I'd be lying if I said the potential of meeting someone that'd been intimate with Kyle wasn't weirding me out a little, but it was true… I understood he had a past. I had one, too. I could either accept it or let it eat me alive so I chose to accept it.

"Come on," he said looking me over and nodding himself. "It's hot as fuck out here."

"I know that's right. I'm not much of a fan of the daystar."

"Yeah?" he asked.

"Worked mostly on a sort of swing shift so I could avoid it."

He dragged open the back door and held it for me, "Oh yeah, what does someone on the lam do for a living?"

"I don't know about anyone else, but I'm a tattooist."

"Oh yeah? No shit?" Trigger asked, looking up from his phone.

"Got any of your stuff with you?" Reaver asked. "Like your drawings and shit?"

"I suppose it's as good a way as any to pass the time." I went for my messenger bag.

The two men circled almost like sharks, grabbing and setting up a dusty card table and planting a couple of folding chairs around it. I pulled the rolling desk chair across the cracked cement floor and parked it before up ending my bag on the table, letting them pick out a sketchbook to thumb through. I set about folding the clothes Kyle had bought me and decided that if I were going to be staying a while, I might as well unpack a little. I took the neatly folded garments with their price tags still attached over to one of the workbenches.

"When did you do this one?" Reaver asked and I shrugged without looking.

"I dunno, look at the date."

"There isn't one."

"Then it's probably the first book you've got, does it have the Nine Inch Nails sticker on the front of it?"

"Yeah."

"Then it was done in high school. Probably '98 through 2001 or so."

"Good likeness," Trigger commented and I turned around to see Reaver holding the book out to him. I blinked and realized it was the book I thought it was and, of course, realized too late the sentiment attached to some of those early drawings.

"Yeah, well, I'd been drawing a long time by then, since late elementary, maybe early junior high. I started dating everything in the next book. Seemed important."

"So like, these are your diary?" Reaver asked and I gave another shrug, going back over and dropping into the desk chair.

"I guess so."

"Oh, weird…" he closed the book and set it down like he'd just been caught going through my underwear drawer. I laughed.

"What's this?" he asked, picking up a small, black velvet bag.

"My old pocket knife."

He slipped the old red Swiss Army knife out of the bag and opened it up, wrinkling his nose as he tested the edge.

"I see you took care of this about as good as Trig says you took care of your daddy's gun." I frowned at him, but Trigger barked a laugh.

"I don't think that thing had been cleaned since your dad bought it," he remarked.

I snorted, "My dad didn't buy it," I said. "He either won it or stole it. My dad wasn't really in the habit of holding down an honest living or, you know, buying things if he could lift 'em or cheat 'em out of somebody."

"Apple fell far from the tree, didn't it?"

"Only because Kyle and his folks got to me and intervened. They did what they could to teach me the right way to do things and I've probably struggled with it ever since." I was watching Reaver by now, who was going through his many pockets, my poor, old, little pocket knife that hadn't actually cut anything in years open on the table in front of him. He gave an 'ah-ha' and produced a little whetstone out of one of his pockets.

"Got any oil on you, Trig?"

"What? Yeah, gun oil."

"That'll do for this, I think."

I sorted through the rest of my meager belongings, stacking my books, setting my art supplies near them, and generally just moving things around when Reaver stopped me again, thrusting his chin out and asking, "And what's that?"

"God, you're nosy, aren't you?" I teased.

"Maybe, now what is it?"

"They're my Tarot cards. Kyle bought them for me when we were," I rolled my eyes and my breath left me in a rush as I tried to remember exactly how old we were. "God... fifteen?"

"Oh yeah? You any good with 'em?"

"I dunno... You tell me." I unwrapped the deck and set it in front of him. "Shuffle."

He raised an eyebrow and looked over to Trigger who grumbled at him, "Don't look at me, asshole," without even looking up from the sketch he was absorbed in. I frowned slightly.

"You're looking at that thing like it's the map to the holy goddamned grail," I said.

He glanced at me over the top of the book and said, "It's good work, your lines are clean and your design well-thought-out. You as good with a needle as you are a pencil?"

I held out my arm and said, "What do you think?"

"You did these yourself?" he asked, leaning forward to scrutinize my forearm.

"Just the forearm, here. Awkward as fuck to reach the rest, so once I was sure Djinn had it down at the shop I used to work at, then I let him do all of the rest, but this one was important and the watercolor style isn't easy."

"It's a pretty new thing, that's for sure. Not many people do it."

"Which is exactly why I kicked its ass. Women love it."

Trigger nodded to himself and went back to my sketchbook. I turned back to Reaver and raised my eyebrows goading him on, "You gonna puss out over a deck of cards or are you gonna shuffle already?" I asked.

I was genuinely curious as to what the cards would tell me and so I didn't feel too bad about the slight manipulation to get him to pick them up. He set aside my tired old pocket knife and his tiny whetstone and swept the cards off the edge of the table into his long-fingered hands, shuffling them deftly. He was as light with the cards as he was with his knives, even pulling some dealer's tricks with them, shuffling them all fancy-like.

I gave a wry smile as he passed them back to me and said, "Going to do a simple three-card spread. Past, present, and future. Cool?"

"Cool," he agreed and scratched the side of his head.

I laid out all three cards face down in the proper order, let out a breath and focused inward, opening myself up to that space inside myself that let the energy *flow*. Opening myself up for interpretation, which I didn't do often for other people.

Okay, here we go... I thought to myself as I turned the first card like the page of a book, carefully over to see what was on its face.

"The Knight of Swords in reverse," I murmured, studying the card and feeling my heart sink a little.

"What's that mean?"

"Remember, this is your past. The Knight of Swords traditionally symbolizes intellect and thinking clearly. He is a Knight, so he stands for authority, however, in this case, he is shown reversed or in the negative."

"Okay, what's that mean?"

"Again, remember this is your past, and the interpretation that I get from this card isn't that it stands for *you* per se, but rather someone that was close to you. Reversed like this is harsh. I see a tyrant, an abuser. Someone who the very definition of kindness is anathema to him. It's definitely a 'him', too. I think you were raised by or around a man who it was best to get out of his way as much as possible. Does that sound right?"

By the way he was leaning back in his chair and the way his fingers gripped the edge of the table, mottled with the force with which he held on, I'd say I hit the nail on the head. I could sympathize. My dad seriously had his moments, but this? The overwhelming miasma of negativity emanating from that card told me that the depths of pain and brutality that he'd grown up with... well, my dad's moods didn't hold a candle by comparison.

"You said the next card is the present?" he asked, jaw tightening and I let the past go. Let it sink back into the dark where it belonged. I nodded and took a deep cleansing breath, shaking off the last card before I turned the next.

I turned it and blinked, "The Lovers, also reversed," I said, staring at the couple on the card. While in the negative, the feeling I got from this card wasn't nearly as ominous.

"Shit, is that bad? That's bad, isn't it?" Reaver asked and I smiled.

"Maybe not," I reassured him. "I get the feeling this one is more of a warning. The Lover's in negative like this typically means a misalignment with a loved one. Core values or perceptions may be skewed, leading to misunderstandings or unhappiness. A break up may be coming unless corrective action is taken. I'm going to seek clarification." I set down the deck and arched them in a neat fan in front of him.

"Choose a card."

He slid one from the fan and handed it across to me. I set it down on the corner of The Lovers and turned it over carefully.

"Hm, Ace of Cups, also reversed."

"Jesus H. Christ, could it get any worse?" he asked, but the laugh he attached was strained and nervous. Trigger had stopped looking over the sketches and was looking at his friend, worry etched in his expression.

"Not if you listen to what the cards have to say and take the corrective actions needed. Anyways, the Ace of Cup reversed typically stands for blocked emotions. One or the both of you are feeling stagnant. That's not the end of the world, buddy. That's flowers and a night on the town for most people, although I get a sense of anxiety here."

I blinked and sat back and looked up at him sharply saying, "I don't mean to be indelicate here, but the Ace of Cups reversed also sometimes means something else. Something more physical... are there problems with fertility?"

Reaver let out an explosive breath and even Trigger uttered a surprised, "Whoa."

"Yeah, I uh, I can get it up just great but my little swimmers... well let's just say they're no Michael Phelps..." he said, and I looked back down at the two cards, running my finger lightly across their surface and around their edges.

"It's you," I said. "Not her."

"What do you mean by that?" Trigger demanded, frowning.

"When it comes to the infertility, you need to let that one go," I said. "It's not her. It's you that is making too much of it. I get the feeling she's upset about something else. Something big, but back here..." I tapped to the left of the cards indicating the past but not nearly as far back in the past as the Knight of Swords... that I distinctly had the feeling was in his childhood. The way, *way*, back as opposed to just back when.

He nodded and let out a harsh sigh, "I know what you're talking about." He sounded sure of it. As sure as the knowledge that the sun would rise in the morning, so that meant my work was done with these cards.

"Good, if you know then knowing is half the battle. You can go and fix things. I get the distinct impression that the suit of swords coming up first wasn't an accident. That even though the Knight of Swords isn't *you*; that the suit *is*... Swords is the suit of intellect and cunning but also action. I'm confident that whatever this card is," I tapped the final unrevealed card denoting his future, "you already have a handle on it. Are you ready?"

He looked grim but finally nodded. "Do it."

I turned it over and smiled, "See, that's not bad. That's not bad at all. The Empress upright."

"Yeah, I'm reserving judgment until I know what it means," he said and I smiled.

"The Empress in her upright position stands for a lot of things. In this case, I get the impression that she represents a person. She can stand for beauty and abundance and typically relates to fertility but I don't get that she's doing so in a physical sense this time. She's a rockin' omen for a good and stable relationship, so that tells me that you definitely aren't taking this lightly and have every intention of taking some action here and heeding the warnings."

I tapped a fingernail at the base of the present's cards and Reaver nodded emphatically. I smiled and said, "Pick another card. I'll see if I can get anything else for you, this one feels like it's just laying the groundwork; like there's something more to tell."

He drew the final card from the fan in front of him and handed it over. I turned it and nodded, "See, Strength in the upright position. This screams that whatever is going on right now with your relationship to her, it's going to be fine. Strength like this reinforces the final meaning of The Empress which is harmony in the home. Strength upright like this points to compassion, endurance, patience… all the things a long-term relationship thrives off of. Bottom line, this card is telling you that you have the power to make the changes necessary to ensure survival but it's encouraging you to do it with love rather than force."

"When it comes to a woman, is there any other way *to* do it?" Trigger asked.

"Nope," Reaver stated and leaned back in his seat. He was seriously mulling it over, his icy blue eyes roving from one card to the next to the next, head bobbing slightly as he considered each one in turn.

"Thanks," he said finally, shaking himself as if waking from a dream.

"Hope it helps," I murmured and gathered the cards up letting the edges slide between my fingers into a neat stack once more. I silently thanked them for their service and glanced to Trigger and asked mostly out of politeness, "Want to have a go?"

He shook his head and I nodded. He seemed to be at solid peace with himself and his life. Like he had it together. I honestly didn't think that the cards had much to tell him. I put them away and sighed.

"Now what?" I asked.

"Now, we wait," Trigger said and I sighed.

"These kinds of things," Reaver said, dragging the edge of my pocket knife through oil against the stone. "You spend ninety-eight percent of your time being bored." He closed one eye and looked down the edge of the blade with the other, testing it with his thumb.

"And the other two percent?" I asked.

Trigger answered, "Wishing you were back to being bored."

I smiled and shook my head, pulling my newest sketch book across the table towards me and retrieving my roll of pencils from falling off the edge of the table and onto the floor.

"Good thing I was an only child," I said. "I have no shortage of ways to keep myself entertained."

"I know that's right," Reaver said and Trigger looked at him over the edge of the book in his hands again.

"You grew up with Shelly, motherfucker."

"So. I was still technically an only child. She's my cousin."

I shook my head and opened up to a blank page and listened to their affable bickering. The atmosphere a little lighter since the reading. I didn't know what to make of that, but I would take it.

16

D^{ata...}

I returned to Point Nowhere with food enough for myself and everyone there. It was late; much later than I wanted it to be. Not my first choice, not by a long shot, but the clubhouse's security needed a little more attention than I thought it did. It'd fallen into a little bit of disrepair in the last year after a couple of hardcore storms had swept through and toppled some branches that'd held cameras and downed lines.

Everything was up and running smooth as butter now, but really, what needed the attention was Point Nowhere. That was the next project over the couple of days or so. Once that was accomplished, it was going to be a long haul of springing the trap and slamming energy drinks to make sure that our prey was lured in hook, line, and sinker.

Mali was standing in the doorway, practically humming with the need to come out into the dark and touch me and I couldn't get the fucking bags of teriyaki off the back of the bike fast enough to get to her.

"I told you not to wait up," I called and reveled in the smart-assed little smirk that painted her lips as she shot back, "And I do what I want."

"Can't argue with you there," I said softly pulling her into my arms and kissing her intently.

Her arms twined around me and I felt like given a chance she would climb me like a fucking tree, and fuck if I didn't love the shit out of her passion... Not to mention return it like a thousand-fold.

"Dude, is that food? I'm fuckin' hungry!" I heard Reaver call out and I held out the two bags of Styrofoam clam shells out past Mali through the door. The weight of the plastic grocery bags was lifted from my fingers and I took the sudden freedom to fill both hands with Mali's ass, hauling her tight up against me. She smiled and laughed where her mouth was pressed against mine, the giggle making my heart soar and I don't know how long we spent like that, suspended in our self-made moment of happiness.

We had to grab them while we could and exploit that shit for all it was worth. I don't think either of us was keen on taking our mere presence within each other's reach for granted. At least not anytime soon.

"I missed you," she murmured and I trailed fingertips from her temple to her chin. She closed her eyes and kissed the pad of my thumb and my cock went from half-mast to all the way erect faster than I ever remembered it doing before.

"Yeah? The natives been restless?" I asked.

"A bit, but nothing I couldn't handle..."

"Come and eat before this shit gets cold," Trigger called and I reluctantly let her down from her toes to stand flat-footed in front of me.

"He has a point."

"As soon as we can send them packing, I'm blowing you," she said. I laughed and followed her into the building, despite the surge of surprised unease her proclamation gave me.

We sat around a card table that'd been erected, Mali shuffling her sketch books into a neat stack in the center of it to give us room. It looked like she and Trig had been drawing while Reave had been meticulously sharpening every blade in Mali's old pocket knife. I gave a low whistle and reached across for it and he handed it over.

"Never thought I'd see this again, I'm kind of amazed you've still got it."

"I didn't get to hold on to much, just what I could carry, and you can never underestimate how much having a good knife can mean in so many situations."

"On that, we can agree," Reaver said with his mouth full and held out a fist to Mali to bump. She grinned, pleased and bumped knuckles with him. I handed the little knife back over.

"So what's the plan?" Trigger asked.

"Got to get this place up to code with cameras and shit the next couple of days then I cast a line and see what we can hook."

"Sounds like a plan," Reaver said smiling a little too enthusiastically, shoveling more food into his face.

Mali, however, looked grim. She sighed and said, "I just want this to be over… Kind of can't believe it's going to be, you know?"

"You been livin' it for seventeen years, babes. I don't think there's a light bright enough for the end of a tunnel that long." Trigger gave a gusty sigh and she nodded, spearing more chicken on the end of her fork.

"Yeah, I hear that," she agreed.

The rest of dinner went by pretty quiet, the gravity of the situation weighing each of us down, each of us for our own personal reasons.

Soon enough, the guys were done eating. Trigger gathered up their empty food containers and shoved them away into a spare plastic sack.

"Pack these out for you," he said and I nodded.

"Thanks, man."

"No worries. We'll see you tomorrow. I'm going to have to leave part way and get back to the shop… I've got clients."

"No worries," I repeated him. "I appreciate everything you've done, everything you're doing."

"Ain't nothin' you ain't done for me, brother. It may be easy for citizen motherfuckers to forget when they've been done a good turn but isn't that part of why we're in this life, to begin with?"

I nodded, "Too true, man, too true."

"All right, get a good night's sleep."

"Not a problem."

I embraced him and Reave each on their way out, the rush of water going off behind me causing me to look over my shoulder. Mali was drawing a bath, and I had to wonder if I smelled, suddenly secretly self-conscious about it. I'd been sweating my balls off just about all day resetting and fixing cameras around the club's compound so it was likely.

"Enjoy," Reaver said with a wild grin.

"I know *that's* right," I shot back and he ducked out. I shut the door behind them and it was like an almost physical shift, the way the energy of the building, the mood, changed. Like I'd suddenly just hermetically sealed me and my girl into some much-needed solitude together despite the clear rumble of the bikes starting up outside.

I went over to Mali who was running her hand through the water filling the trough. She straightened and let me pull her close. Her mouth still tasted of the sweet, sticky teriyaki sauce and I smiled against it.

"Need to brush your teeth," I murmured.

"Fuck you, then you need to brush yours, too."

"Hmm, grab our shit and meet me back here?"

"Yeah, where you hiding it?"

I chuckled, "Figured you would have gone through my things out of sheer boredom by now."

"Hey, just because I have no shame or real expectation of privacy doesn't mean I don't value other people's," she argued.

"Fair enough, baby."

She was right. She didn't care what people thought of her and she had no need for secrecy when it came to material things. I knew that much and more about how she operated. She didn't keep objects as secrets. All of her secrets she kept locked away inside of herself and if she didn't want to share, she wouldn't. Still, that being said, I didn't ever remember a time she didn't share her secrets with *me*. Up until she disappeared, that is.

I pulled my tee off over my head and kicked out of my boots. I felt naked without my cut, but it was locked away safe in the footlocker at the base of my bed in my clubhouse room. None of us liked going incognito, the Sacred Hearts had always been a force to be reckoned with and it felt disingenuous to all of us to hide our colors. Still, we had more to think about than just our own skins and if anything happened to the women or children…

I shuddered. I'd been a prospect when the shit had gone down with Tillie and the rest, and I didn't ever want to see that kind of thing happen again. I got into the trough, easing down into the hot water, muscles starting to tighten up and get sore on me already. Mali dumped the last two bath bombs in and set the rest of the soaps and shit onto the stool to the side of the tub within easy reach.

"Bottle of water there," she said indicating it and the tooth brush and paste next to it.

"Get in here," I demanded and she smiled.

"Thought you'd never ask." She stripped down slowly and stepped in, gasping. "A little hotter than I expected." She sank down between my knees and eased back against my chest, sighing in contentment as I put my arms around her, cradling her close.

I closed my eyes and just relished the feel of her in my arms. The tub filled slowly around us, wrapping us in warmth and soothing aching muscles. I don't think a single one of my dreams compared to the reality. Not even close. She sighed lightly and relaxed completely and we didn't have to speak. It was like all those times, under our tree. We would lay there for hours, listening to the leaves rustle in the breeze and never even had to say a word. Yet every time we got up to drag ourselves reluctantly home, I got up feeling like it was the best conversation we ever had.

She cuddled back into me and I smoothed my hands along her skin beneath the water. She groaned and sat up, turning off the tap before settling back against me and without the cascading sound of the filling trough, the echoing silence in the building resounded.

"It's supposed to storm tonight," I murmured and she didn't say anything, just gave a faint "Mm," in response. I smiled to myself and chuckled lightly, letting my hands sweep over her in a gliding touch beneath the surface, kissing the side of her neck. She sighed out but it didn't sound like a good thing; if anything it sounded frustrated as all get out. I frowned.

"What's wrong?"

"Ahhhh," she groped for what to say, and I kneaded her shoulders, patiently waiting her out. "You're all grown up..." she said finally and I wasn't catching whatever double entendre she was putting out there.

"And so are you..." I said tweaking a knot in her back. She gasped and made an adorable growly sound that quickly turned exasperated.

131

"Fine, I was trying to be subtle and save us both some embarrassment, but since you won't get with the fucking program I'll just come out with it!"

"Yes, please do. I wouldn't have it any other way."

"Your fucking junk is bigger than my poor pussy can handle."

I froze, and then couldn't help myself, I burst out laughing. Mali growled again and that only made me laugh harder. She turned around and splashed me, irritated and I threw up my hands to fend off her onslaught.

"I'm sorry! I'm sorry! It's not funny, but oh man, it's *really funny!*"

She was smiling to belay any notion that she was really irritated and I wiped tears from the corners of my eyes. I must be a little out of it with fatigue or something for this to be that funny, but I couldn't help it. It just struck me as hilarious for some reason.

"Why do you think I was sayin' I'd blow you?" she asked defensively, and the laughter died, right then and there, and I pulled her to me and kissed her soundly.

"You don't need to go there with me," I whispered against her lips and she broke eye contact and stared fixedly at the side of the tub.

"I want to," she said and I studied her face. Everything about it said she did but that she was scared or nervous. Mali had been handed a shit hand in life, and a set of the cards she'd been dealt was that she'd been bullied hardcore in school. I usually was there to diffuse some of the situation. I mean, no one, for some reason, really had a problem with me... but Mali, being poorer, being from the proverbial wrong side of the tracks... She'd been stubborn, had fought back time and again. She'd faced suspensions, had even whooped some ass in some real scrapes but that hadn't stopped the three ringleaders of her little bully squad from sexually assaulting her.

The twisted fucks hadn't thought it was rape, I mean, they wouldn't dare stick their dick in Mali's crazy... at least not in her vagina. They'd beat her to within an inch of her life during homecoming of Junior year and had forced her to fellate every last one of them. She'd spent a few days in the hospital and as far as her dad knew, it'd stopped with the beating... but like most secrets, Mali had told me all of it.

I'd gotten my cold hard revenge. I'd hacked into the public records department and set some nuclear time bombs in her three assailant's lives. I'd set death certificates to issue for all three of them around their early twenties. It was sure to cause them no end of headaches, proving to various companies and government agencies that no, they were indeed still alive. Probably would fuck them out of graduating college on time, and I know, in at least one case, it was a years-long nightmare.

Still, it wasn't enough. I was super disturbed that it still affected her this deeply, but sadly, not really surprised.

"You don't have to do anything with me that makes you uncomfortable. You tell me to stop, I stop. It's as simple as that."

"I know that," she said, rolling her eyes, but she stopped when I gripped her upper arms intently. Her gaze lasered in on mine but cooled the instant it met my stare's intensity.

"You tell me to stop, I stop, Mali."

"Okay," she murmured and swallowed uncertainly. I didn't mean to rattle her, but her knowing I valued her was important to me. I don't think she'd probably had many lovers who did. I didn't know. It wasn't something we had talked about much, yet... the in-between time. So much about each other was left a mystery and I hated that, but if there was something I knew about Mali, she didn't let people get close. Not like me, not like us... I didn't know why I was the special one, but I thanked whatever powers that be that she had chosen me. I held myself to a lofty standard, and I knew she could trust me. Which is why the separation that was to come was killing me inside.

"I love you," I whispered, the approaching rumble of thunder nearly drowning it out.

"I trust you," she said and twisted fully to straddle my lap. "I don't offer things like that up unless I do…" She rested her forehead against mine and cradled my face with one hand. Slowly she lowered her lips to mine and kissed me, a gentle contact of lips. I kissed her back, but let her go at her pace.

"I don't like thinking about it too much," she confessed and I nodded.

"Consider the subject dropped."

"Can we not bring it up again?"

"For now, but I'm not going to let it go back into the dark completely," I said honestly. "Eventually we've got to drag some of these demons into the light and let the light kill them."

"Therapy?" she asked, and she made it sound like a dirty word.

"No, just you and me, like we've faced everything else. We just didn't really get the time back then to deal with this particular monster under your bed."

Her gaze flicked down to the shimmery water of our bath and fixed there. She sighed and it was heavy and asked, "One thing at a time, yeah?"

"We've got the rest of our lives to figure it out, baby. I promise."

Her hands came up from beneath the water and fixed one on top of the other over my mouth. She frowned at me as I let out a surprised and muffled "Mmph!" and she glared at me accusingly.

"Don't you dare jinx us, Kyle Cochran," she hissed and I smiled slightly against her palm. I was wondering when my superstitious gypsy girl was going to show up to the party. I put my arms around her waist and raised an eyebrow, her hands slowly lowering from my mouth.

I resisted the urge to wipe the water dripping down my chin away and said honestly, "I have the ultimate good luck charm this run, baby."

She rolled her eyes, "Better be one big fucking rabbit's foot."

I grinned, "Try about a dozen badass motherfuckers. It's going to be fine."

"Yeah," she said, drawing in a shuddering breath, "Famous last words."

"Don't do that," I said sharply and she looked at me.

"What?"

"Quit trusting me now."

She stopped, jerked back as if she'd never considered the notion then said after a peal of closer thunder, "Metal building, metal tub, let's get you washed up and get out of this thing before we become fricassee."

I laughed, "Sounds all right to me."

17

A malia...

Fifteen hours. That's how long it took for them to reach us from the time Kyle switched on my laptop and connected to the internet. It'd been around nine o'clock after two intense days of getting the piece of property we were on set up and ready to rock and roll. We'd gotten eight hours of sleep, the guys that were staying with us taking up scattered cots around the available space, which had pretty much put the kibosh on Kyle and me getting it on. I wasn't *quite* that level of exhibitionist.

Eight solid hours of sleep, then we all got up and took our positions. Kyle was behind his keyboard and mouse, eyes on multiple screens and camera angles. I was at his side marveling at the amount of technical know-how he'd amassed since we were kids. I mean, he'd always been into computers, but this was nuts, way above my pay-grade. My messenger bag sat at my feet fully packed and ready to go, as the plan was as soon as the shit went down and we were through it, I was supposed to go with Reaver to a nearby safe house. I was okay with that, but only because I was going to see Kyle later on.

Anyways, seven hours after the guys took position, the first alarm went off. Kyle clicked a couple of keys and the mouse once, and the biggest screen was suddenly splattered with a view of the road, and three black SUV's climbing into the hills.

Trigger came over the radio, "Tint's too dark to make out how many, but they damn sure out-number what we've got on the ground."

Dragon came on and I looked up at him standing just inside the door to the building, "That's what we got you for, not to mention the home-field advantage. I wouldn't panic just yet."

"Got six of 'em moving through the woods," Archer came over the radio and his voice was low, careful.

"Oooh, it's show time!" Reaver sounded excited. Kyle was pointing out movement on screens and I slipped my dad's gun out of my waistband just to have it ready, just in case.

"Keep it silent, boys. Also, keep it last minute if you can, taking these fuckers out might tip off the rest o' their clan."

"Copy," Archer muttered over the line.

"You suck," Reaver pouted.

Some tall grass and a branch thrashed in the corner of my eye on one screen and I looked, a man with an arrow through his throat sliding, face first, back out of view.

"One down," Data murmured.

"Two," Reaver grunted.

"Three," Trigger muttered.

"Four." Archer.

"Five." Reaver.

"Six." Archer again.

"Any deviation?" Dragon asked.

"Nope," Data said and added for my benefit, "This is how we do it. Smooth as butter."

I punched him lightly in his well-developed shoulder and hissed, "Don't jinx it!" But he wasn't paying me any mind. Instead, he called out, to the team both here and over the radio, "Second wave incoming."

His voice was all business, in total control, and reminded me of how he got when we'd played video games as kids. It was one of those moments where it was a cross between being adorable and having such terrifying overtones it left you speechless and grim. I rolled my lips together and breathed in deep, letting it out slow, anxiety and the urge to *do* something, to be *useful* somehow, making my skin crawl.

"They aren't slowing down," Trigger stated and Dragon cursed.

"So pump the brakes, Big Man. You're the only one who can," he said into the radio.

The SUV's were coming up the driveway, and the first one, movie-perfect, which was really what this felt like seeing it play out on the screen like this, had a perfect hole develop in the windshield over where the driver's head should be. The car swerved and went into the split log and wire fence at the side of the sloping field leading up to the building we were in.

"Start pickin' em' off," Kyle ordered, and I realized that this wasn't Kyle anymore. This was the man seventeen years in the making, during my absence. This was Data... a cold, calculating biker who could casually order the cold-blooded murder of men he didn't know. I swallowed hard, and let the guilt swamp me, rush over and through me, swirling once inside before I ushered it out the back and focused on getting both him and me out of this situation alive.

I turned him into this... I realized, and it wasn't a good feeling.

"Get what I can, but I ain't got a bead on most of 'em," Trigger said before I heard rounds popping off just outside, *loud*. Louder than I expected.

"Take cover!" Zeb shouted in his thick accent through the radio.

"Shit! Fuck! Goddammit, they're gonna breach!" Rush shouted and I pulled on Kyle, dragging him out of his chair and to the floor, Dragon echoing the movement, just as whoever was outside opened up on the building with an automatic weapon.

Sparks and plastic shards flew from the equipment on Kyle's desk. Shouting, screaming, some of it mine echoed in my ears that suddenly felt as if I was hearing everything from under water. A ringing took up in them and I shoved Kyle down.

Dragon and I made eye contact from across the cracked cement floor and I was galvanized. Action, we needed action or this was going to be much worse.

I think Kyle shouted, his fingers scrabbling over my jeans-clad leg, and slipping over the leather of the back of my boot. I got up into a low crouch and skittered across the floor and, breath pistoning in and out of my lungs, chest cramped hard with dread, I ducked out the swinging door and out into the yard and the blazing sun and shot the first man standing.

"Keep one alive!" Dragon shouted and he was next to me. The one I had shot went down like a felled tree, clutching his throat.

"Zeb is hit!" Rush screamed and an arrow whizzed, taking another man low, in the hip. He went down, eyes wide behind his ballistics mask clutching at the wound and I didn't think I just acted. I scrambled low across the dirt and grabbed him by the shoulders of his vest and hauled him towards the open door behind me. Dragon was covering us, popping up from behind the hulk of car we'd rolled in front of the door in preparation for this and shooting. Rush and Zeb were behind two more we'd set up as a barricade, and while Zeb was on the ground, pale and panting, he was *still* reloading his gun, leaning out and firing.

The man I was pulling on was reaching for his gun and I dropped him, ripping off his mask and without thinking just started smashing him in the face and head with the butt of my daddy's gun. He was trying to fight back, a glancing blow skidding along my cheek as the cacophony of gunfire raged around us. Some of the men in their tactical gear were folding like cheap paper, others falling back and ripping at their gear, surprised to find they weren't dead.

The man and I struggled, his gun cleared the holster and I grabbed his hand, forcing it down, screaming in impotent rage that he just wouldn't give up! He was forcing my hand, I couldn't stop. It was him or me and I pointed the barrel of my dad's gun down and pulled the trigger, his blood and brains painting the ground, my boots, and part of my pants leg in a sticky, crimson starburst pattern.

Hands grabbed me from behind and hauled me into the building and I screamed, turning the gun; my wrist was grabbed and forced up; the weapon went off, harmlessly away from everyone else, thank god; and Kyle's face entered my vision. I stopped resisting and he pulled me inside, Dragon following, and I caught one order from the older man.

"Let them advance!"

The trap was set, Kyle mouthed 'trust me' and I did; so I followed orders, I fell back, and even though it went against everything I stood for, I let the men take the lead…

18

D ata…

"Go with Reaver, baby." I held her face between my hands and kissed her forehead which was salty from sweat and her smeared tears. She didn't take killing a man lightly, even though she'd done it twice and wouldn't hesitate if it came to it again. Strong, brave, but so very human and with a heart… some of the qualities I would forever love about my girl.

"Soon, I'll see you soon, right?" she demanded and I felt the bitterness of the lie on my tongue, even as I spoke it anyway.

"Yeah, I'll see you soon."

"Okay… okay…" we'd taken two alive, and both of them were on their knees, bleeding from superficial injuries that were about to get a whole lot worse. Some of the rest of the club were already on their way out to begin a rapid clean-up. Doc was among them to tend to Zeb, who'd taken a shot to the outside of his thigh, more substantial than a graze, but nowhere near the femoral artery and it didn't look like he'd broken the femur.

Still, Rush was with Zeb as he grunted and huffed, and tried not to scream as Rush tightened the tourniquets high up, dangerously close to Zeb's nuts.

"You catch one of the boys in this medieval torture racket, we ain't gonna be mates anymore, yeah." He said and Rush laughed.

"Don't be a fuckin' baby," Archer grunted, lighting a cigarette.

"Come on, Queenie," Reaver said, adopting the nickname given to her by Revelator. "We've gotta go." He hefted her messenger bag, plastic bits from my slaughtered systems and glass from some of the monitors slipping off its red vinyl top flap to tick and tinkle against the cement floor.

"Right behind us, right?" she asked, and I nodded saying, "As soon as we clean up this mess."

She followed Reave reluctantly. They had a bit of a hike through the woods to get to where the bikes were parked and get the fuck out of here. I watched them go, kissed my fingertips and held them up and out to her. She did the same, and then she was out the door.

I turned grim, went over to the first guy and pulled the gaffing tape off from over his mouth. He instantly spit in my face and I punched him right in his fucking mouth, his teeth scraping my knuckles and taking some skin. His head snapped back and he groaned, and when it fell forward again it was right back to the tape over his lips. Fuck that.

I pulled a bandana out of my back pocket and wiped away his spit and went to the next guy.

"Now I got some questions, we all do, and if you answer them, this might not go as badly for you as it's going to go for your friend... you feel me?" I asked.

I'd seen these interrogations more than once in my life since joining the club, but this was the first time I'd taken a willing step off that ledge and into the abyss of no return. I couldn't think of a better reason on this good, green earth to do it than for Amalia Rose, either.

The man looked wary and nodded slowly. I smiled and I knew it wasn't friendly. He'd picked the wrong boss to work for, and I wanted to know exactly who that was. I was much nicer about peeling the tape off of him. A little kindness in these scenarios went a long ways.

19

A malia...

I followed Reaver through tall grass and trees, his pace rushed, taking the terrain in long, ground-eating strides that left me struggling to keep up, not to mention out of breath, but my pride refused to let me ask him to slow down. I was my father's daughter that way, and if I had to have a cardinal sin to rule me, it was a toss-up between pride and anger.

We reached the bikes, parked off an old dirt country backroad in a clearing. He got astride his, holding out a helmet to me. I put it on as he put his on and put on some eyewear. He handed me a pair of women's sunglasses and I put them on, knowing that my eyeliner hadn't run, being that'd I had permanently tattooed some of it on me, only using the actual cosmetic when I wanted a thicker line or a different look.

"Get on," he ordered and I did, settling myself behind him, wrapping my arms around him.

"How far is it to the safe house?" I asked, and I should have realized right then by his answer that something wasn't right.

"We'll get there when we get there, Queenie," he called over the sudden roar of the engine starting.

I swallowed hard, trusting in Kyle, and held on as we lurched out onto the pitted dirt track out of here.

Six Weeks Later

~

20

A malia...

Something like nine or ten hours after the showdown, we pulled into some fucking town I'd never heard of, Ft. Royal, fucking *Florida*. I'd been *pissed*; but now, six weeks later, the place *almost* felt like it could be home except for one thing.

No Kyle.

Like I said, I'd been fucking *pissed* when we'd gotten here. Angry with Reaver, pissed off with this new set of biker assholes The Kraken, and ready to fucking punch something. That something had been Reaver at first, but that hadn't quite worked out, then to add insult to injury, the Kraken Prez's ol' lady, Hope had stepped up.

She whooped my ass before I could snarl anything about her ol'man having a flaccid cock. I'd been on the ground quicker than lightning, in a joint lock that could have – and would have – busted my elbow if I'd moved and that'd cooled me off a bit. When they'd disarmed me and were sure I wasn't going to try anything, they'd let me up.

I didn't cry, but it was a near thing. I was just that angry.

They'd put me on a secure face time call with Kyle who looked like he was so full of hurt, fear, and regret, my anger had chilled the rest of the way, which just turned it back on itself and pissed me off a whole new way.

"Mad at me?" he'd asked, and I'd felt utterly defeated in the face of it. He knew. He'd always known. The only man, the only person on the planet who knew me better than I knew myself and he still had it… even after all that time.

A blur of turquoise and white dropped onto the low rock wall next to me, blurting out, "Hey, whatcha thinkin'?" I startled and knocked off my sightless staring and looked over at Faith, the ol' lady to The Kraken's VP.

"About the night I got here."

She grinned and knocked her shoulder into mine and sighed, "And?"

"Still pissed," I said wrinkling my nose impishly. It'd become a running joke now, but I still felt bitter and tumultuous over it. Mostly because I *missed* him. It wasn't fair. We'd only just found each other again to be separated and I *still* didn't know how to feel about the fact that he didn't trust me enough to tell me the plan. *"But he was right."* the little voice, ever-present in the back of my mind, whispered.

Of course, he was. Still, it didn't mean I had to fucking like it.

"I love you, baby, but I need to focus on this part…"

I closed my eyes. We hadn't been able to talk much since that night. Mostly when we did talk, it was via text messaging, again, through secure accounts and shit. The setup on my end had been provided courtesy of The Kraken's technically inclined guru, Radar. I kind of had to admit at that point that these bikers weren't assholes either.

"Sorry," I muttered, realizing I'd gone back inside my own head and had completely missed whatever Faith had just said to me.

"It's okay," she murmured, always patient, always kind.

I sighed harshly and shook my head, "No, it's really not..."

"It is!" she insisted, sweeping her long, blonde, beachy waves over one shoulder and pulling them through her hands. She smiled at me, "I have a hard enough time being away from Marlin when he goes on a fishing trip longer than a day without me, I couldn't imagine six weeks away from him."

I nodded, then shook my head again. "We only just found each other." I sighed and apologized again, standing up. "Sorry, I'm really just not in the mood or the best company right now," I told her.

"Hey, no, I get it. I still have my bad days, too." I could believe it, her turquoise eyes the color of the water around here, were always slightly haunted. Her sister Hope had filled me in some on that over one too many beers one night. While I couldn't exactly relate, I could relate; if that made sense. While free, I'd still been in an extended captivity, and I knew what sexual assault felt like, even if I didn't classify what'd happened to me as *rape*, it was... I mean... yeah. I tried to cover up my deep and dirty thoughts with some forced levity.

"One of these days I'm going to get you to 'fess up and tell me, 'Yeah, Mali, you're totally being a whiny bitch!'"

She laughed, "Well, not today, I'm afraid."

"I'm going to go for a swim."

"Sure, dinner should be up in an hour or so, though."

I nodded and trudged through the soft sand down to the shore. When I got there, I unknotted the sari wrap at my hip and let it flutter to the sand. Kicking out of my thongs, I walked barefoot the rest of the way into the water.

Swimming helped to both pass the time and keep me fit, and while I would have never swum in the Chesapeake back in Indigo City, that was mostly due to the combination of the water temperatures being too cold and the fear of pollution, being near a major metropolis.

Speaking of Indigo City, in a major twist of fate and fat irony, three weeks back it'd been plastered all over the news. The Boyle Irish crime family had all but fucking collapsed. Arrests were being made left and right and there was a mountain of state's evidence against them. Everything from drug to human trafficking. I'd had to shake my head. Leave it to my dad to fucking hide us right under their damn noses... Of course, if you really wanted to hide something, you had to do it in plain sight.

Still, having them arrested was only part of the equation. The Italian crime bosses had proved, time and time again, it was just as easy to run a crime syndicate from prison as it was from anywhere else. Kyle assured me they were working on it, and to be patient. Meanwhile, I sat here and grew more and more frustrated with the whole damn situation. I was still hiding, I still wasn't safe, but hey, at least I knew what I'd done to incur this life sentence. Apparently, the kid I'd shot had been Danny Boyle's only son.

I dove under the water and swam deep until my lungs burned and I was forced to return to the surface. I'd been able to stay down longer and longer, which I was happy with; my endurance was improving. I kind of felt like I needed to stay on top of that still. Like I was going to have to make a run for it any minute. It was one of the reasons I still kept my messenger bag always packed. One, I didn't know if I was going to have to run again but more importantly, I never knew when I was going to need it to fucking *go home*... Wherever that was, anymore.

Where it is, is with Kyle and wherever he *is...* my traitorous brain whispered.

"Hey, Mali!" the masculine voice was faint, drifting out over the water, and I bobbed, treading the waves and turned back towards shore. Cutter stood on the edge where sand met the sea, waving his arm above his head. I gave him a chin lift, realized he probably couldn't see it and made strong, sure, strokes towards shore.

I got my feet under me and marched the rest of the way out of the low waves calling out, "I thought dinner was in an hour."

"Dinner's in about a half an hour now, Darlin', but I figured you were gonna wanna see this." He held out a towel to me with one hand and an iPad in the other. I scowled and took the towel, my fingers itching for the news. I wrapped my body, and tucked the end under one arm and snatched the device as soon as I felt I wouldn't get it all wet.

Danny Boyle Dead! I blinked and looked up to Cutter.

"As in the head of the Boyle crime family?"

"That would be the one," he declared grinning.

I scowled and let my eyes tread over every word in the article, which wasn't much. He was shanked in the middle of a prison cafeteria riot, died of his injuries before anyone could get help. I swallowed hard and let my eyes rove over the image of a shrewd old man in a suit, eyes glowering from beneath substantial white brows as he leaned in at his last court appearance to hear what his lawyer had to say.

I handed the iPad back and looked up to Cutter's beaming smile and warm, smiling brown eyes.

"I need a beer," I declared.

"All right! Now that's what I'm talkin' about!" he declared and I walked side by side with him up the beach. He bent and scooped up my wrap and sandals and held the things out with an arched brow, silently asking if I wanted them.

"No, I'm good," I said, but I wasn't. At least not really. So much was going through my mind at once and I couldn't put any of it into words if I'd wanted to. In the end, I had to shrug... so he was dead... in the grand scheme of things, it didn't make a difference. I was still here, Kyle was still there, and I still felt like I was on the run. I mean, I guess it just wasn't real yet.

"Got a lot going on up in that head of yers, ain't yah?" he asked.

"Yeah," I agreed, but I didn't expand on it. One of the things that was nice about Cutter and his crew is they didn't try too hard to make me. At least most of them. Cutter was particularly good at letting it go.

"Go on and wash up, supper should be on the table by the time you get done."

I nodded and took my unhappy ass upstairs. I grabbed a few things out of my bag and shut myself into the bathroom. A hot shower was made to order to rinse all the sand away and the seawater out of my hair. I'd dyed my ends again, a deep, sea-blue fading into a teal-green. I wondered if Kyle would like it the next time we video chatted. Then I wondered if he would even be able to see it. Most of our chats happened at night, typically in the dark, just the blue-white light of whatever screen illuminating us.

I rested my forehead against the cool tile, the steam rising around me, and sucked in a few deep breaths, letting them out slowly. I was *not* going to lose my shit. I was *not* going to cry... but of course, the second I thought that was the second I felt my face crumble and the hot rush of tears. Of course, this was the only safe place to let it out so I sat my ass down in the bottom of the tub and choking down on making too much noise, I let fly. If I didn't, I *was* going to lose my shit, completely, and I couldn't. I wouldn't. My father hadn't raised a weak little girl, but he'd sure left one behind, buried deep inside.

I hated that about myself. It was one of my deepest, darkest secrets and the one I hadn't even let Kyle in on. I didn't know if I would ever let that one out to see the light of day.

A knock fell at the door, a man's voice, sounded like Marlin, calling out, "Mali?"

"Yeah!" I called back, voice strong, no hint of the tears I turned my face into the spray to rinse off, letting it at all go down the drain. I was fine. I was hard, solid, a force to be reckoned with.

"Yeah, dinner's on the table. Come and get it."

"Cool, thanks!" I called back.

I got my ass out of the shower, dried off, pulled on the short-shorts I'd had donated to my woefully inadequate wardrobe and threw on one of the loose tank tops that Kyle had bought me. This one was black with silver writing on it that said 'Believe' with a couple of stars around it, the ones made from intersecting lines with one central focal point, not the five-pointed kind.

I whipped a brush through my hair, snarling at my reflection when it caught and pulled but I wasn't trying to waste everyone's time, either. I whipped it into a braid over my shoulder, tying it off as I descended the last couple of stairs into the dining room and kitchen. Looked like dinner was outside tonight, on the stone porch through the back sliding door.

I went out, the patio lit by citronella tiki torches and froze. I had to blink several times to make sure I was seeing things right. I mean, his back was to me, the patches of his cut faded and dirty, but the vest and jacket they rode on was well taken care of. His hair had been cut, which was a good idea, I mean, it was hot down here.

Nervous chuckles went around the table and he turned around, and of course, as it had ever been between us, I blurted out the first thing that came to mind.

"You son of a bitch!" Kyle grinned at me, joy filling his warm brown eyes, and I declared, "I missed you."

Couldn't stop these tears, they came out of nowhere, blurring my vision as he closed the gap between us and crushed me against him. I shuddered, an irritating broken little sob escaping into his shoulder as I wrapped my arms around him and held him so tight I didn't care if it hurt.

"Awww," Hope, Faith, and Charity chorused and there was some feel-good masculine laughter.

"I missed you, too, baby…" he pressed his lips to my damp hair and cradled my body with one arm, his other hand pressing my face into his shoulder to help hide me from the onlookers. Goddammit, he knew me so well.

"Guys, give us a minute?" he asked gently and chairs scraped against the stone, the slider opened and the tread of booted feet moved past us while I shook in his arms. The door slid shut, and I managed to hold my shit together for a few heartbeats more but then I lost it.

It was real. I was free. I was *home*.

21

D ata...

"Shhh, I've got you," I murmured against her ear, but I didn't try to stop her. This was Mali in a storm. I'd only seen it once before, when she confessed what'd happened to her way back when, and it scared me as much now as it had then. I knew, though, that when she broke this thoroughly, when she lost her shit this completely, it was just temporary. When she came back, it was stronger and better than ever.

"You lied to me," she warbled into my cut and I smiled but it was a sad thing.

"I know, I'm sorry, and I swear it will *never* happen again."

"What happened to no more games? Not between us?" she cried and her pain was almost more than I could bear.

"I am so fucking sorry, baby. I didn't want to but I knew you would never agree to this long apart."

"You *promised!*" she shuddered and broke down some more and I had to hand it to her, as well as I knew her, as much as I loved her, she still surprised me. Things I fully expected her to be upset over she shrugged like it wasn't anything. Things I expected she would shrug like it wasn't anything would stick with her and bother her to no end. I hadn't known where this one would fall on the spectrum, but I knew now and it predictably, crushed me too.

"I know, baby, I know and I am so sorry."

She thrust herself back from me and hit me – granted, ineffectually – twice, in the chest, pushing me back, and screamed at me, "You can't *do* that to me, Kyle!"

I knew this about my Mali Rose, too. She couldn't fight against the things that were really turning her upside down and inside out, so she was picking the thing that she could rage about; the fight that she could win. She was pouring all of the rage, frustration, and pain into that, and I let her. It was like using a thermonuclear device to kill termites, total overkill, but I got it. I got her, so I did what I was supposed to. I let her have what she needed; I let her win.

She stood there, shaking, trembling like a leaf in a storm and when I was sure that she wasn't going to try and hit me for real, I went to her and pulled her in again. Cuddling her close, I kissed her temple and breathed her in and swore to her, "Never again."

She nuzzled into me miserably and I smiled, knowing I'd been forgiven, even as she asked weakly, "Promise?"

"I promise."

I waited for an accusing *'you promised last time'* but it didn't come, and that's the point I could tell I was forgiven. It wasn't precisely a game, but it was. One that I played dutifully, and had since we were kids, and one she didn't even know she had a piece on the board for. She really, genuinely, didn't know she did it.

"I hate that you know just what to say, sometimes," she grumbled and I laughed and tipped her face up to mine.

"You love me just for that reason, too," I chided and she frowned.

"Ass," she muttered, but she didn't stop me from kissing her, and all was right in our world again. Truce declared.

I had to guess the guys of The Kraken sort of guessed the coast was clear because the sound of the back slider opening up interrupted our kiss, which to be honest, had gone on a little longer than was polite anyway, so I couldn't be mad about it.

"Y' all right, darlin'?" Cutter asked and Mali nodded, the blush barely there under her deep, dark tan.

"I'm fine," she grated.

"Good," Marlin declared. "Means we can eat."

I met their VP's eyes and gave a silent nod in thanks. I'd asked in my initial email if they could make sure to eat dinner every night at the table, like a family, for Mali. I knew it meant more to her than she let on; it was another thing I'd known since we were kids. The shaggy blond man lifted half his lips in an awkward smile and gave a nod back. A silent, 'no problem.' Mali looked from him to me and I smiled at her and knew I was busted. She didn't call me out, though. She just shook her head and slipped out of my arms, her hand slipping down my jacket sleeve, fingers tangling with mine. She dragged me gently to a vacant seat next to hers and we sat.

"So how long you stayin'?" Cutter asked, and it wasn't in any way a pointed way of saying 'get thee gone, motherfucker' but a genuine open invitation to stay as long as we'd like, just curious as to how long that would be.

"No more than a day, two at the most," I said. "We have a life to build back home."

"Fair enough," he said, adding, "Welcome to stay as long as you'd like, take a load off, by the looks of you, you've earned some R and R."

I exchanged a look with Mali and the look she gave me back, plus the tightening of her fingers through mine told me clearly, she just wanted to go home. I smiled down at her; even as tired and absolutely wrung-out as I was, I couldn't deny her. This homecoming shit was seventeen, going on eighteen years in the making.

"Thank you kindly, Cutter, but I think we'll get out of your hair."

"Not at all, brother," he said passing a large bowl of salad down the table towards us. "What're friends for, after all?"

I smiled and said, "You need anything, you damn sure know where to call."

He grinned and shook his head, looking down the table at Mali, "Pleasure was all mine."

She blushed again and wouldn't make eye contact, which told me that she'd probably been a difficult little shit. I grinned and loaded both her plate and mine.

"I THOUGHT THAT WOULD NEVER END," she said as I shut the door on the outside world and gave into that feeling that I'd grown to love. Like it was just me and her, hermetically sealed into our own space, shutting out the wild and oppressive energies out there. Turning ourselves over to the peaceful, symbiotic energy of just her and me in the same space, finding our inner peace.

Mali was a different person when it was just her and me. Like she could shake off this invisible yoke of responsibility, like she shed a cloak and let her wings unfurl. It was beautiful to watch, too. The tension and pretenses draining from her until she was just as raw and vulnerable as the next person... and that she was that way just for *me*.

"Come here, beautiful," I murmured and her shoulders dropped, the tension draining from her body as she stepped barefoot and perfect across the carpet. She pushed my jacket off my shoulders and I let her take it, her eyes never leaving mine as she carefully reached out and hung it, cut and all, on a hook in the back of the door.

She got it, the respect that my colors and my brotherhood deserved; and I loved her more for that. I drew her to me, hands slipping along the light, airy fabric of her tank, appreciating how her nipples pressed against the thin material, the outline of the jewelry adorning them shimmering alluringly through it.

"I really like this," I murmured, tracing a thumb over one pert bud.

She shivered under the light touch and pressed her thighs together, saying, "Oh yeah?"

"It's hot, and a good look for you."

"You know just what to say to turn me on," she replied, her voice gone a little breathy.

"C'mere," I whispered, my own desire rising to a slow simmer in my bloodstream. We both gravitated toward one another, making careful, unconscious baby steps into each other's intimate space. Her lips were soft and warm beneath mine.

I smoothed my hands along her body, my hands finding the slight curve of her ass, and I gripped the back pockets of the tiny scrap of shorts she had on. I pulled her tight against me, kneading through the fabric and wishing like hell they weren't there, no matter how long and elegant they made her legs look. The mere thought of those stems of hers twining around my hips brought my dick to stand at attention and I remembered the last time we'd made love.

I was determined not to break her this time, which just meant there needed to be a lot more foreplay, a lot more care in making her ready to take me.

She whimpered against my mouth and I marveled at this woman, this beautiful and fantastic creature. So fierce, hard, and sharp when it came to the outside world but so willing to love me and trust me behind closed doors; in the world of our own making. So willing to be soft and yielding in my arms. A real hellion in the streets and an angel in the sheets. The opposite of what most men wanted, but so very perfect for me.

"Kyle," she whispered her tone halfway between breathy and begging as I played my lips along the side of her neck, sucking the spot behind her ear and relishing the shudder she let loose against me. She responded to my touch so beautifully and it had been a gaping hole left in my damn heart, my soul, these past six weeks that I couldn't wait to begin to fill with all things Amalia.

"Put your legs around me, baby," I breathed into her ear, and hands on her ass encouraged her to give that little leap. She did and the feeling of our sexes pressed together even through the layers of our mutual clothes was enough to damn near drive me insane.

I carried her to the bed and sat her on the edge, burying my fingers in that tank top I'd bought her what felt like ages ago, sweeping it up and off her sweet body, over her head, discarding it on the floor. I could tell by the heat index in her eyes that she wanted skin on skin contact as badly as I did, her hands balling in the front of my own butchered black band tee. I reached behind me and hauled the offending material over my head and let it join her shirt for some sexy times on the floor.

I loved the little sharp inhale she made when my body was revealed to her. Loved it, even more, when she didn't hesitate, and went right for it, her lips pressing against my stomach, her tongue licking a long, hot wet line up one set of abs before moving to the other side. Tasting me like I was her fucking dessert. I let my head tip back and my breath escape in an appreciative rush, my hands capturing hers as her fingers fumbled with the button on my jeans.

"I want to," she said, voice sure and stony. "Please don't stop me."

I stared down into her very serious eyes and slowly took my hands away from hers. She swallowed hard and continued her mission to free my throbbing cock from my pants.

I balled my fists at my sides as she swept the cotton of my boxers and the rough denim of my jeans down my legs. My boots and socks lay forgotten somewhere in the living room downstairs, so they weren't in my way, but still, I didn't want to move, didn't want to do anything wrong to scare her, or trigger any unwanted memories, so I held very, very, still and let her do what she wanted.

"Holy shit," I muttered and dug nails into my palms, as without much preamble, she took me into her mouth and immediately to the root. I swallowed and my breath came in surprised pants. I hadn't expected that, but oh, goddamn, did it feel good.

She bobbed her head gently, her small velvet tongue trailing up and down my frenulum, teasing it lightly, swirling around my head in a way that made my heart damn near seize up in my chest and my eyes roll back.

She got her long, elegant fingers involved, wrapping them around my shaft with just the right amount of pressure, stroking rhythmically along with her mouth's attentions. I swallowed hard and moaned, planting my palms flat against my lower back and ass to keep from doing what I really wanted to do, which was touch her head.

Instead, I fought the rising urge to do it by speaking, saying, "Oh yeah, baby… that feels so good. Just like that." I sucked a breath in between gritted teeth and fought down the urge to come. She had me on that fucking razor's edge, man; and I didn't know if it was okay or not. I hated to kill the mood by asking, so instead, I went the route any other red blooded alpha male would. I stopped her, gripping her upper arms lightly and pulling my cock from her mouth by drawing back my hips.

"Stand up," I ordered and used a tone that should brook no argument, but with Mali, you never knew.

She got to her feet, like a puppet drawn by strings and oh god, that turned me on. Knowing I was the damn puppeteer to a woman who was as fierce as she? Goddamn. Power flooded my veins and I ripped open her shorts and sent them cascading down her legs, my balls tightening, my cock twitching at the sight of no panties.

I pushed her back onto the bed and she collapsed willingly with a dark smile that spoke to my own. I let it rise and fill my eyes, wrapping my arms around her thighs, dragging her body so her ass was at the very edge of the bed, the glistening flower of her sex begging to be defiled, but that was a game for another night. Right now, I wanted to worship my woman for the goddess she was, so I went to my knees instead.

Her scent was heady and intoxicating, her flavor like nothing else I'd ever had cross my tongue as I lapped at her center, finding that jewel I knew would spark fire in her eyes and teasing it with the tip. I wiggled my tongue back and forth over it to send pleasing vibrations through her core. The passion in her eyes deepened, the glow of her desire something else to behold until she couldn't stand it anymore, her head tipping back and a deep, throaty sound of satisfaction escaping her long and lovely throat.

Her legs twitched, spasming to either side of my head, telling me I had her close. I delved my hands up underneath her back, cradling her in my arms as I drove my tongue into her pussy, lapping at her. She cried out and arched into the support of my arms, her fingers digging into the bedspread, balling it into fists to the side of either hip. She was gonna come, so I took a deep breath and flicked my tongue over her clit one more time, twice, and it was like she was an arrow let fly.

I expected it, but it was still pretty satisfying. Her legs snapped closed around my ears and her body writhed. I let her have my tongue, laying it flat against her as her writhing hips did all the work for me, running her sex, top to bottom, bottom to the top against it.

Jesus fuck, I could eat her pussy all day if this were the kind of reaction I would get. She lay serene, her fingernails scratching against my scalp lightly, fingers tangled in my hair and I stood, knees cracking loudly, climbing her body with elegant little kisses until I could lay over the top of her and whisper in her ear, "How do you feel?"

You know you've done your job when all she can muster in response is a throaty little laughing moan ending on a whimper. Of course, I upped the ante by bodily manhandling her onto the bed laying on it length wise so I could fuck her.

I went into the pocket of my jeans and came up with the three condom chain I'd kept handy just for this eventuality. I knew she was on the implant, but she'd already had a late period when she'd come down here. Like over a week late, and concerning as all get out. She'd eventually started, but for a second there, I thought we'd be starting our family sooner than I'd like... I mean, I didn't know if I really wanted kids. I know that when we were teens, Mali hadn't wanted kids, but she could have changed her mind sometime in that seventeen years. At any rate, she chalked up being late to stress, which I could believe, and we had agreed on condoms from now on.

I tore off one of the foil packets and she writhed a little on the bed in anticipation, watching me slide it on. Another conversation we'd had as teens... a detail that'd stuck with me. She said she thought she'd think it was hot, watching a boy put the condom on himself before sex. That she didn't know why, but she always fantasized about it. It'd instantly become part of every fantasy and every sexual encounter I'd had since.

I rolled it down my length, making sure it was snug against the base of my shaft, and lay over the top of her, bodies pressed tightly together, her breasts pressed flat against my chest, her barbells digging just a little and I liked the sensation. I looked her in the eyes as I slid into her, slowly, deliberately, and it was seriously like coming home.

22

A malia…

He had me so wet it drove me wild, and filled my pussy slowly. God, he was thick, pressing out against my walls, it was almost hard to grip him. Laying on top of me like he was wasn't oppressive by any means, in fact, it was quite the opposite. It was so full of love, light, and safety… he felt like *home*.

"Kyle," I gasped and he smiled.

"Anything for you, baby, just name it," he growled.

"Kiss me!" His mouth was gentle against mine and we were deep into the kiss when he began to move, slowly, gently, careful of me.

It was a slow burn, every careful thrust growing in intensity, but not speed, oh no. No matter how much I whimpered, whined, and begged, Kyle was taking this at his pace and of all the times I'd ever gotten it on with somebody, no matter how hard I'd ever fucked or been fucked, I *never* felt as thoroughly *ravished* as I did right now under the love of my absolute life.

I wrapped my arms and legs around him, my hips rising off of the bed to meet his, my body fine-tuned and on that razor's edge and it was *killing me*. I wanted to come again, I was *so close* to coming again, and he just expertly *held me there*. Smiling against my mouth and moaning *mm-mm*, to every request, every time I begged, every demand I made. Goddammit, he would just *not* be swayed.

You would think that as much as it frustrated the hell out of me it would piss me off, but no. Instead with every plea, every whining begging vocalization of what I wanted, I found myself giggling and laughing absurdly. My heart lighter than I ever remember it being, Kyle laughing and giggling back, our mouths pressed together, the tickling sensation of our laughter against each other's lips just caused us to laugh and giggle even more.

It was the most fun I could ever remember having during sex, ever... and I realized it wasn't just sex, it wasn't just a fuck, this is what love felt like... this is what loving your best friend, what giving another person all of you and having them accept it unconditionally felt like, and it was a sobering thought.

I stopped laughing, and Kyle drew back just enough to look at me, stilling, brushing a stray hair out of my eyes that'd escaped my braid to ask, "What's wrong?"

"Nothing," I gasped, eyes welling. "Nothing's wrong... I just love you so damn much."

He smiled and it was the most perfect thing in the universe, dipping his head and pressing his lips to mine, the tone of everything suddenly shifted and I stopped caring about having it my way and started caring about just accepting what he was trying to give me and it opened up my eyes... not the ones I physically used to see, but emotionally, my heart, the windows to my very soul were thrown wide and I invited him in wholeheartedly.

He looked into my physical eyes, his so full of love, trust, and happiness that the tears of wonder in my own escaped and with a smile that could melt your heart he kissed me, his hips rolling into motion again. I gasped and gave myself over and stopped *resisting* and *oh my god...*

Euphoria lifted in the center of my being, lighter than air, swirling out subtly at first, gently creeping like mist over a pond until I was completely enveloped in it. I drowned in Kyle's attentions and had no desire to come up for air as he smiled serenely and whispered *"That's it, baby..."* against my ear.

I clung to him, and let it happen, the build torturously, sweetly, *slow*. My breath escaped in an impassioned plea. He rolled with me then, and suddenly I was on top, astride his body and I was determined to give him as good as I'd got. I placed my fingertips gently over his heart and closed my eyes, slowly rolling my hips, finding that sweet, sweet, spot inside me that I never could really get to with a partner outside this position.

There.

It felt like the tip of him nudged it just right *there* and I moved my hips accordingly, my head bowing, lips parting and voice spilling heavy into the dark of the room in a satisfied groan as I managed to take what I needed while simultaneously giving Kyle *all of me*.

He watched me, expression glowing with love and light, hands on my hips gently encouraging, thumbs sweeping in the hollows there, at my front and I found myself in that blissed-out state where you just wish that you could hang off the moon among the stars forever... and Kyle was both my moon and my stars. My lover, my best friend, my rock, my support and the greatest thing to have ever happened to me.

"Oh god, I'm close," I gasped. "I'm so close!"

"Take your time, baby... I could do this all night," he said, but his voice was strained, a tell, he was lying but at the same time, I believed him. He would do this for me all night, for as long as I needed, *because* I needed him too.

It was an unexpected tipping point that sent me straight into the fall of orgasm. I jerked, pussy spasming around him and he cried out, hoarse, cock twitching in counterpoint and we both fell together… just like we did *everything* else.

Together… forever…

Forever was a really long time, my hazy mind thought out… but then… *Still not long enough to make up for lost time…* and that was the truth.

~

THE MORNING LIGHT streaming through the blinds fell across my eyes, waking me. I was warm, far too warm, and fetched up against a hard body. I lifted my head, groggy and opened my eyes to Kyle's smiling, warm chocolate gaze.

"Morning, baby."

I felt a slow creeping smile cross my lips and said, "Hi," almost shyly. It wasn't the first time I had woken up beside Kyle. It wasn't even the first time I'd woken up beside Kyle after a night of incredible sex. Still, there was something incredibly fragile about this moment and how shiny and *new* it felt.

"How are you feeling," he murmured, concerned, and I felt a slow, lazy smile spread across my lips.

"Mm, deeply satisfied… whole… you?"

He chuckled and whispered, "Pretty much the same, but that wasn't what I was asking… I didn't hurt you again, did I?"

"Mm-mm, no."

"Good," he pecked me on the tip of my nose and I crossed my eyes to look. He laughed for real then and I felt my smile grow brighter. I loved that I could make him laugh, I loved that I made him smile, I loved that I could finally *love* him and not hide it behind a bunch of teenage insecurities.

Speaking of which, I felt *young* again. I mean, I know I wasn't exactly a bitter old hag at thirty-five, going on thirty-six, but all of this... I felt seventeen again. Pre-all the garbage that had taken me away from him.

He pressed his lips to my forehead and murmured, "We went at it for a *really* long time. I was a little worried this morning."

"Mm, nothing to worry about here." I closed my eyes and laid my head back down on his chest and he chuckled deeply.

"You ready to head for home?" he asked.

"Are you? I mean, you only just got here and it's a long ride..."

"Came down in my truck, figured it'd be easier on you."

"Explains why I didn't hear you arrive."

He chuckled and kissed the top of my head again, "Snuck up on you pretty good, huh?"

"Yeah, you did," I said and I was glad it came out brightly, I was glad it felt bright.

"Need some time to pack?" he asked and I shook my head.

"No?"

"No... I kept all my shit ready to go."

"For the last six weeks?"

"Yeah."

"Okay... okay..." he held me tighter, the way he said 'okay' like he was trying to digest this bit of information.

"I just want to go *home*, Kyle... this isn't home and I don't want to stay."

"Back to Indigo City?" he asked carefully and I looked up at him, frowning.

"Don't be stupid," I chided. "*You* are home. You always have been and you always will be."

He chuckled then and snuggled me closer, "Sounds about right to me, babe."

We spent another lazy hour or so in bed, but then we had to reluctantly drag ass out of it. The ten-hour or so drive back to Kentucky wasn't going to make itself. We showered together, caring for each other in a new, simple way... although I was a shower girl at heart, I think I would always prefer bathing with Kyle in a tub. I was a little sad that we likely wouldn't be able to as comfortably as in the damn horse trough, though.

Our goodbyes were sweet, and I found that I really would miss this charming little sea side town and the men and women of The Kraken. I had started learning from Hope and the lessons would be missed. Still, I was confident enough that I *might, might, might* pull at least one fast one on Reaver and I was hoping the opportunity would come up. I owed him a touch of light-hearted revenge.

"You take care now, y'hear?" Cutter asked, and I smiled at him, hugging him back.

"I promise," I said and he grinned.

"The broken find their way to Ft. Royal, but they rarely, if ever, leave the way they came. They always go home better. You come back anytime you should need us," Faith murmured and she hugged me tightly.

"Leave it to my ol' lady to find just the thing to say. Couldn't say it any better m'self," Marlin smiled at her and it lit up his whole world.

"We'll totally take you up on coming back to visit. Might be a while, though. I think we're both looking forward to getting back home and rebuilding our lives... together this time," Kyle said.

"Thank you for hiding me, I don't think it's a kindness I could ever repay," I murmured.

"Think nothing of it," Hope said. "I'm just disappointed I didn't get to really kick someone's ass. I feel like I am getting all kinds of rusty."

"Heh, you want I'll be your Huckleberry," Cutter offered and she gave her mate a savage grin.

"You're on, always ends up us fuckin' anyway."

"Too true, too true!"

There was laughter and I said, "Say goodbye to Galahad and Charity for me?"

"Of course," Marlin said.

"We're going to miss you!" Faith came in for another hug and I hugged her back tightly. You would think Hope and I would have gotten along like a house on fire but I honestly think were a touch *too much* alike. Faith and I, though? We'd damn near become best friends over my stay.

"You all will have to meander up north for a stay," Kyle said and Cutter said, "Sounds like a fine idea! Been a minute since we've taken a club ride. We'll see about settin' somethin' up in the near future."

"Sounds good," Kyle shook hands with him and we turned for his 4Runner.

"Y'all drive safe, now!"

He took off his jacket and cut and laid it across my lap with a wink, before shutting me into the passenger seat and then came around to the front. A weight I hadn't realized rode me lifted from my shoulders as we headed out of town.

"Homeward bound," he declared and I smiled nodding.

"So where is home?" I asked.

"Well, for tonight, it's at the club. The boys and the ol' ladies are dying to see you, meet you for real and roll out the welcome mat properly. We'll stay in my club room, and tomorrow we'll head on over to the house."

"Your house?" I asked.

"No, baby… the house… I kept it for you."

"Wait, the house you grew up in, as in your folk's place?"

"Ah, yeah…"

I leaned back in my seat, a little stunned, my fingertips absently petting the patches on his vest.

"Can't we go straight there?" I asked, suddenly eager.

He laughed, "Tomorrow, babe. I promise we'll get you all moved in tomorrow."

I nodded and turned to face out the window, my fingers suddenly itching for my tarot cards in my messenger bag in the back cargo area.

We drove in silence for a couple of hours, and I appreciated that he let me think. At the next rest stop, he pulled off and asked, "Do you think you can drive for a couple of hours?"

"I don't have a driver's license, I never got one. Just a fake ID as Lexi."

He pulled into one of the spaces in front of the rest stop facilities and turned his head to look at me, eyes a little bit wide, and then flipped through the folds of leather in my lap. He pulled out a thin stack of cards, all rubber-banded together, and handed them to me. On top was a Kentucky driver's license with my photo. With trembling fingers, I moved the blue rubber band aside to reveal my name… my *real* name.

Junix, Amalia Rose

It had all the right information, hair black, eyes brown, but the address... I looked up at Kyle and asked, "Your folk's place?"

"*Our* place," he amended.

"Is this real?"

He nodded, "Keep going."

I blinked and moved the license aside to reveal a crisp, new, social security card with my real name and real social security number. I still had mine, and my real birth certificate, tucked into an envelope in my bag... but he didn't know that.

Behind the social security card were two other cards, one was a debit card, the pin number taped to the back, Kyle's birth month and day, and the other was an actual credit card, something I had never owned before with a credit limit that far exceeded any amount of money I could *ever* pay back in my lifetime.

"You did all this?" I asked, and he nodded solemnly.

"I did," he said.

"How?" He smiled and it was a little bit devilish and a little bit mysterious.

"I have my ways. You *can* drive, right?"

"Yeah, I mean, I *learned how* and I drove on occasion as Lexi, but I didn't really need to in the city. I took transit and stuff."

He got out of the car and came around to my side, opening the door. I handed him his jacket and cut and he smiled at me.

"She's all yours, you're going to need her when we get back home. Things are too spread out for transit to be very effective for you. I have the bike, so that'll do until we get something you like."

I went around to the driver's seat and got in a little numbly, stashing the new cards, complete with *insurance* in the cup holder.

"Try not to get pulled over, just keep going the way we're going, wake me up when you start seeing signs…"

His voice buzzed a little, blurring as I scooted the seat forward and buckled my seatbelt. I nodded, catching what he was saying, but just flummoxed that he managed to get all of this together, that he thought to, before coming to get me.

"Mali, you okay?" he asked and I shuddered as if waking from a dream, but this dream was real.

"Yeah, yeah! I'm fine, I guess it's just becoming real, you know? Like really real."

He smiled at me and leaned his seat all the way back, covering himself with his jacket.

"It's as real as it gets, baby."

I put the 4Runner in reverse, and carefully backed out of the space he'd pulled into. It'd been a while since I'd driven, but I wasn't at all intimidated by the prospect. I was more intimidated by the real me being all over the documents in the cup holder between us. It was just so surreal.

A few hours later, we switched again and I ended up napping for a time. I woke to winding country highway and a limited view due to the creeping darkness.

"Hey, we're almost there," he said softly, voice velvet in the dark. I shuddered and sat up, pushing his jacket and vest down into my lap and sitting the seat up.

Around twenty minutes or so later, he got into the center lane turning left and steered us through a menacing, but open, iron gate. We traveled up a steep, newly blacktopped drive that ended up spilling into a gravel and dirt lot. He parked over in line with some other vehicles and killed the engine.

A bonfire was going somewhere behind the low cinderblock building, the shifting orange light bouncing off of the underside of the surrounding tree's leaves ringing the property and I let out a breath I hadn't realized I'd been holding.

"It's okay, everyone is looking forward to meeting you."

"I feel like I turned their lives upside down for a minute, I mean, one of you was shot, they all have families…"

"No one's mad. No one's upset. Mali, we're a big family here and we do for each other, that's how things are."

I swallowed hard, nodding, popping the door open, the dome light startling me. I couldn't ever remember being in a car nice enough to have a working one. Kyle got out and went around to the back to grab my messenger bag and the two reusable grocery totes of expanded summer wardrobe from Florida that the Kraken girls insist I take with me.

He shouldered everything and refused to let me carry anything, nudging me in the direction of the clubhouse's front door. I steeled myself and walked across the lot, Kyle close on my heels, and dragged open the club's front door.

"There she is!" Trigger crowed and a rowdy cheer went up. I winced at the ear-splitting whistles and put up a hand, curling my fingers in a weak wave. An even weaker "Hi" escaped my lips and people rushed forward to greet me. It was more than a little overwhelming.

"Awright! Awright! Let the woman breathe!" Dragon boomed, and Kyle said close to my ear, "Be right back, going to put this stuff in my room."

I turned to tell him he wasn't leaving me, not for one minute with all of these people but it was too late, I was being swept into hugs, handshakes, and introductions before I knew it. I swallowed hard and smiled nervously for half of them before I realized that this was like anything else and needed to be taken head on. I pulled myself up by the bootstraps, just in time for Kyle to rejoin me.

"Mali, this is my Sunshine girl, Ashton." Trigger was all loving smiles, the way Kyle looked at me, and my respect went up for him a notch.

"Nice to meet you," the diminutive woman said, reaching out to me. I didn't know what else to do so I bent to her level and she kissed me on each cheek, which was weird, but okay. I could deal with weird.

"Nice to meet you," I said.

It was a lot to take in. I guess after the no-nonsense way the boys handled things at the building Kyle had dubbed Point Nowhere, I hadn't expected them to be so boisterous in their... I didn't even know what to call it. Off time?

It wasn't long before the women were dragging me over to a table, chatting and exclaiming over my tattoos. I looked back over my shoulder to find Kyle at the bar looking my way smiling, talking to the person behind it, the tall, skinny brother covered in ink from neck to fingertips... Dizzy, I think his name was.

A platinum blonde woman sitting at the table I'd been brought to asked, "What'll you have?" I eyed the offerings of booze behind the bar and sighed, it was a good question. They had a lot of variety.

"Jameson, neat."

"A girl after me own heart," I turned to the woman with the thick Irish brogue and raised an eyebrow. She raised her whiskey glass in salute and sipped.

"You must be Everett," I said and stuck out my hand.

"Aye, excuse the accent, comes on when I've been drinking."

"We've all got our quirks," I said with a shrug and the platinum blonde rocking the adorable pixie cut yelled my drink order at the bar across the room. She dropped into her seat and grinned at me.

"So glad I finally get to join the fun now that we've quit with the fuckin' baby-makin' for half a damn minute." She grinned, her blue eyes sparkling and it hit me. I sat up a bit straighter, suddenly thrust into that zone of awkward when you feel like 'oh, shit' because you've just met your current's ex.

"What're you lookin' at me that way for?" she demanded and I shook my head.

"Nothing, it's nothing… you, uh, you must be Shelly… right?"

"Oh, goddammit, Reaver!" she yelled and he looked over from where he was playing pool, frowned and demanded, "Whhhhhaat?"

"You, not keepin' your fuckin' mouth shut, that's what!"

I laughed as he shooed her away like a fly and went back to talking with whoever he was talking with. Shelly scowled, steamed a little, and muttered, "Asshole…"

"It's honestly, nothin'," I said, "We all have our pasts."

"Aye, but it's still different when that past be starin' ye right in th' eye." Everett sipped her whiskey and a glass appeared over my shoulder.

I looked up into Kyle's guarded expression and took the glass. "Everything all right?" he asked.

"Just peachy," I told him and tried to give him a reassuring smile.

"Need to check on a few things in the fishbowl."

"Cool," I said, tight-lipped. I had no fucking idea what the fishbowl was and didn't want to look stupid for asking.

"Okay," he leaned down and kissed me and I kissed him back, drawing it out a little longer than necessary, you know, marking my territory in

177

case any bitches around here wanted to get any ideas. Truthfully, though, I got why he picked Shelly. She maybe didn't look a fucking thing like me, but she *was* hot and she kind of reminded me of me, personality-wise.

I let my gaze linger on his back as he marched over to a glass room in the corner with curtains on the inside. He went in and swept them open, revealing a massive setup of computers, monitors, and even a rack of servers. I felt my eyebrows go up in surprise, but I really shouldn't have been. I mean, it was Kyle, and I knew he came by his road name honestly. *Data...* I would probably never call him that. It felt... weird.

"This moment of awkward brought to you by the letter 'R'..." Shelly muttered, glaring daggers at her cousin.

"Want me to kick his ass, later?" I asked. "I mean, if it will make you feel better."

That got a laugh from around the table which dwindled and a short woman with shoulder length dark hair cocked her head to the side, studying me with jade green eyes. Her vest read 'Doll' on the front and the nickname tickled the back of my brain. I raised an eyebrow and sipped my whiskey as she took a breath to say something, frowned, and then frowned harder.

Whatever she was going to say disappeared and was replaced with, "You're serious aren't you? You'd scrap with him."

"Have before, didn't come out any worse for wear. Not gonna lose again, though."

Nervous glances were exchanged around the table and Ashton laughed with the emotion painted all over her face like a Rembrandt, "That's, um, inadvisable..." she said and I shrugged.

"He ain't bad," I said and more looks were exchanged.

A redhead exchanged a significant look with Everett and said, "You're either very brave…"

Everett finished her thought, "Or certifiable."

"Certifiable," a teen-aged girl said, laughing over the rim of her wine glass.

"You even old enough to be here?" I asked.

She laughed, "I'm nineteen, and Nox's ol' lady. My name is Maren," she held out a hand and I shook it.

"Nice to meet you, Maren," I shrugged, didn't give a fuck, I was drinkin' before her age. Hard to throw stones living in a glass house.

Another woman with hair as black as my own and blue eyes looked me over. "She's both," she said judiciously and I laughed. I liked her.

"And you are?"

"Dani, Red-Thirteen's ol' lady."

"Nice to meet you, Dani."

A woman came out of the dark back area pregnant belly just starting to show round beneath her blouse, her hands pressed to her back, and dropped into a seat heavily, "Thank goodness, he *finally* went down."

"Aw, Hayley, you have to consider the source," Shelly said grinning.

"He is certainly his father's son," she said rolling her eyes. The women around the table laughed.

"Just a bit of teething," Red said and there was a tinge of concern at the edge of the look she shot Hayley.

"Thanks for the help," a blonde woman that'd introduced herself as Melody said. "I don't know why Chandler took to you like he did, but I am not complaining. Besides," she said with a wink. "It's good practice."

"No problem," the dark haired woman smiled putting both her hands on her stomach. "I'm sure I'll find out soon enough and you're right, it's good practice." She turned to me saying, I'm Hayley," and held out a hand.

"Amalia, Kyle calls me Mali, though…"

"Which do you prefer?" she asked.

"Mali, to be honest, but if you can't get me to answer to that, try Lexi. I've been Lexi for the last twelve years, so Mali sometimes doesn't feel like it quite fits anymore." I downed the whiskey and glanced in Kyle's direction, he was sitting in his desk chair, back to the computers and monitors he was supposed to be checking. Dray was leaning against the open doorway looking this direction, arms crossed over his chest, talking, but not looking at Kyle. His eyes were fixed on me.

I raised an eyebrow and he grinned savagely, made a remark to Kyle, who laughed and said something back, all of it lost to the general din in the room caused by conversation and loud music.

I turned back to what Ashton was saying and said, "I'm sorry, what?" and rejoined the flow of conversation. The women were nice, welcoming, but I still felt like the odd woman out. I especially kind of tuned out when they started talking about their babies. I didn't want to become a parent. Not with knowing just how fucked up shit could be. Plus, I didn't think I would be any good at it. I hadn't changed my mind in the last, shit, twenty or more years on the subject, but honestly, just because I didn't want any kids of my own, didn't mean I wasn't open to the idea of parenting… just not in the traditional sense of the word.

I didn't want a *baby*… I figured if I was going to do it, I'd rather get into it with a pre-teen or a teen that needed help. Every-fucking-body wanted a baby and there were some kids out there that would never have a shot because of it. That was me, rooting for the underdog every damn time. Hard not to, when you've been one your entire life.

Eventually, women had to peel off and go check on toddlers or babies, some were dragged off to get hardcore fucked by their men, which I could appreciate, being attracted to both ends of the gender equation, and sometimes in-between. Shelly asked if I wanted to go check out what was going on out at the bonfire and I looked around and realized the bar had emptied out a fair bit.

"Cool," I nodded and ducked into the room Kyle had dubbed the fishbowl to tell him what was up.

"Really?" I asked and he paused his game of Diablo, *old-school* Diablo.

"Hey, you looked like you were having a good time, I didn't want to interrupt."

"Right, well, Shelly and I are going out back."

"Bonfire?" he asked.

"Yup."

"Beer?" he asked.

"Fuck, yeah. Even better."

"Meet you out there," he said jerking his head that I should go. I grinned and leaned down.

"You're the best, baby," I murmured, giving him a kiss.

"You and Shelly cool, you know, with…" I smiled.

"Good choice, she gives *me* a lady boner."

He laughed and gave me a swat on my ass saying, "God, I missed you!"

"I missed you, too," and something about my tone, that it was oh-so-serious, that it was hushed, I don't know… but it brought his head up with a sharp look. He drew me down into his lap and I went willingly.

"You sure we're cool?" he asked.

"If you're asking if it's a little weird I'm hanging with a chick you used to bone on the regular, yeah... it's a little weird, but she's cool people and I don't fault you for it. Shit, not like I spent the last seventeen years pining for you nonstop, locked into a life of celibacy."

"Celibacy? No, the pining for me part, though? The thought was nice."

I smiled and I knew it was sad, "Okay, so maybe I was lying about that part. I used to dream about you just about every night. You know?"

He shook his head gently, the same sort of sadness descending on his features, "No, I don't know, but it's a conversation for another time, baby..."

"Yeah, you're right," I agreed, nodding.

"Kiss me before you go," he said and it wasn't an order, but it wasn't a request either. I smiled and brought my mouth to his.

"You're the *only* guy I let boss me around like that, you know?"

"Makes us even, baby," he whispered against my lips and the kiss was pretty much just as fantastic and exquisite as our first.

He broke it first and reluctantly at that, "Go on out, I'll grab us a couple cold ones."

"You got it," I said and just before I went out the door to his little command center he called out, "Try and stay out of trouble? I know that swagger."

"You call it trouble, I call it fun!" I called back over my shoulder and he laughed, shaking his head. I shot him a grin and followed the sounds of voices through the dark hallways, ignoring the sounds of sex and the angry wail of a kid that either wanted to be fed, or was having none of the experience of their first teeth coming through, as I passed by doors.

Outside, the air had cooled off, signifying that it was pretty much so late it was early. I was starting to feel the fatigue of our long drive, too.

The nap I'd had in the car long since worn off. Fuck my second wind, I was hoping for a third or a fourth at this point.

I went up the grassy berm to the fire pit and impressive array of pergolas with swinging seating attached. There was a fucking *television* on out here, replaying the UFC fights on it. I blinked and shook my head in amazement. Reaver wandered over and said, "Put 'em up!" and brought up his fists playfully.

I grinned savagely and said, "All right, let's go," taking the stance that Hope had taught me.

Booming laughter came from around the fire and I could see that we had everyone's attention. Reaver grinned and threw a mock punch. I whipped out a hand, caught the back of his wrist, stepped in and turned, lighting quick. He scrambled, twisting last second and I didn't quite get the throw off, but that was okay. We were circling.

"Oh, shit! Data's girl has some crazy!" I heard someone call out and I felt my lips curve into a smile. Reaver may have been drunk, but he sobered in an instant, those cold blue eyes filling with a winter that would have rivaled the shit on Everest.

"Oh, it's on now!" someone called.

"Better check yourself before you wreck yourself, Queenie!"

He lunged, but I was ready for it, I twisted, blocked, stepped, turned and *I got him*! He went up, over my hip just as I heard the snick of one of his switchblades open. I had him on his back, gave the arm with the blade the proper twist, added a little torsion and straddled his hips.

We were nose to nose and I smiled, murmuring, "Fool me once, shame on you. Fool me twice, shame on *me*..." Then I threw his words back in his face from our first encounter, "Make better choices, Reaver." I pecked him on the nose as he had done me and plucked his knife from his fingers.

He knew he'd been beat, that a little more pressure and I could, and would, snap his arm. Still, *I* knew that I would probably *never* get one over on him again, so I didn't push it. I got off of him and reached a hand down. He looked me over warily, but the predator didn't see prey anymore… he saw another predator. He reached up a hand slowly and I clasped it, hauling him to his feet.

Someone made a comment I didn't catch and all of the guys laughed. Reaver nodded, "That's good, Queenie. You did good," he conceded. I went to hand him his knife back and he took it, bouncing it against his long, slender fingers.

"You know, this here is my very favorite knife…" he said and I smiled.

"Oh yeah?"

"Yeah," he said solemnly and I realized he was serious; that something important was happening.

"I want you to have it. I think you won it fair and square."

"You're serious."

"Very."

He held it out to me and I plucked it from his grasp, "Maybe when you've got time, you can teach me how to best use it."

He grinned and said, "You bet!"

A cheer went up and I looked up from the very nice switchblade in my hands, meeting Kyle's gaze which was a mix of surprise that was completely outshone by pride.

He came up the berm and handed me a cold bottle of beer, "Always taking on the baddest motherfucker in the school yard, aren't you?" he asked.

"You know me so well," I said winking and taking a long pull from the bottle in my hand. A loud cheer went up and the guys, predictably, started giving Reaver a ration of shit. It was cool, though… They weren't being major dicks about it, if they were, I would have called them out.

Reaver pulled his wife under one of his arms and held her tight to his side, she murmured something up to him and he grinned, looked down at her and said something back. She smiled and he kissed her, and I thought back to the card reading I'd given him. It looked to me like he'd listened.

I caught Shelly's shocked gaze from over near her man and gave her a one-shouldered shrug, "Told you I'd kick his ass." Her eyes shone brightly in the firelight and she threw back her head and laughed and laughed… I think that was the point I really made a new friend.

23

Data...

After Mali's spectacular display of seriously *hot* physicality, I was ready to take her back to my room and let her manhandle *me* to her heart's content, but that would have meant missing my favorite part of these club gatherings. The part where everything started winding down and mellowing out and just a few brothers remained outside by the fire. This was the point I would usually come out of my nerd-cave that was the fishbowl and rejoin them.

I was, for the most part, a mellow dude. While I liked a good party, *this* part was my idea of a party. I didn't go for the rowdy stuff. That was all Mali's department and I was totally cool with leaving it as a sort of *more for her.*

I was proud of her, and it was fantastic seeing her come out of her shell tonight. If anything, she'd certainly cemented herself as totally belonging. The thought made me smile as I rocked us idly on one of the swings. I had my booted heels up on a round stump of wood, gently bending my knee to give us some momentum. Mali was curled on her side, head on top of one of my thighs, eyes closed but awake and commenting from time to time on the conversation. My arm lay across her where she was snuggled under my jacket and cut, my other hand raising my second or third beer to my lips. I was sipping on it; nursing it pretty well. I wasn't in the mood to be drunk, but it was pretty refreshing and I didn't feel like switching to something less flavorful, like water or sugary, like pop.

"So what have you thought about doing, then?" Revelator asked and it was actually fitting that he, Trig, Reaver, and Disney were the ones out here.

"Guess I'll find something so I can rebuild my supplies. I mean, probably no chance in hell I'll get my portfolio back. I mean, I disappeared for *two months*. I don't think Joey is going to be apt to forgive that," she said and gave a gusty sigh.

"Fuck that, man!" Reaver crowed, "Your whole tattooing *life* is back there."

"Artists are fuckin' flaky by nature," Trigger agreed. "Any good shop owner will keep that shit the minimum required by law."

She snorted, "You're assuming Joey is a *good* shop owner, but yeah, maybe." She shifted uneasily and I scraped my lip between my teeth.

"Place have security cameras?" I asked her, taking another casual sip.

"Yeah, of course, it does; any business in Indigo City would."

"Want to check and see if it's still there?" I asked.

"What, you're going to hack into Indigo Ink's security systems and check?" she asked. "Just like that?"

"What company do they run through, do you know?"

"Shit, no… but there's a sticker on the front window. Jesus, I looked at that thing just about every damn day. You would think I would remember what it is."

"It's okay, I have a trick for that, too," I told her and said, "Hey Trig, let me see your phone."

He brought it over and I opened up Facebook and typed the name of the shop and location muttering as I went through the pictures, "Nope, not there…" I opened up Yelp next and nodded. Google street view sometimes sucked for clarity, so I tried social media first.

"What's that look like to you?" I asked Trig and handed it up to him.

"Same company I run through, Advanced Guard Services."

"Want me to grab your laptop out of the fishbowl?" Disney asked.

"Nah, this is going to require the big rig." I declared.

"It's past quittin' time out here anyway." Rev declared and woke Mandy who was sleeping against his shoulder, murmuring, "C'mon Red, it's time I put you to bed."

Sunshine had already gone in, telling Trig to take his time and Reaver simply lifted Doll saying; "I'll catch up."

Mali groaned, "This means I have to get up, doesn't it."

I chuckled, "Just enough to let *me* up. You don't have to come in."

"Fuck that," she said rolling off of my lap and landing in a crouch. She stood up and managed to do all of it without letting my colors touch the dirt. I'm telling you, she was made for me and me for her.

"Help piss on this," Trigger muttered and let fly. It was a cheap and dirty way to put the fire out, but between him, me, and Disney, we got the job done.

"Boys are gross," Mandy muttered as she leaned on Rev and made her way sleepily down the berm to his club room. Mali just laughed.

"Join you if I could, but I'm just not built that way. Meet you at your mini-command," she leaned over and kissed me and I shook it off and packed it back behind my zipper, laughing.

We went back inside, and I went to my well-worn and comfortably broken-in desk chair, dropping into it. A swipe of the mouse, and a few clicks of the keyboard and I was in business. I was going through the motions, getting settled into binary and back servers when she slipped into my space. She was like a key in a lock, a custom fit and meant to be there. She didn't pull up a chair, but rather sank to the floor beside me on her knees, her eyes skating over the screens and lines of code that might as well be alien translated into Greek to her…

She put her hands on my leg, folding them one on top of the other and I closed my eyes for half a second, drawing her energy in, holding it close even though I couldn't hold her. I opened my eyes and refocused my own energies on getting this accomplished for her. I nudged under firewalls and moved through the web as if I'd spun it myself and found myself in the directories of the security company for Indigo City.

"You're really good at this," she murmured as the camera views for the place flickered to life in all their night vision glory on the high-def screens and monitors.

"No, he's the *best,*" Trigger said from the doorway.

"You are not lying, brother…" I murmured flicking through screens onto the big screen for her.

"That's my portfolio," she said, pointing to one in a line on the front counter, off to one side.

"Which one's your station?" Revelator asked.

"That one," she pointed at a back wall of the shop. I went through images until I got a decent close-up.

"Someone's been using the shit out of it, but that's all my stuff," she declared, rocking back onto her heels.

"Well then I say we get some sleep, we've got a long ride tomorrow," Trigger declared.

"Wait, what?" She turned to take in each of our grave expressions as Reaver walked up.

"We riding?" he asked.

"Looks like it," Rev declared.

"Gotta be tomorrow," Trig stated. "We got clients the night after. It'll be tight, but doable."

"Woah, woah, woah…" Mali chimed in. "We *just* got here!"

"You can't let that shit go, Queenie," Revelator declared and he was right. Every tattoo she'd ever done was in that portfolio. The proof of her abilities. It would take *years* to rebuild that and her reputation? She was already back to square one with it. With going back to her original name, Lexi Duran didn't exist.

She looked agonizingly torn and I knew why… She just wanted to go *home*.

"I have to think about this," she hedged.

"Better think fast, baby," Trigger threw in and she looked at me, hopeless, helpless, and I understood. It was a big decision.

"Why don't you ask them cards of yours?" Reaver said, smiling but not unkindly.

A look, almost of relief crossed Mali's face and I would do anything to keep it there, to give her peace of mind and so I asked her gently, "What am I after?"

She didn't know where my club room was. She looked up at me and hesitated for half a second and finally said, "In my messenger bag, wrapped in the purple silk scarf. I need my tarot cards."

It was late, we'd been up nearly twenty hours, but I wouldn't deny her anything. I nodded, got up and took myself down the hall quickly and fetched what she asked for. When I returned to the common room, I found her at one of the tables, eyes closed, head bowed; waiting and, I think, finding her Zen or whatever.

I set the carefully wrapped pack in front of her and she sighed. I stood apart with the guys and let her do her thing. Watching her with the cards was something different, something new. I had bought them for her, for her birthday, mostly because I had loved the artistry of the deck and I knew she would, too. Also, because she had been super into her heritage that year. You know, as a gypsy… being descended from the actual culture, her dad filling her head with all these stories growing up when he wasn't being a bag of dicks. I guess it was only natural she should want to find herself.

Apparently, this was one of the things that stuck. Mali had never, not once, expressed any interest in religion when we were kids, but she was spiritual. A deep, hidden kind of spirituality, but there and solid none the less. She'd always believed what she'd believed and fuck anyone who tried to gripe her ass about it.

I watched her carefully turn and study each card. Watched her frown over some, nod over others, and generally do her best to find her way. Finally, her shoulders sank and she gave an exhausted and defeated sigh.

"Looks like we're going backward to move forward," she said.

"Right, get some sleep, talk to your women, and meet back here. Say," Trigger checked his watch, "No later than noon tomorrow?"

"Sounds good," Revelator declared nodding.

"You know I'm in," Reaver echoed.

"Cool."

"Thanks, guys," I muttered, a little blown away by their willingness to ride eight or nine hours in a single shot, only to turn around and ride it right back over a single booklet of images. I got it, though. That, and I *know* they knew what it meant. Shit, it was both Rev's and Trig's livelihood too.

"I just want to go *home…*" Mali repeated with a long suffering sigh.

"You *are* home," Rev said and he didn't get it.

"No, man… she means my place, *our* place. The house we pretty much grew up in."

"Thought you lived in an apartment," Reaver said wrinkling his nose.

"No, man… I live in the house I grew up in. The one my folks left to me when they died."

"No shit? I thought you lived in an apartment or something, too." Trig looked surprised.

"Enough of this," Revelator said. "If I'm going on a long ride, I need some fuckin' sleep and y'all do, too."

"Right, night all." Trigger left, I held out my hand to Mali and she put her cards away. She fell into step beside me as I led her to my room. She didn't say anything, just tucked her deck away and stripped out of her clothes leaving them in a messy pile on the floor. I didn't even care. I did the same.

We got into bed and she immediately fitted herself against my side, her head finding that perfect spot that was both shoulder and chest.

"I know you're disappointed…" I started and she sighed.

"Yeah, I am, but they're right and the whole Lexi thing happened and is just as much a part of me now as being Amalia was when I was Lexi. I am never going to get those years back, but I can't just erase them either. I should have taken the damn portfolio… I didn't think."

"We'll get it," I said and kissed her forehead.

She laughed a little and said, "Yeah, we will."

I would leave the question hanging for now, even though I wanted to ask, *and what do you want to do after that?* I knew she wasn't thinking that far ahead, and that was okay. We had forever in front of us.

24

A malia...

"Oh, god," I groaned getting off of the back of Kyle's bike. I looked up to the dilapidated exterior of the motel Archer had made our reservations in.

Kyle and I had been woken up that morning to Reaver jumping on the bed. I swear to god I was going to find that stash of energy he had and steal some. He'd bounced and bounced crowing like a fucking rooster and I damn near hoofed him right in the junk for it. We'd gotten something like six hours of sleep, which after the drive we'd completed the day before coupled with the hard partying? Yeah, not nearly enough.

We'd gone out to the bar area of the club and had found Archer on the phone and poring over maps. He'd hung up, declared the reservations for this motel were made and handed Trigger a sheaf of papers including a map. I'd looked at Kyle and asked if Trigger was coming with but he's said something about it being Archer's job as Road Captain, whatever that was.

Now we were here, getting checked in, the evening wearing on toward night. As soon as we had our keys, we were supposed to go straight to the shop and get my shit. I didn't care about the furniture. I just cared about the ink, needles, my other two guns and the grand prize: my portfolio. Any other incidentals I could make off with were just a bonus after that. Each guy had one cleaned-out saddle bag on their bike in anticipation of pack-horsing my shit back to Kentucky.

Kyle caught my elbow and pulled me around to face him. He sat down on his leaning bike and pulled me between his knees, settling his hands on my hips. His quick brown eyes caught mine and held them as he dipped his chin and gave me a contemplative and searching look.

"What's bothering you? It's not like you to drag your feet on anything and you've done nothing but on this one."

I turned away and fixed my gaze on the faded teal blue paint on one of the motel room doors.

"I used to fuck Joey," I said finally and turned back to look at him. He was smiling which confused me.

"And? I used to fuck Shelly and you dealt with it just fine, you don't think I can do the same?"

"Not you I'm worried about," I said honestly.

"Oh yeah?" His expression became a little guarded and he waited me out. Sometimes I hated when he waited me out and this was one of them. I gave a harsh, impatient exhale and swore.

"Joey can be a little intense, but he's a good guy. I don't really feel like breaking his heart."

"You guys were close, I take it?"

"Yeah and no."

"Yeah and no?"

Damnit, he wasn't going to let me get away with vague. I rolled my eyes and tried to turn but he kept me rooted to the spot, his hands smoothing around to my ass and pulling me closer. I sighed and looked down at him where he was sitting and came clean.

"He was the closest I ever let anyone get beside you. He thought it was serious, I knew it was getting serious, and I broke it off. He still doesn't know he was getting all involved with a total lie. It hurt him, then my dad died, then I disappeared – " I threw up my hands and let them crash to my denim-clad thighs. He didn't get it, and I didn't want to say it out loud. That Joey was in love with me and I had let it happen because I'd been excruciatingly lonely. That I had let him fall in love with me with absolutely no intentions of ever returning it. *God, what kind of a fucked-up bitch did that make me?*

"You had a life as Lexi, baby. I get it."

"Yeah, *you* get it, Kyle but Joey? Joey's not going to…"

"Problem?" Trigger called down from the second floor of the motel, over the railing.

"No," Kyle called up.

"If there's a problem, I bet I can solve it," Reaver called down with a wicked grin.

"Fuck you, no! You're not solving anything," I called back.

Reaver cackled like a maniac in response and shot forward, disappearing into his and Trigger's shared room. It was him, Trigger, Disney, me and Kyle on this run to Indigo Ink. Revelator had a wife and kids which made it harder for him to break away. He'd wanted to come, though. Was a little intent on it, actually; something wasn't quite sitting right but hell if I knew what it was.

"I say let's get it done, get a few hours of sleep and take our happy asses back home," Disney said and I felt bad.

"I appreciate you coming," I said and he smiled taking the sting out of his next words.

"Then let's go get your shit already. Faster you get it done, the sooner you ain't never got to pretend you're someone else or look back."

He had a point, but still, it was never a fun thing breaking someone's heart all over again which I was bound to do here. Joey wasn't going to take my disappearance, sudden reappearance, and subsequent vanishing all over again really well. He was bound to not take me pitching up with four unknown bikers from Kentucky real well, either.

"Why does this bother you?" Kyle asked quietly and I sighed.

"Not exactly a shining example of my finest hour, you know?" I said.

"No, I don't know… why don't you explain it to me?"

"Later," Trigger called out and he and Reaver were back down from the rooms. "Let's get this over with, grab a few hours and head back."

I sighed and felt my shoulders slump, nodding wearily and we headed over, the five of us, on four bikes. The shop was lit with its familiar blue neon and was as busy as ever. It was the middle of our day and I felt a huge pang of guilt. I mean, I guess it was better than me being dead which is where I thought I would be at this point, but nobody needed to know that.

Disney went in ahead of us, Kyle held the door for me, and I slipped through. He was right behind me, followed by Trigger and Reaver and the first thing I did was pick up my portfolio and slip it to Disney. If it were the only thing we got out of this, then let it be so. I didn't know what kind of reception I was about to get.

Kit looked up from her computer screen and froze, her pink bubble gum she'd blown into an expert bubble, snapping. She took a full two seconds to pull it off her lips with her tongue and suck it back into her mouth.

"Hey, Joey!" she called and her tone wasn't friendly, but it wasn't exactly hostile, either. More of an 'oh, shit... I don't know what to do with this one' which was fine. I wouldn't have been so uncertain, though. I would have been pissed off.

The guns in the shop stopped buzzing, people looked up and surprise flitted across Lissard's face; Djinn looked nonplussed, but this was Joey's shop and as the king, it was his job and his place to deal with me. Joey rolled across the checkered linoleum floor and his green eyes burned.

"And just where the fuck have you been?" he barked and I tilted my head. His voice was barely restrained and I knew this was going to be a knock-down drag-out.

"You wouldn't believe me if I told you," I said and let out a pent-up breath slow and controlled. "I don't want any trouble, I just want to get my shit and go."

"No! Fuck that Lexi! You owe me a goddamned explanation!"

"Fuck," I muttered.

"Which one's yers again?" Trigger asked. I turned to look at him, standing behind me just inside the door, chewing on the end of a black e-cigarette.

"Back wall, central station."

"No, fuck that! Who the fuck are you?" he demanded.

"We're her new friends," Reaver answered and followed Trigger to the back. They had a couple of tool boxes that would hold my shit, but that fit nicely in their saddlebags. Disney held a third in case they needed it.

"I don't care about the gloves and saran wrap and shit. Just get my ink, there should be a rotary gun in the drawer, and whatever other essentials," I told him.

"Lexi, seriously, what the fuck?" Djinn demanded from the corner.

"You disappear for a couple of months, no call no show on your clients, then just show up here rip out your shit and *leave?*" Joey demanded.

"Like I said, you wouldn't believe me if I told you. I'm sorry, but this is really for the best. You won't hear from me again. I promise."

"Not good enough," Joey came out from behind the counter and said, "Kit, call the cops!"

"What for?" I demanded.

"For robbing the place," Joey said defiantly.

"Oh, fuck *you*, Joey. All that shit is *mine* – bought and paid for with my own fuckin' money!" I shouted, outraged. He grabbed my arm and made to haul me in but Kyle stepped between us, a gentle hand on Joey's chest.

"Don't touch her."

"Who the fuck are you?" Joey demanded and hauled off, and I got in it to win it then. I caught his wrist, stepped past Kyle and landed Joey on his ass. He slid back into some of the waiting area chairs, shoving them into the front window which shuddered with the impact but thankfully, didn't break.

"Woo hoo hoo! She got me with that one last night!" Reaver cried. God, had it really only been last night? Too much shit was happening too fucking close together. That felt like days or weeks ago already.

Out loud I said, "No, different move," adding dryly, "You're not helping!"

"Sorry," Reaver muttered.

Joey looked up at me like I had a forked tongue and I shook my head, "You don't touch him. These guys are the least of your fuckin' worries. You don't have a clue who I am or what I've been through but he," I pointed back at Kyle, "is everything. Now sit the fuck down and shut the fuck up. I don't owe you *anything*!" I turned to Kyle to check and make sure he was okay while Joey climbed to his feet. Kyle looked amused but what came out of Joey's mouth made me freeze.

"The fuck you don't! I *made you*, Lexi Duran!"

I turned slowly and spat in his face, "No, *I* made Lexi Duran. She doesn't *exist*, asshole! She never did. This whole time, this whole thing is all a fucking *lie!* So suck on that, why don't you!"

"You fucking this guy?" he demanded, and of course, it always devolved into that, didn't it?

"Yup, every chance I can get and while the sex wasn't half bad with you, it's fucking mind blowing with him!" I stared Joey down and if looks could fucking kill… I didn't give a shit, though. I'd broken up with Joey to try and spare him some pain, but shit… this was all my fucking fault. The anger, the bitterness, the rage in his face was all a demon of my own summoning. Not my finest hour. Not by a long fucking shot. Didn't matter what I did or who I was with, it always turned to shit despite my best fucking intentions.

"Shit, fuck, goddamnit!" I muttered as pain replaced the anger in Joey's eyes. They glassed over and I stared at the fucking ceiling and counted to ten. I couldn't and wouldn't ever fault someone for feeling a depth of emotion for someone else but the person he loved wasn't *me*, she was a lie.

"You owe me *something*," he said and I nodded.

"Yup, I do… but I can't give it to you." Guilt ate at me as Trigger and Reaver filed out, they'd pillaged my shit, filled all three of the tool boxes while Joey and I bickered and he shook his head, helpless.

"Why are you doing this to us?" he demanded and I swallowed hard.

"I'm not, there was no real 'us' and you can't know how sorry I am for doing this to you, but it's over. I'm done, and I'm going now. I hope you wind up with someone worth more."

Kyle's hand landed on my shoulder and he squeezed. It was like breaking up with Joey all over again but on a monumental scale.

"Fuck, well, if you're not Lexi Duran who the fuck are you then!?" he screamed as we went out the door. Sirens were fast approaching and I didn't answer him. I was hoping like hell it wouldn't be an unanswered question that haunted him the rest of his fucking life, because the look of betrayal on his face? It would damn sure haunt mine... At least he was still alive, though. At least I'd managed to do that right.

25

D ata...

"Don't do this to yourself," I said softly when we were safely shut into our motel room. Disney was sharing the other bed, but he was giving us some privacy, smoking a joint out front. She sighed out and looked up, her expression bleak and I knew exactly what she was up to. Blaming herself, taking it all on her shoulders and bearing the brunt of everyone's pain with a heaping side of guilt.

It was something that was quintessentially Mali. I just didn't think it was something she could turn off. I dropped onto the end of the bed beside her and she looked over at me and just sort of keeled over, resting her head on my shoulder. She sniffed, and I let out a breath I hadn't known I'd been holding. I'd rolled the dice. She could have flown off the handle at me, vented some of that rage at herself and maybe some of the pain she was feeling. She was always super sensitive about hurting other people. Hated it, but sometimes, like now, it couldn't be helped.

I put my arms around her and just held her while her eyes leaked and she shuddered silently against me. I didn't know how she could do that, sob without making a sound, but when she did, I could tell just how much she was hurting. The crying jag in Ft. Royal was her angry crying. When she wept with no sound, she grieved.

"Who we mourning, baby."

"I don't know," she said, her voice feeble and water logged, "Lexi, I guess."

I could see it. I nodded and held her tighter, kissing her hair, breathing her in, saying the only words of comfort I could for this impossible situation, "I'm sorry."

"Don't be, it's stupid…"

"It's not stupid," I rejected the notion out of hand. "You built a life as her, relationships, and that's a pretty powerful thing."

"But I wasn't her, it was all a lie," she argued pathetically.

"May have been a lie, but you definitely *were* her. I wish I could make this one better."

"You do, I'm just… I'm just scared. I don't want to hurt you, or *anyone*, like that again." Then she said the words that send my insides heaving, "I totally didn't expect you to show up. I thought I was as good as dead when I posted that message."

It hit me, like a stone dropped into a well, a leaden rock of reality disturbing the surface of my neat little pond I had constructed in my mind. I choked it down and sucked in a deep breath, letting nothing show on the outside how deeply and awfully her confession affected me.

"Not on my watch," I chided gently and then I held her close and closer because I really didn't want to have to imagine a world without Amalia in it.

I hadn't realized she'd lost hope that hard, had never in a million years entertained the idea that my proud, brave, strong, woman would ever contemplate giving up. Shit, it fucking rattled me to my core. Scared me like no other, and made me feel helpless that it'd been that close. A near thing... but not on my watch. I'd swooped in and saved the day, but fuck. *Fuck, fuck, fuck... at the last fucking second!*

"I don't know what I would do without you," she said tearfully and looked up at me.

I pursed my lips and searched her beautiful face and committed as hard as I had ever committed to her before when I said, "You don't ever have to find out."

She threw her arms around me and I held her back and realized that for as strong as Mali was, she indeed had a breaking point and we were fucking at it. I needed to take her *home*.

SHE WAS SOMBER and somehow *less* the whole ride back. One word answers or noncommittal grunts were about all she could muster to the rest of the guys. Disney had helped by giving her a joint and standing outside the room with her as she smoked it. I watched them talk softly and a new friendship was tentatively born. Out of all my brothers, Disney knew a thing or two about hiding who he was.

We didn't sleep well. I think both of us were thinking too much, but neither one of us were really in a place to talk about it. At least not yet. I was still reeling from her admission. I knew she harbored a darkness in her. I think all of us did; me included. It was a very different animal all together knowing that she had thought about it. That it had been more than a mere moment of what Dani called 'L'appel du vide.' Those little self-destructive, fatalistic thoughts we all held inside of ourselves. Like standing on the edge of a cliff taking pictures and suddenly thinking that you could just take that one last step and it would be over and the thought of that is appealing... Even though you know you would never do it.

What had led my beautiful, strong, brave, Amalia Rose into such a line of thinking looking at that blinking cursor on that thread? I wanted to know. What made her actually type the message? What made her click send, thinking it would bring almost certain death upon her and what made her *okay with that?*

The stark reality that I could have lost her, were I not as good as I was at what I did, well, it gnawed at me, chewed me down to the raw, bloody, bone. When did things get so bad for her that she decided to answer l'appel du vide, which literally translates to 'the call of the void'?

I shuddered, thinking back to the conversation that Dani and I had had that late night when she had left Thirteen sleeping and had come out to the bar. She'd been having nightmares again but hadn't wanted to wake him. I had been up at my systems doing work for a client. She'd poured a generous measure of alcohol and had sat watching me and we'd talked... and it was one of those rare moments I had felt Amalia with me because the feeling had been eerily the same. Dani, confiding in me, while I'd listened and just been there. It'd been so starkly reminiscent of the times with Mali under our tree, I could almost hear the distant rustle of the breeze through the leaves.

I split off from my brothers when we reached the town. They looked up and over at my unexpected change of plans, but I gave Trig the hand signal for 'home' and he raised a hand, giving me the okay. Mali perked up a bit when I made the turn and settled in again against my back, but I could feel her damn near vibrate behind me in counterpoint to the bike. She didn't know what was up and I could feel her tension over it. Still, she didn't shout any questions or make any demands as to our destination, choosing to trust me, and for as tense as she was, the fact that she trusted me, even now, to do right by her, made me relax.

When we turned onto my street, she jumped slightly. A lot had changed in the neighborhood over the years, so I figured between that and the deepening twilight, she didn't readily recognize some things. When we got to the house she'd gone very still. I turned us into the driveway, the garage trundling open. The doors were new, automated, and something I had put in. There was a sensor that knew it was me by Bluetooth and my particular cell phone drawing near. My own design, actually.

I pulled into the cavernous space and turned the bike around so it faced out and killed the motor. Mali got down groaning, her body likely as stiff as mine. I got off with a grunt of my own as muscles ached and screamed from too long kept in the same position. Neither of us was getting any younger, it seemed, but neither were we old and used up. I kind of dreaded this just being a preview of coming attractions.

"You're quiet," I observed and she turned, working the chinstrap on her helmet loose.

"It's different," she said. "From the outside, it's the same house, but not quite how I remembered at the same time."

I nodded. "New garage door, new, more energy-efficient windows, and it's been painted."

"The inside isn't going to be the same at all, is it?" she asked and she sounded almost sad… disappointed.

"No, but some things are. I promise."

She took a deep breath and steeled herself. I held out a hand and she reached out, our fingers tangling together. I hoped she liked it inside, but I'd had to change things. Make the house mine and transition it away from being my parent's. I was living alone in this giant space with these old ghosts and it wasn't healthy. I needed to make some changes, but I'd been pretty resistant to some things. Some things I kept as close to exactly the same as I could. Mostly, those were the spaces Mali and I had spent the most time in.

"I guess I'm ready," she declared. "If that's what you're waiting for."

"No, just soaking up the moment. I mean, you're here, you're home with me, and I can't really tell you how long I've waited for this."

I swept a hand through my hair, chasing it back in front and out of my eyes. She nodded, her eyes traveling over my face and she smiled. "I've been waiting just as long," she said and her voice was light, not judgey, not accusatory, just a gentle and sweet reminder. A reminder that though I'd felt alone all that time, she'd been with me in feeling the same things wherever she'd been at in the world.

We still had so much catching up to do... Now we were finally in a place where we could do it.

"Hungry?" I asked, leading her up the steps and into the house. She stopped inside the door, standing in the entry hall and gazing toward the living room, her eyes roving the familiar room with its unfamiliar furniture.

"There are more pictures on the walls," she said softly, turning to look at the hall walls and past the banister to the stairs to the walls beyond it.

"More living happened. You know my mom and pictures."

"Yeah."

She went to one, drifting away from me, her fingers slipping from mine and I let her go to it. She touched the frame with a gentle fingertip and her eyes grew wet with a light mist.

"I remember this. We went to the carnival, what were we?"

"Seven, I think."

"Your dad bought us cotton candy, and you wanted to go on the Gravitron... that ride that used centrifugal force, remember?"

"Oh, god! Don't remind me!" I groaned and clutched my stomach. She laughed.

"We came down off those panels and you staggered outside and barely made the trash can!"

"Everything was blue and I freaked out."

"Never made fun of you for crying, though."

"No, you never did…"

"Your parents were so cool about it, too." She looked wistful and I went to her, pulling her into my arms. She rested her head on my shoulder and her arms dipped beneath my jacket and cut, close to my body, taking advantage of the warmth and closeness. I laid my cheek on her hair and twisted gently, back and forth, rocking her and she worked through some of her sorrow. I know I was working on mine. The grief of lost time, lost memories, mourning the death of what could have been…

"You didn't answer my question," I said softly, after a time.

"Not hungry," she whispered. "Just so tired…"

"Bed, then?"

"Yeah. Sleep sounds really good. I wish I were up for something else but…"

"Hush, plenty of time for all of that, later. Right now I'd be good with you naked against me and like a solid week's worth of sleep."

She groaned, "God that sounds so good. I mean, is it always like this with them? Go, go, and go, all the time?"

"No. Wasn't my first choice either, baby; you can trust me on that."

"No, no, I believe it," she let her breath out in a huge rush of warm air, "Just… I'm tired."

"I get it, come on up."

She let me lead her to and up the stairs to the second floor and paused, touching the door to my old bedroom. I smiled and opened it up for her and I felt her shoulders slump with relief. This was a room I hadn't changed. Nothing. Not a thing… but I also didn't sleep here anymore. The twin bed definitely insufficient.

"We'll revisit later, yeah?"

"Yeah, okay," she agreed.

I led her down to my parent's old room, the master suite, and she followed. I shut the door tightly behind us and she sighed, looking around relieved. This space was all mine, the new me, the 'me' that I'd been without Mali here, suffering daily through her absence. This room was very grown up and with her in it, almost felt foreign now.

She took everything in, the muted masculine colors I preferred; the modern furniture, and slid out of my old jacket slowly. I took it from her and hung it on the coat tree in the corner by the closet, adding mine beside hers. I stared at the two coats, side by side, hanging innocuously there and felt a stricture around my heart ease marginally. She was here, really here with me in this space, but it still sort of felt incomplete. I didn't know why, and when I turned, I saw it reflected in her eyes, too.

Maybe time? Maybe we just needed to get through a small grace period before things started to feel right. It was just so incredibly new, shocking almost, even though it was what both of us wanted so badly.

She sank down carefully on the side of my bed and leaned over, working the laces open on her boots and disengaging the zipper on the inside of each leg, lowering them to the floor. I pulled off my own and set them at the base of the coat rack like I did every time I took them off when I was home. She looked around with uncertainty and scraped her bottom lip between her teeth. I went over and took her boots from her and took them over and set them next to mine, beneath her jacket.

"I feel so out of place," she said and looked at a loss when it came to saying more. I went to her and held my hands out. She obliged me and took them, letting me draw her to her feet. I pulled her close, twining her arms around my waist and cradled her face between my hands.

"You're right where I want you to be. You're right where you belong." I lowered my lips to hers and her eyes drifted shut. She kissed me back, slow, sweet, and in no rush. We savored each other, our bodies relaxing, tension easing from muscles even as our mutual breathing picked up.

"Clothes *off*," she breathed and I hauled on the back of my shirt, up over my head. She gripped the hem of hers and they both drifted to the floor forgotten as we reached for one another, pulling each other tight.

"I thought you were tired," I teased when she went for my belt.

"I am, but I need you to put me in a coma."

I laughed, "Yeah?" The smile melted off my face when she looked at me and her brown eyes were nothing but somber. It killed my boner, and I smoothed my hands up and down her arms.

"Talk to me, baby," I murmured and didn't care about the pleading that'd crept into my tone.

"I'm a magnet for disaster, Kyle," she said helplessly. "I hurt *everyone* I come into contact with. I feel like a regular Typhoid Mary and I'm all of a sudden not so sure that this was such a good idea."

"It's the best idea," I said.

"I'm *really* not so sure. What if I fuck this up like I have everything else?" She grimaced and I held her tight.

"You didn't fuck anything up, Mali. You shot the son of a crime boss who was trying to shoot your dad. You defended the only piece of family you had. If that's on anybody, it's on your pops. Not you."

I knew I was treading on dangerous ground. Mali was as loyal as a person could get where her dad was concerned. When we'd been kids, she'd come up with every excuse for him under the damn sun when he'd lose his shit and do something awful. She craved so badly to be loved and accepted by him; and on the surface? He tried to make it look good in front of other people that she was the apple of his eye, but I don't think he was honestly capable of anything deep. As my momma used to say, that man was as shallow as God made them.

I waited for her to make an excuse, to take up for him now, but she surprised me. She didn't say anything in his defense, instead, she murmured, "Maybe I just need a good night's sleep. Maybe, I'm just tired and will feel better in the morning."

I nodded, "I have a thing tomorrow for my day job, but I think you're right, baby. Sleep is the order of the day."

She stepped back reluctantly but I beat her to unfastening her pants. I went to my knees in front of her and slid them down her legs, taking her panties with them. I took them off, then slipped off her socks one by one. I stood, trailing fingertips along her curves and supple skin. Learning her body by touch like a blinded man learning braille. I guess, in some ways, I was blinded when it came to Mali. I knew she had flaws but to me, they were nothing compared to her light and I was dazzled by that. I was so in love with her, I took seventeen years out of my life to find her and did things in that time that most men would call me crazy if they knew.

I *was* crazy. Crazy about *her*. Always had been and always would be.

I stood slowly, letting my fingertips drag along her body as she stood there, eyes closed and barely breathing. I was inside her space, drinking her energy in long before my lips touched hers for a physical taste. She whimpered against my mouth and the hard-on that'd lost interest was suddenly back and all about it. I unfastened my own jeans, shoving them and my boxers off my hips, Mali's long, sensual fingers came out of nowhere, wrapping around my length, stroking me from root to tip. Her other hand rested on my hip, fingers digging, subtly begging for me to come that much closer.

I held her face between my hands and concentrated on kissing her and she took a half step back toward the bed. I followed, staying in her space, unwilling to let her go. Her talk of being toxic bothered me, made me afraid that she might try to leave again in a bid to protect me from my own heart's deepest desire: that she stay. That she would live with me and be with me like this until we were both old and gray like we'd talked about so many times before, when we were kids.

She stopped, pinned between me and the bed. She broke our kiss and turned in my embrace putting her back to my chest. My arms locked around her body and my hand found her chin. I pinned her against my body, playing lips and teeth against the side of her neck. She gave a throaty gasp as I let my cock find its way between her ass cheeks, pressing it snug between them as I growled in her ear harshly, "What you do to me…"

"God yes, I want you to use it," she moaned back.

"Hair down," I ordered and her hands immediately moved to comply.

Her fingers unwound her braid and worked the mass of her tresses loose. I gave her a shove and demanded, "Lay down on your stomach."

She climbed up onto the bed and lay on her stomach and the fact she complied was a heady cocktail of power and desire in my blood. I started low, kissing her calves, moving up her legs, steady, my heart rate and body heat climbing as I settled over her, hands on her ass and opened her up, I wanted to make love to her, but more importantly, I wanted things to be *intimate*.

So I played with her body, causing sensations, doing everything I could to make her melt, make her *relax*, and bring down the invisible walls between us. I would take all night if I had to.

26

Amalia...

I wanted him inside me, *badly*, but he wasn't about to let me off the hook. He kissed me at random, a soft touch of lips, a hot, wet lick up my spine followed by the cooling sensation of him blowing on it. His hands kneading, teasing out the knots until I was as wet as a woman could get, aching for him, but at the same time calm. My anxiety, my guard, dropping to let him in all the way.

He was so in tune with me on that deep level, the soul-bound one that no one except maybe Joey had come close to... Who was I kidding? That was the guilt talking. The sex with Joey had been good, but I could never fully let my guard down or bring down my walls with him. Not like I could with Kyle. I never felt safe enough or comfortable enough to give up my control over anything like I could when I was with Kyle. It was a special kind of bond to have with another person to trust them so fucking completely.

"Hold still," he demanded and his hand fell onto the back of my neck, pressing me to the covers. I froze and closed my eyes, fighting my body's natural reaction to buck, to fight him off, even as his thumb tenderly caressed, pressing in that spot of tension at the base of my skull, his fingers digging slightly into the muscle running along my neck telling it to loosen. It wasn't about to listen, but he was on the right track. It felt good.

His other hand smoothed down my back, over my ass in a caress, he pried me open, and I went to open my legs, give him access. That hand disappeared and came down in a slap on my ass.

"Keep your legs closed," he ordered sternly and I swallowed hard. I wasn't used to bossy Kyle, but I was beginning to really like him. I gripped the covers at my shoulders and held my breath as his fingers delved between my cheeks and he went looking for the entrance to my pussy.

"No butt stuff," I said. "At least, not tonight."

He chuckled darkly and said, "Not what I had planned but good to know it's on the menu at some point." He worked a couple of fingers inside me and I gasped, hips lifting off the bed. He pressed me down harder by the back of my neck, the heel of his hand pressing at its base near the shoulders and that was *hot*.

I couldn't help myself, I writhed a little against his hand and he chuckled again, a low growling, purring sound that went straight to my core and caused my pussy to give a little throbbing ache. *I wanted more.*

His hand disappeared and he got up on the bed, straddling my thighs like he was going to give me a fucking back massage but then he went questing for my entrance with his cock and my brain went out for drinks without me. I let out a throaty gasping moan and my hips raised up, my back bowing down low, tits pressed to the bed. I was offering myself up to him like a fucking cat in heat and it was so *hot*. He didn't disappoint me, either; sliding himself right inside like he owned me... and maybe he did, but only because I wanted him to.

Holy shit!

The angle was beyond perfect for us. I think I found my new favorite position because the way he moved inside of me forced the head of his cock right against the roof of my vagina, you know if I had been laying on my back. Except in doing so, it went *right over that spot*. His hand left down below, pulling out from between our bodies once he was sure he wasn't going to slip out and joined the other at the base of my neck, his fingers curling over my shoulders, thumbs easing the tension out from between them.

"God, baby you feel so good," he crooned and then it was like he lost all sense of mercy. He gripped my shoulders and pulled back on me as he thrust forward with his hips and I cried out in a combination of surprise and a little bit of fear. I'd never encountered any sensation so *intense* before and it both shocked and awed. He paused as I tried to figure out if I actually liked it or not and when I took too long to give him a response one way or the other, he did it again only this time he didn't let up.

Oh my god, he knew me so well! He flexed his body against mine and rode me expertly and I could only think to myself, *be careful what you wish for* before my brain switched off completely and I just gave myself over to the new and different sensations he wrought. I'd told him to put me in a coma and he'd taken me at my word; *Jesus!*

The orgasm was seriously like one of those time lapse photos of a flower bursting from bud to full bloom. One moment you're looking at a bud swaying gently in the breeze then bam! A riot of color, petals, or in this case, pleasure, unfurling from my center. Only instead of withering away, the petals burst from the stem swirling on the wind and through my veins like one of those stylized anime movies while the somber characters went through their angst.

It was a perfect feeling. Deep wrought and full of meaning, all of the emotions I kept bottled filtered through his love until I felt like I could breathe again. Oh, I was sure they would be back and that I would feel as if I were drowning again, but for now? For now, Kyle gave me precisely what I needed. A physically blissed-out fucking coma.

I came around his cock I don't know how many times. My body was wet and ready, taking every punishing thrust and releasing a little more emotional hurt with each one. It was probably the most cathartic sex I had ever participated in and I can't even remember if he got his own.

It was still dark when I woke. I was laying on my stomach and sucked in a sharp breath, a firm but gentle touch smoothing my loose hair out of my face, back behind my ear. Kyle was dressed, and he leaned down to kiss the edge of my ear and say into it reassuringly, "It's just me."

"What time is it?" I groaned.

"Pushing five-thirty," he said and crouched beside the bed to bring himself eye level.

"What the fuck?" I moaned.

"Didn't want to wake you, just wanted to kiss you goodbye."

"Where are you going again?"

"Deal with a client, it's an hour drive, more with traffic and in the city. I should be home by around ten or so."

I groaned and let out a string of swears in Romani. He laughed, and I forgot, I'd taught them all to him. It was one of the things my dad had taught me. The language, but it's not like I'd had much occasion to use it. He'd done something or other to get himself outcast from them and I was, by default, an outcast with him. It was part of why we'd depended on each other so hard through everything... I was, quite literally, all he had in the world and I knew it.

Now he was gone, but I wasn't alone. I had Kyle back, and there was another major difference. I had a loving relationship full of respect. I turned my head away and said, "Be careful, I want you back in once piece."

He chuckled and smoothed his hand appreciatively down my nude back. I shuddered with desire and he tucked me in, kissing the back of my shoulder before pulling the sheet up over it.

"I love you," he murmured and I closed my eyes, the first tears slipping silent down my nose, staining the pillow case in front of it.

When I could trust my voice not to betray me I let out a muffled, "I love you, too. I mean it, be careful."

"I will," he said and with that, he slipped out of the room. I groped to his side of the bed and dragged his pillow into my chest. I buried my nose into in and breathed deep his smell and I couldn't hold any of the grief and overwhelming emotion in any longer. I had myself a deep, good, cleansing cry.

27

D ata...
     I felt a little guilty, spying on her like I was. I mean, she didn't know the extent of my security systems in the house and I'd tell her, but right now I was so worried about her I couldn't help myself. I'd brought up the bedroom before I even got into my 4Runner to see her clutching my pillow to her chest, sobbing brokenly into it.

Shit.

She was falling into a quagmire of guilt and she didn't have fuck all to be guilty about. Confused about? Sure. She even had plenty to be scared and uncertain about. Starting over wasn't easy, no matter how many times you've done it before. I started the 4Runner and drove into the city after stopping at one of Everett's new coffee stands, *Sacred Grounds*. I'd need her special brand of fucking jet fuel to get through the next several hours.

Predictably, those hours dragged, and my thoughts weren't far from Mali during every fucking second of them. I managed to stay focused enough to take notes on what this particular start-up was looking for out of me, and I think I flew under the radar. They didn't seem to know I was as distracted as I was, so at least there was that.

The whole drive back, I worried. My mind going a thousand miles an hour. I hoped she'd found her stuff and had resisted the urge, by a narrow margin, to violate her privacy any more than I already had that morning.

I stopped by the club. I'd let her eat breakfast and had swapped my SUV for my bike before we'd taken off, back for Indigo City. Unfortunately, the plan had been to spend one more night at the club but I'd deviated, so while she was at home with no car, her shit was here. I went through the club's front door and was stopped by Dragon in the common room looking up over his paper and saying, "What the fuck you all dressed up for, boy?"

I smirked. "Meeting with a client in the city this morning," I told him and he raised an eyebrow. "What? Got to look respectable and shit sometimes when charming the citizens."

"Mm, what about your girly girl?"

"Back at my place."

"Thought you were supposed to come back here."

"Yeah, me too," I went over. He was being awfully chatty, and since he opened the door... Well, I could use the unsolicited advice that was burning in his gaze. Okay, maybe it wasn't advice that was there, at least not yet, but the curiosity *was* and Dragon was always good for some pretty sound advice when it was called for.

I dropped into the chair across from him and waited for the inevitable leading question. He and I were always good for a game of mental chess over any given situation and, I think, it was one of the reasons we appreciated each other. I know I was one of very few men that could, on occasion, out-fox our president. It made me both useful to him and gave us a unique friendship outside of some of the other guys, including, every once in a while, his own son. Although, the rift in their relationship had been steadily healing over the last couple of years.

"Stopping by to pick up her stuff?" he asked and I nodded, not breaking eye contact. His teeth showed white in his salt and pepper beard, despite how heavily he smoked. "Right," he nodded, "I'll cut the bullshit this time."

"Appreciated," I said.

"How's she doing? What's got you worried?"

I sighed, "I don't even know if I *should* be worried. I've seen Mali go through some shit before and she's always bounced back pretty hard and pretty fast, coming back better than ever but…"

"But?"

"But she's never *given up*, not once, not *ever*…"

I told him about her admission in the tattoo shop to Lexi's ex-lover, because, let's face it. She may have been boning that guy, but he didn't have the first fucking clue as to who or what kind of woman Mali really was. I was dead certain *I* was the only one privy to that information and selfish me, I didn't mind keeping it that way for the time being. Not that I wanted to keep her to myself completely. Not that I wanted her some kind of *dependent* on me… it was just nice to have that specialness back. At least, for right now.

I hoped, that eventually, she could feel and be herself around at least the club. She needed badly to expand her world, but I also didn't want to push her past her comfort zone too fast or too fierce. Mali burned hot; she was a pressure cooker of emotion and wildness, and right now, to me, she felt like she was on a tightwire, striking a fine balance in this major life transition of hers. If she took her eyes off the prize, she was going to slip and I *was* going to lose her to the void… forever.

I sighed and looked at Dragon plaintively, "I feel like we're in this wild, dangerous place where the call of the void isn't just some whisper out of the dark. It's a fucking siren's call and that scares the shit out of me, D." He looked somber and nodded.

"She's been through a lot of shit, that's for sure, brother; but now she can't run from it. It's the end of the line and it's got her backed into a corner and she's got to deal with it."

It was a grim proclamation, and one I had expected. Still, I was none too happy to hear it. We'd been apart for so long, we'd lived separate lives, and now I wasn't sure if I knew what to do. I said as much.

"Take it a step at a time," Dragon suggested. "Definitely do *not* deal with it all at once."

"Jesus, there's so much, I don't even know where to *start*."

"Best you *don't* start at the beginning. Maybe start with the here and now and work your way back. You feel me?"

I nodded slowly. "Get her set up and stable, that way she feels secure."

"Right. Gotta give her the high ground, make the teeming horde bottleneck and work their way up to her, so's she can cut 'em down one thing at a time."

"She lets herself get overwhelmed," I said.

"So, use the dick god gave you and distract her with it."

I laughed. Couldn't argue, it had worked last night, even if it had been a short reprieve and sex *was* a great stress reducer.

"Thanks," I said getting up.

"No problem."

I got up, and shook the man's hand out of respect, and went to collect Mali's things. When I got back to the house, I found her right where I'd left her, racked out and exhausted in my bed. I stood there for I don't know how long, just staring at her. She was like a dream made flesh. Everything I had ever wanted, everything I had ever wished upon stars for, or prayed to whatever god, whatever powers that be – fate, karma, the universe – fuck. I didn't know what was out there, but whatever it was, I had begged and pleaded with it for her and here she was.

Who said dreams didn't come true?

Of course, I'd been a realist about it. I knew she wasn't going to come back to me completely undamaged, completely unbroken. She'd always been the stronger of the two of us on the day to day, but I guess now it was my turn to really hold her up and hold her together. I'd relied on her plenty of times growing up to take care of shit I was ill equipped to deal with… Feelings weren't always her forte, so I guess it was time for a bit of a crash course.

One thing at a time… I reminded myself. *Baby steps.*

I set her things off to the side and quietly stripped bare, going around to what I guessed would be my side of the bed from now on, and slipping between the sheets. I cuddled up to Mali's back and drew her into the curve of my body. She stirred and mumbled something unintelligible.

"Shhh, go back to sleep," I whispered.

"Mm. Mm-hm," she murmured and her breathing evened and deepened. She was *exhausted* and I couldn't say I blamed her. I was pretty much right there with her. So I closed my eyes, breathed her in, and slept right along with her.

28

A malia...

It was night when I woke again. I vaguely remember Kyle coming home and curling back up with me, but now I was finally *awake* and not only did I need to pee, I was fucking *starving*. I was also alone in the room, but not in the house. Don't ask me how I knew. Practice? A sixth sense? Who knew, but I knew he was somewhere in the house with me, down below.

I pushed myself up, body feeling stiff and abused, as much from all the riding as from the brutally beautiful and powerful lovemaking last night. Also, I think, maybe, *too* much sleep. I sat up and found one of Kyle's black tees at the end of the bed waiting for me. I pulled it over my head and went into the bathroom in here, used it, and splashed some cold water on my face to wake myself up. It was refreshing, and once I'd blotted it off with a nearby towel and finger-combed my hair into some semblance of sanity, I went in search of my man.

I found him in his dad's old den, which wasn't old anymore and had been transformed into something out of a sci-fi nerd's wet dream. I leaned against the doorway and stared at him, illuminated by the blue glow of multiple computer screens as he read through what looked like emails. Only Kyle could make that shit look sexy. He sat in a super comfortable-looking desk chair in a pair of black drawstring lounge pants and a black wife-beater.

He let out a breath in an explosive sigh and leaned forward, his long fingers playing over the keys of an ergonomic keyboard, which I couldn't stand those damn things, no matter how good they were for your wrists.

"Hey handsome," I said softly and he jumped slightly, but didn't seem too startled. He gave me a side-eye glance, finished typing his thought without looking, quickly checked it and hit 'send' before turning.

"Hey, sleeping beauty," he said back and I pushed off the door jamb and padded down the two steps, into the room. The carpet was light, and plush under my feet as I went to him. He reached up, hands smoothing around my waist and guided me into his lap. I put my arms around his shoulders and leaned down to kiss him and it felt like my broken shards were grinding together.

I loved how the simple act of having his lips against mine eased the grinding ache of emotion. It soothed some of the hurt into a dull roar instead of the clamoring cacophony of an angry metal concert that it'd been since the confrontation at Indigo Ink.

I cradled his cheek in the palm of my hand and rested my forehead against his, just soaking up his calm. Grateful that after all these years apart, he still had it. That cool, collectedness to him that soothed the crazy I almost always had going on inside. I mean, for real, no one I'd encountered before or since had such a tranquilizing effect on my inner crazy. Not like Kyle did.

"I missed you so much," I breathed and his arms tightened around me.

"I missed you, too, baby," and the way he said it was a shot right to my heart. Like he'd been missing such a significant part of his life for so long and that the missing piece was finally fucking *here*. The tide of guilt started rising again and I was so fucking sick of it. Just tired of it. It was mentally and emotionally exhausting and a damn near constant companion.

"I'm sorry," I whispered.

"For what?" he demanded gently and I let out a pent-up breath and came clean.

"I feel like I broke us, and I don't know how to fix it."

He chuckled and shook his head, leaning up and pecking me on the tip of my nose. He met my eyes with his, decided the cute move wasn't enough and kissed me gently, then deeply. I drew back and held him off.

"I'm serious."

"You didn't break us, Amalia Rose. The Boyle family crime syndicate did."

"I still can't believe I murdered a crime boss' son. That's like the plot line of one of those really bad action movies we watched all the time as kids."

"You didn't murder him, baby. You defended your deadbeat cheating huckster of a father, and I know he's your dad and you loved him but that doesn't change that he was a real piece of work and that he fucked you over entirely too much and entirely too many times."

He rushed all that out, heading me off and I harrumphed, "I want to argue with you, take up for him, but I think we're past that now." I wasn't a kid anymore. I was old enough to know better, and I did. I knew Kyle was right. My dad was a piece of work. A real piece of work.

"Didn't stop him from being your dad, and doesn't stop you from loving him, but if there's anyone to blame for you being taken from me, it's him and I'm going to be angry. I can't *not* be angry... but don't you dare try to take that shit on yourself. *You* didn't do anything wrong." He captured my face between his hands and I ripped my eyes from where I had fixed them on his fancy, modern desk. His burned with such a fierce sincerity some of my resolve weakened and it was like a chunk of *something* I had no name for broke off and fell away. My soul felt slightly lighter than a moment before.

I changed the subject. I'd never been awesome with feelings, and to be honest, I'd been punished for them so much as a kid, that it had become worth it to just bury them and ignore them for the most part.

"Got anything to eat around here?" I asked.

He smiled brightly and said, "Oh yeah, I've got something."

He gave me a little nudge to let him up and I stood. He followed suit and guided me in front of him out of the study, down the hall, to the kitchen. I stopped and stared at the little dining nook in the corner by the windows, by the back door.

It felt like a real blow to the center of my chest. I mean, this had been the central hub of our childhood lives. This was the table of science projects and dinner every night. I went over to it and touched the old wooden tabletop and turned.

"Told you it wasn't all different," he said softly.

We'd never eaten at the fancy dining room table except for special occasions. Thanksgiving, birthdays, Christmas… that sort of thing.

I sank into 'my' chair and Kyle smiled from across the kitchen.

He got into the fridge and microwaved a couple of plates. Midway through the second plate, the aroma reached me. I blinked and sat up a little straighter as he grabbed napkins and silverware and brought the two plates over.

"Made it special for you. Found her recipe for it after she died…"

"Mom's Mac and Cheese." My vision blurred and I looked at him and sniffed. "Fuck you," I said savagely and he laughed and came around,

226

kneeling by my chair and gathering me up while I broke down in fucking girly-assed sobs.

So many things came swarming out of the dark place I kept them and it was like I couldn't stop them. I didn't want to feel all of this mess, but I couldn't stop it. I felt pitched into a storm-swept sea and I was drowning in the black, but then there was Kyle. He was a rock to cling to as the tides ripped at me and tried to drag me into their undertow.

"I've got you, baby. It's okay," he murmured and I believed him. I trusted him implicitly and knew that if anybody had my back in this life or the next, it was him.

"I'm so sorry I wasn't here for you!" I cried and it was true. It killed me that his parents, who might as well have been mine for all they looked after me when my dad was off scheming, had died and I had missed it. I had missed being there for him. Of course, it was also news to me and hadn't been something I'd had a lot of time to process. Even when I was down in Florida, I think I'd had myself fooled some. Was living in denial. There was no denial to be had, sitting here in 'Mom's kitchen, without her in it.

"It's all right, I look at it this way. I needed to get over it, come to terms with it, so when it was your turn like it is now, I could be strong for you. It's all good, baby. Trust me, it's all good. You're home, with me, and that's all that matters now."

Leave it to Mr. Rational to have an answer for fucking everything. His words should have made me feel better, and they did, so why did I feel like I dropped like a stone further into the depths of despair?

29

D ata...

"She doing better?" Dragon asked me a few days later. I blew out a breath between gritted teeth, my cheeks turning into bellows to force the rest of the air out and took the half a second my mouth was occupied doing it to think.

"Yes and no," I said finally, into the phone.

He'd called me, but his question had been his version of a greeting. It was one of the things I liked about him. He was to the point, didn't waste people's time or treat the important things like a game, not when hearts and minds were on the line to this degree.

"She around you?" he asked.

"No, I'm out on a gig." I sat back in the borrowed desk chair while my laptop ran through the diagnostic code on its screen, hooked up to the client's mainframe trying to figure out why the fuck it was doing what it was doing.

"Where's she at?"

"Home, why?"

"She settling in?"

"Again, yes and no."

"She's the active type," he said judiciously.

"Yup."

"Think it's time to find her a job or something?" I chewed my bottom lip. "Data?"

"I'm thinking," I said.

Dragon grunted on the other end of the line, "You didn't hear it from me, but Trigger is impressed. Hasn't shut up about her artwork."

"Shit, yeah, he has her portfolio, doesn't he?"

"Might want to take her by the shop. A familiar setting, even if it's different, might do her some good. Break her outta that funk you were complaining about."

"Was honestly waiting for her to say something about being bored," I said with a smile. "Don't want her to rush into anything. She's good at that."

"Boy, please. She's a work-horse type, needs to be involved in something. You can tell her type from a mile off."

I smiled to myself, he wasn't wrong. It was probably time to put out some feelers and see if there was something I could get her into, even if it was only part time. Sometimes all you needed was something to focus on.

"Thanks for checking in, D."

"You got it, what brothers are for." he said.

Yeah, sometimes I just needed the reminder. My laptop beeped and I looked up, "That's my cue. I've gotta go."

"See you this Friday?"

"Yep."

"Keep the shiny side up, brother."

"You too, man. Bye."

I hung up and set my phone down, muttering to myself, "Now why the fuck would you do that?" at the technology in front of me, letting *my* work suck me under and roll me.

∽

MY BRAIN FELT the consistency of fried mush when I got home, but the sound of Mali striding quickly up the hall and appearing in nothing but one of my shirts definitely perked me up some. She practically crashed into me, greeting me enthusiastically, and I let my laptop bag slide to the floor so I could get my hands on her.

"I missed you," she murmured into my mouth and I pulled her in tighter, urging her, with my hands against her thighs to give a jump and wrap her legs around my hips. She complied, and I carried her to the first available surface my tired brain could come up with.

Just so happens, that surface was the granite kitchen countertop. I set her down and she squealed, writhing declaring "Goddammit, Kyle, that's cold!"

I laughed and she did too, and it was the first one I'd heard from her in a few days. I was glad this was a good one for her. I looked her in the eyes and said, "I'm going to do you against this kitchen counter, then I want to take you somewhere."

"Oh, promises, promises," she declared, but she was already working buttons loose on my black shirt. I grinned and covered her mouth with mine. She kissed me with some of that fire of hers and pushed my shirt back off of my shoulders. I pulled it off and let it hit the floor, intent on getting inside her.

She sucked in a sharp and appreciative breath when I hauled my undershirt over my head and let it fall next. I gave her a smile that said she was in serious trouble and her eyes grew hungry.

That gave me an idea.

"Lay back," I demanded and she did. I went to my knees between her legs, using an arm as a bar across her hips to keep her from bucking or writhing, I nipped the inside of her thigh. She giggled and tried to squirm, but I wasn't going to let that happen.

I tasted her and God, she was good. Her whole mood immediately downshifted with the touch of my tongue and she went from giggling and squirming to letting out a sharp, throaty moan, her fingers grabbing the edge of the counter as she sat up abruptly to watch me.

I met her suddenly so-serious gaze and teased her clit with the tip of my tongue, sucking it into my mouth slowly. She closed her eyes and moaned faintly, her knuckles turning white where they gripped the edge of the stone countertop. I draped her long legs over my shoulders and went to town, determined to make her come at least once to make sure she was wet enough, ready enough, to take my cock.

She shuddered and I worked a finger inside of her, curling it up, stroking that slightly rough patch on her roof. She cried out, shaking, fighting to keep her legs from wrapping around my head and finally she lay back.

"Oh, ow!" she cried and I looked up sharply.

"You okay?" I demanded.

"Ohhhh no! I just cracked my head really hard!" She sucked in a sharp, pained breath between her teeth and I stood up. She had both hands wrapped tight around the back of her head, lifting it from the counter.

"Shit," I muttered and helped her sit back up.

"Oh my god, so stupid!" she cried and I gently pried her fingers away so I could look. She bowed her head and I probed the spot gently with my fingertips. She yipped when I found the swelling goose egg and I bowed my head and tried not to laugh at the sheer absurdity of it.

Fuck, I felt so bad. It clearly hurt her and was swelling pretty quick. She made to get down and I stopped her, my hands on her knees.

"Stay right here; I'll get you some ice." I went to one of the drawers and pulled out a Ziploc freezer bag and dispensed some ice from the fridge. She watched me, half wincing, half trying not to laugh and I felt my lips twitch.

"You *do* think it's funny!" she accused.

"Well, yeah, kind of hard not to, but I feel bad you're hurt."

She laughed, "Of all the stupid fucking things to do…"

"Hey, it's okay," I twisted around so she could see the bulge in the front of my slacks. "Even slightly maimed you're still sexy as fuck." She lost it then while I wrapped the makeshift ice pack in a dishtowel and brought it to her, easing it onto the back of her head.

"Mm, note to self, eat you out on soft surfaces only."

"You're really good at it," she said knocking her shoulder into mine.

"Yeah?"

"*Oh, yeah.*"

We laughed and she smiled, gaze roaming my face. It was an intense look, and one I didn't readily understand so I asked, "What?"

"Just… I love you. More than anything. More than life itself," she said.

"Mali…"

"No, I mean it. If anything happened to you because of me –"

"*Stop.*"

It came out harsher than I meant it to and she looked vulnerable, uncertain, and for the first time that I could ever remember she looked that way about *me.*

"Are you mad at me?" she asked and the hurt and uncertainty in her tone was so far off her baseline it *scared* me.

"No, I'm *scared* for you, Mali."

"Scared?" she echoed in disbelief.

"Yeah. You as good as told me you were trying to *kill yourself.* That you *gave up.* That's not my Amalia Rose, baby. That's some other girl. This," I waved my hands in front of her, "constant melancholy. This isn't *you.* You can't let what happened to you *break you* like this. I *need you.* You mean *everything* to me!"

Her eyes dropped to her lap, and her listless hand there. She lowered the other with the ice pack from the back of her head and rolled her lips together. She didn't say anything. I mean, shit, this wasn't the way I wanted to handle it. Fuck, did I just fuck up? Did I just chase her back down deep inside herself?

I fought the panic clawing its way out of my chest and up my throat as I worried, *did I just turn into every other guy she'd ever been around or been with?*

"I don't know what to do with this…" she said and I blinked.

"The ice pack?"

"No, *this.*" She waffled her hands back and forth. "I have all these damn feelings and for the first time ever, I don't feel like I have to keep a lid on them and not all of them are good, you know? It's like the dam has busted six ways to Sunday and the water's out and I can't get it *back in…*" She looked up at me, her eyes misting and asked, "What's wrong with me? What do I do?"

I grabbed her and pressed her into my bare chest, my arms going around her, her breath hissing out as I touched the back of her head to hold her close and comfort her. The enormity of the moment causing me to forget what'd started us down this damn road in the first place.

Fuck, U-turn. How do I get us back out of this mess?

"I need to know you aren't going to try anything. That you aren't going to hurt yourself."

"Of course I'm not!" she warbled.

"Promise me, baby. I can't face a fucking world without you in it. I've never had to before and I don't fucking plan on it."

She looked up at me sharply and sniffed, searching my face. "You really never gave up on me, did you? Not once."

"Not even for a minute, not for one second," I affirmed.

"How did you know?" she asked, dubiously.

"I didn't, I just never gave up."

"I'm sorry I did," she said and sniffed.

"I get why you did, but you can't ever again. You promise?"

"I promise." She held up her pinky finger and I latched onto it with mine.

"Never let me go," she said and cuddled close to me.

"Never gonna."

"Good, because it's all I ever wanted."

"Me, too."

"Glad we had this talk," she snarked and I laughed. I couldn't help it. That was Mali, that was my girl… she raged, cried, did whatever she had to in order to let it out, and bounced back at the speed of light stronger and better than ever.

30

A malia…

I legit had a headache for two fucking days after cracking my skull on the damn counter. Didn't stop me from having sex with him on the couch that night, but I'd begged off going anywhere. I still felt as fragile as blown glass and needed time to cool properly after my raging shit storm of a crying jag.

God, I hated that shit.

Now we were at his clubhouse on a Friday night and the boys had all come back to get the little women and children out of what they called the media room. Gag me with a spoon, but being on the domesticated end of the spectrum was so not my thing.

Kyle came in behind Trigger, caught one look at the sour look on my face and started laughing.

"Everything all right?" Shelly asked, catching the same look. Man, my mouth wasn't the problem. It was totally my face that needed some sort of deliverance.

I told the truth, couldn't help myself. "The mommy shtick is so not my scene."

She smiled and nodded, one of the kids was teething, and I knew it wasn't their fault but the damn crying set my nerves on edge and made me antsy.

"It's okay, I totally get it," she said. "I always wanted my own kids but other people's kids? Not yours!" she shot a look at Red who was looking over amused, Melody echoing the look beside her. "Like stranger's kids. Like to drive me up the wall!"

"Yeah, it's no offense," I said wincing as another one of the toddlers started in after getting beaned in the head with a block.

"Come on," Kyle said laughing, holding out a hand. I took it and he hauled me off the end of the couch. "We're out!" he called.

"Man, now I feel like I'm being shitty!" I groused as he pulled me out the door.

"No, trust me, they aren't in the cult of mommy, they get it. They signed up for it, you not so much."

"Amen," I said. "Not disappointed are you?"

He shook his head, "No. I can live without the baby phase."

I laughed, "Okay, all right."

I knew it was a conversation we had before, but people changed their minds, you know? I had to check and see every once in a while. I knew I took bullheaded to a new level, but not everyone made a decision and stuck to it like I did. Kyle was in this, too and his thoughts, his feelings on any given subject, meant the world.

We went out the back and up to the fire pit area. I sank onto one of the benches and Kyle dropped onto it next to me, his arm automatically lying across the back of the seat and curving around my shoulders.

"Your kid is crying," Revelator called out from behind us towards Ghost who was crouched and trying to get the fire lit.

"Yeah, so's yers," Ghost said absently.

"Go on, the both of you. I got this," I said getting up and Rush called out, "Sit down all o' you! Before you go an' fuck up my fire pit!"

I snorted but sat back down gratefully, putting myself closer, tucking myself tight into Kyle's side.

Bailey, Rush's girlfriend and apparently Dray's cousin on his mama's side, had two beers each in her hands. She stopped in front of Kyle and held two of them out to us with an arched brow.

"Thanks," Kyle said and took them from her.

"Just doin' what you asked," she said with a wink.

"And he's expressing his appreciation, Bailes!" Dray called out. Bailey and I exchanged a look and rolled our eyes in unison.

"Jesus, I heard that all the way from over here," Everett called as she and Dray took a seat across and one swing to the left of us. Cue some good-natured laughter.

I liked this. I felt at home – like I might actually *fit* here. Even more so when Kyle's arm tightened around me, dragging my temple to his lips where he pressed them for a kiss that took two seconds longer than was polite. Of course, that's because I knew he was breathing me in. He liked the smell of my shampoo, or so he said, which I found funny because I hadn't used the same stuff more than twice since we'd landed here. I kept raiding his stock of stolen hotel shampoos and conditioners and it was *killing* my color.

Even though there were other men and women of his club around, I felt comfortable. Like we might as well be out here alone, so I asked the question that'd been burning the shit out of me for a couple of days, now.

"Where were you going to take me the other night before I so gracefully tried to give myself permanent brain damage?"

He snorted and laughed and hugged me a little closer, but before he could answer, Trigger did it for him.

"Was supposed to bring you by the shop."

I frowned and echoed the word questioningly, "Shop?"

"Yeah," Disney said, showing up to the fire with his arm around his boyfriend. "Our shop."

"As in tattoo?" I asked.

"Asking about if she wants the job?" Revelator asked, coming up bouncing his son. The boy had finally stopped with the crying and was sucking his thumb, his tear-stained face dull and sightlessly staring from where it lay on his dad's shoulder. Lost in his own dreamy little imagination, the kid was tuckered out and two seconds from racking out completely, and I felt a pang of almost, *almost*, wanting one of my own.

I had no doubt that I would be completely cured of the notion as soon as he started screaming again. I just *did not* do screaming child well at all. They sent my damn blood pressure through the roof and made me want to punt a puppy or something.

Yeah, my 'mommy' was *definitely* broken.

"What job?" I asked, suspicious.

"We get a lot of transient talent to fill spots for a few weeks here and a few weeks there, but we have a station we'd like to permanently fill," Trigger said, looking across the licking flames at me.

"Seriously? Just like that, you want to give me a job?"

Revelator laughed, "No, not just like that."

"You forget we have your portfolio?" Disney asked, grinning.

Yeah, I actually had… Fuck.

Out loud I said, "No, but I didn't expect you all to go snooping, thought that wasn't y'all's style."

"Oh! Listen to her! Losing that city girl accent already," Rush grinned.

"I was a Kentucky girl long before I was a city anything," I reminded him. Kyle nuzzled the side of my neck and I got the hint. *Cool it down, he didn't mean anything by it.*

"Couldn't help myself," Disney declared. "Good art begs to be looked at."

"Spot's open, but it's a limited time offer," Revelator said but he wasn't being a dick about it. He stared into the fire, rocking his body back and forth, shifting from foot to foot and bouncing on his knees a little and the tyke was almost out.

"How limited?" I asked.

"As in not on the table for long," Rev said.

I rolled my eyes, "Do I have to decide right this second, or can I see the shop first?"

"I'd hope you'd want to see the shop first," Trigger said grinning.

"When?" I asked coolly. I didn't want to seem over-eager.

"We're open tomorrow," Disney declared.

I nodded slowly, thinking it over. I mean, did I *really* want to put *all* my eggs in one basket? I settled against Kyle and sheltered close to his body while a tempest of thoughts raged in my head.

Living with him, being a part of his life was becoming as natural as breathing. Granted, I was restless as fuck and wanted to go back to work, but did I want to work for his club brothers? Was that a good move? I mean, I was *sure* there were other shops in the area that could use some talent. I mean, if I had to leave, working for these guys would make it that much harder to bolt at a –

I startled so hard at my revelation I physically moved and Kyle's attention snapped to me.

"You okay?" he asked slowly and gave me some serious side-eye when I answered too quickly.

"Yeah, fine. Random cold shiver."

"It's in the 70's out here and we're in front of a fire," he said flatly. I hung my head, and he took a pull from his beer. "Come on, let's go somewhere we can talk."

Well, I wasn't getting out of this one, but granted I wasn't trying very hard to either. He led me away from the fire and away from his brothers over to a copse of trees near the fence line. They made a triangular clearing and there were three hammocks set up over here. The bough of one of the trees hung low enough to screen us from view of the fire and everyone else, giving us the illusion of privacy. I took a drink of my own beer and let the sudsy, hoppy goodness go down smooth.

"Spill," he ordered teasingly and sat down in one of the hammocks, boots planted firmly on the ground so he could swing back and forth a little. I joined him, and we sat under the dim, deepening twilight, rocking back and forth, sipping our beers.

"I just had a rude thought back there is all," I told him, suddenly worried that if I told him, it would hurt his feelings.

"Yeah, about what?"

"I was just letting my train of thought steam on, wondering about working for your friends…"

He interrupted me gently, "Mali, they're your friends, too."

"I know," I said blushing faintly. God, what kind of an asshole was I? *The kind that doesn't let anyone into your circle and guards it like Fort Knox,* my sarcastic self answered.

I let out a frustrated exhale and pursed my lips, Kyle just patiently waited me out. I finally rushed it out, like ripping a Band-Aid off, "I weighed whether or not it was a good option to go there in case I had to make a quick exit again."

He nodded slowly, "I see, and what did you come up with?"

I looked up at him like he'd grown a second head, and when he didn't immediately laugh like he used to, I did what I used to do and crossed my eyes to add to the effect. I got the sought-after laugh, took a deep breath and said, "To be honest, my train of thought derailed right then."

"And now that it's back on track?"

"I'm pretty sure there were no survivors, dude." He laughed again and fell silent, taking a drink from his beer and waiting me out again. To be fair, I used the silence to do what he was silently asking me to do... think about it. I mean, really think about it.

I was so tired of running and I didn't have to anymore. I mean, the problem was taken care of. I knew that. I guess it still hadn't fully sunk in, though. Seventeen years was a long time to be doing any one thing.

"Old habits die hard, I guess," I muttered.

"They say it takes 19 days for any new habit to take."

"And to break an old one?"

"I'd like to think of it as rewriting code," he said.

"Nerd," I accused.

"Jock," he shot back, and I smiled.

We were silent for a long time and finally he asked me, "You don't have to make a decision until you've seen the shop, will you at least go and do that?"

I thought about it and nodded slowly, "Yeah, I'll do that. You coming with me?"

"If you want me to."

"Yeah, I do."

"Then I'll go with you."

More silence, the urge to say something growing in me like a soap bubble on the surface of the water. Growing and growing until it finally burst and the words rushed out, "I'm not going anywhere, you know that right?"

His expression said it all, that *no,* he really didn't know that and I guess I only had myself to blame. I mean, I was nothing if not predictable and I *was* gypsy stock. The nomadiest of the nomads, born with wandering souls… except that must have skipped right over me because all I ever wanted was to put down roots. You had roots, you grew strong. I looked up into the trees and wistfully wished we were under *our* tree. I was half afraid to ask about it, seeing as it's probably been cut down or something.

"Penny for your thoughts?"

"That shit's at least a nickel now if you account for inflation."

He snorted, "More like a buck fifty or more."

I grinned and knocked my shoulder into his, "Doesn't matter now, just a fleeting one. Can't even remember what it was," I lied.

"Uh huh," he finished off his beer and I did the same with mine.

"Not buying it?"

"Nope. It's okay, though. You don't have to tell me *everything.*"

"That's what I love about you," I said. "You make me do what I don't want to do all the time, but only if it's good for me."

"I try," he said with a shrug.

"No, you do."

We lapsed into another comfortable silence, turning at the rustle of dried leaves and someone stumbling, a woman's laugh, and finally, Dani and Thirteen came into view.

"Uh-oh! Looks like our secret hiding place is occupied," he said affably.

"No, it's cool," Kyle said standing up and I did likewise, hastily so I didn't end up swallowed by the hammock.

"You sure?" Thirteen asked.

"Totally, we were just heading in."

"We were?" I asked with a shark's grin.

"We were," he said firmly and I couldn't say I wasn't looking forward to what he clearly had in mind.

"Well, all right then, Y'all have a good night." Thirteen tipped an imaginary hat and Kyle captured my hand, dragging us away, back towards the club. We ditched our dead soldiers in a bin by the back door that was overflowing with them and passed through the open doorway.

"Sure we aren't being anti-social?" I asked and he hauled me up against his body.

"Do I look like I give a fuck?" he demanded.

"That's my line…" I murmured huskily as his lips descended on mine. We made it through his club room's door and kicked it shut behind us, hands grasping and grabbing, pulling and shoving at clothes in a bid to get them *off.*

He, of course, got me naked first. He seemed to have a knack for that, drawing his hips away from my fingers which cradled and stroked his thick cock from root to tip, massaging the hard length in a bid to make him feel good and ramp up the excitement. Apparently, I ramped it up a little too high, a little too fast, because he bodily picked my skinny ass up off the floor and *tossed* me back-first onto the bed. I squealed and laughed and he dove over the top of me, mouth finding mine, kissing down my body, pausing to lavish my small breasts with attention.

"Don't crack your head this time," he growled and went in for the kill, sealing his mouth over my sex and sucking my clit, laving it with sure strokes of his tongue.

My cry was strangled and drowned out by a throaty moan and I gripped the bedding in clenched fists. He held my hips in his hands and when I proved I couldn't hold still against his sweet onslaught, put an arm on them, forcing them down to the bed. He grinned at me from between my thighs, his brown eyes rich like chocolate and holding a dark light as he cracked, "You must be this tall to ride this ride."

I laughed and again he killed it with the skill of his tongue against the most intimate parts of me, but I couldn't care. I just tipped my head back and gave myself over to the sensations.

A warm, tingling rush filled my veins and my body grew wet and ready. That heavy, pure weight of desire settled into my core ready for the long haul as Kyle took his time working me up, bringing me so close, to the very brink, before maddeningly backing off just enough so that I wouldn't come... at least not yet.

He kept me there on the precipice of that warm, sweet abyss for so long I thought I was going to go mad until finally, I started begging. Announcing his name like a plea into the dimly lit room but apparently, he was enjoying himself too much to quit just yet.

I was frustrated, my cunt tight and grasping at nothing, needing just that little bit more to shove me right over the fall, and when I reached the point of aggravation where I was just about to stop him, he slid two fingers inside me and crooked them just right. Instead of shattering, I *exploded*, the pieces of my being so damn small that I might as well have been dust in the wind.

He didn't let me come back down, either. Working that bundle of nerves with light, intermittent flicks of his tongue sending shockwaves of electricity through my system, playing finely with the sweet pain of oversensitivity, the man was a master at his craft. He twitched his fingers, licked me slowly and I tightened around him and bucked, but he had me pinned like a fucking butterfly.

"Oh, god! Kyle please!" I gasped bordering on the edge of panic. Never had I ever lost control of my body and heart at the same time or so completely before and it was honestly so nice, cathartic to do so. I didn't know if I was begging him to stop or to never quit and it was seriously confusing but in all sorts of good ways.

31

D ata...

She begged me, begged God, and pleaded for all and nothing both at once, and I felt a savage grin curl my lips. I gave her over-sensitive clit a break and watched her try to writhe. It was hard keeping her pinned down but worth the effort as I teased her pussy into making her sing for me with my index and middle finger. She panted and gasped and watching the silver barbells in her nipples catch and spark what light was in the room was seriously an erotic treat.

I was hard to the point of pain and made swift work of pushing my pants out of the way when she'd come down enough to hold still on her own. I climbed up onto the bed, kicking my jeans off the rest of the way and put myself between her trembling legs. She reached for me, and I loved that she wasn't shy about tasting herself on my lips. That she wanted to kiss me after I went down on her. Some women were weird about that, and I could respect it, but Mali's reactions... damn, it was like they were tailor-made for me. Everything she did, every look, movement, touch, glance... all of her just turned me on so hard.

She was my teenage wet dream, my every fantasy made flesh, and I loved her so wholly I would do everything to satisfy her, to make her feel so good, so loved, so protected and safe she could put down the roots that I knew she craved.

For now, though, I had to satisfy a craving of my own because my blood was screaming through my veins demanding a satisfaction of its own. She was my perfect drug, my addiction, and my only cure for the deep sense of aching loss I had been living with, without her here. I slipped inside her, and she was so wet, so ready, that at first I barely felt myself go in. That didn't last long, though. She clenched around me and I drove deeper, but it wasn't deep enough. It would never quite be enough for either of us.

I brought her legs up, leaning them against me, hugging them to me, and pressed into her, gauging her expression to make sure it wasn't too much. She pressed her hands against the headboard and her body down onto mine even tighter. A green light if I had ever seen one. I grunted as she tightened even harder around me and bowed my head, closing my eyes, concentrating on the warm, snug, feel of her around me as I tried like hell not to come from it. I didn't want to come too soon, I wanted to relish these moments, draw them out as long as possible. The euphoria she caused to swirl through my body was like the elixir of life itself, my own personal fountain of youth, and greedy bastard that I was, I wanted it *all*. To take every drop of what she was willing to give me.

She panted and moaned beneath me and I could tell she was close, and I wanted it. I wanted her to come around my cock and I wanted to disperse out into the ether right along with her. I was desperate to take her there and would do anything she asked. She gripped the sheets at her hips and closed her eyes, a look of concentration and pure, seductive surrender flickering across her features before she arched and pure, unadulterated bliss took over the both of us. I let go, balls tightening, spine tingling as I lost focus and everything just fell away.

I came back to myself slowly, lying over the top of Mali, cradling her protectively. Our chests heaved into one another as our panting breaths sawed their way in and out of them and when our eyes met, there were stars in them. We laughed, moved, and filled with joy and groaning, I pushed myself up. My legs trembled with the exertion and my abs screamed a little, but the work-out I'd given them was so worth it.

"We need to remember condoms," she said with a face.

"Shit, I am so sorry!"

"Don't be, I didn't stop you," she pointed out. "I'm on the implant, it's just not 100% and I just have no desire…" She trailed off, made a face, and I laughed.

"I know, and you're right. We should be more careful. It's your body," I said leaning forward and kissing her throat. "Your beautiful," kiss, "sexy," kiss, "alluring –" I kissed her again, each kiss in a different spot but she stopped my compliments with an exasperated sound.

"all right! I get it, I get it!" I intentionally kissed her most ticklish spot on her ribs in punishment for stopping me and she jerked in my grasp, laughing. I nipped her there for good measure and rolled her onto her back and started the whole process of making love to her all over again.

LATER THAT NIGHT, I slipped out of the room leaving Mali sleeping the sleep of the sated and exhausted. I used the bathroom and came back out, nearly running into Dragon.

"Woah, hey!" he grunted and I put up my hands, just as startled as he was.

"Sorry, man."

"No worries," he said and with no further segue asked, "How are things doin'? Better?"

"Ah, yeah," I nodded casting a furtive look in the direction of my club room door which was open a crack.

"Don't sound like it," he observed.

"No, no, things are good!"

"Right now," he said dryly. He cleared his throat and said, "You don't mind me sayin', seems to me you need to remind her why she wanted to come back here in the first place. That there's a life here, for the both of you. May not be the same, because let's face it... nothing ever can be, but a life, a good one. An end back at the beginning."

I stared Dragon in the face and let his profound words of wisdom wash over me. Gooseflesh broke out over my skin; there were times in your life you encountered such power in words that you got the chills, and suddenly everything clicked into place for you. I swallowed hard and nodded slowly, a plan forming in my head.

"Thanks, D."

"You got it; what're brothers for?" he asked.

He ducked into the bathroom I'd just come out of and shut the door. I stood in the hall for long minutes and stared at my door. Chewing my lip, I committed to what I wanted to do, a new kind of excitement rising in me. It was a perfect plan...

32

A malia...

I started working for Kyle's boys. I knew it was the right thing to do the moment we walked through the shop's front door. This place was serious business. Right on the strip in Old Town across from The Spot, a bar that'd been popular and a destination dining and watering hole for as long as I could remember.

The place was all black and white checkered tile and a riot of color on the walls. The flash art was serious – all original hand drawn designs by either Trig or Revelator. Some was in the classic Sailor Jerry motif, some clearly geared towards the military, but none of it was out of a book or catalog.

When I stepped up to the counter, my portfolio was already there, except the piece of label tape on its front declaring it Lexi Duran's work was gone, and instead, there was a much shorter strip that simply read 'Mali.'

It hit me right in the feels and I don't know why. It was one of those moments, though. The kind that felt like a gift from the universe and they were so rare, and beautiful, you didn't reject something like that. So I'd joined up, right there on the spot.

That had been 19 days ago. For some reason, the significance of that number tickled the back of my brain, but I couldn't for the life of me tell you why. I leaned back from my customer, a guy that was actually one of Trigger's regulars by the name of Donnie. He had an arctic fox on one shoulder and had wanted some Japanese cherry blossoms and branch work done down his arm to make the shoulder piece into a sleeve.

Trigger had shown him my watercolor style and Donnie had dug it. This was his first appointment with me.

"So I gotta ask, and I'm sure you get asked this all the time but –"

I cut him off, "Am I single?"

"Yeah," he sounded disappointed, the answer already clear on my face.

"You're either very brave or very stupid asking me that when I'm grinding ink under your skin," I said dryly.

He laughed, "Pain is an old friend of mine, gimme your best shot."

"Famous last words," I said teasingly, as I dipped more ink, hit my pedal and dug back in.

He chuckled, and said, "He's a lucky guy."

"Mm," was my noncommittal reply; Kyle wasn't the lucky one. I was… and I knew it.

I ground ink into Donnie's skin for the better part of two hours before his session was up. He looked down at it, his eyes widening a little, mouth down turning in the classic expression of being rather impressed as he nodded.

"You want a picture or anything?" I asked.

"Nah, I'll wait 'til it's done for that. I don't like half-finished shit."

I shrugged and patched him up and launched into the aftercare instructions but he put up a hand, "I know the drill."

"I'm sure you do, just doing my job."

He opened his mouth to say something, but Trigger's deep voice rolled across the shop from his corner, stopping him, "You might want to think about whatever you're gonna say before you open your mouth, Donnie. Otherwise, that tat is gonna stay just like it is. Mali's the only one around these parts that can finish that style."

Donnie stopped, his eyes sparkling with barely suppressed entertainment, and asked me, "When's our next appointment?"

"That's all Sunshine…" I muttered and he went up front to pay and book.

I cleaned up my station and went over to where Trigger was working on a girl's ankle piece.

"Could have handled it," I said. "Not my first rodeo."

He looked up at me and winked, "Yeah, but that's part of doing business under guys like me and Rev; you could have handled it, but in our shop? You don't have to."

I nodded and called out to Ashton, "What have I got on deck?"

"You're good," she called back, "Unless you want to stay in case of a walk-in."

"Nope!" Rev called and got up from his station. He snapped off the pair of black nitrile gloves he had on and tossed them in the wastebasket, shaking out his hands. Picking up an envelope on his counter, he came towards me.

"What's up?" I asked.

"M' lady, you have a quest…" he said and took a flourishing bow. He held the envelope, which was an odd size, out to me.

I frowned and took it from him. It was white, and the flap was on one of the shorter ends on the back side. I stared at the fancy wax seal, red wax, dusted with gold powder and it almost broke my heart that I was going to have to break it. It was a beautiful large cabbage rose. My middle name…

"What is this?" I asked.

Revelator just winked at me, turned around and walked away whistling. Ashton's golden eyes were wide and so there was no help there, while all of a sudden Trigger and Disney were way absorbed in their work.

"Ooookay," I said to no one in particular. I went back to my station and shut out my light. I smoothed the snowy-white, expensive-feeling paper of the envelope between my fingers and sighing, cracked the seal.

It held a single tarot card, not one of mine, but The Fool none the less. Across him, in Kyle's black printing, it said 'follow me…' and nothing else. I turned it over, and on the back, there was an address in silver marker, which showed up much better against the card's dark background.

"What the hell?" I muttered.

I had full use of his 4Runner now, and he'd bought me a cell phone on his plan. It was nice having the little computer with me. One, I knew he could keep an eye on me and that he did… I was learning just how technologically savvy he'd become and it was holy shit impressive. Two, after having been away for seventeen years, I was finding it hard to remember certain streets and how to get around, especially considering back then it had been all on foot or by virtue of a bicycle. The rules of the road hadn't exactly applied, and there were streets now that I could have sworn weren't one-way back then. Not to mention the high yellow curbs in the middle of the road weren't always there, I mean, were they?

I got into the 4Runner in the lot behind the shop and carefully plugged the address on the back of The Fool into the maps feature. I pressed the screen to have it start my route, and followed the directions carefully.

Twenty minutes later I was on a familiar stretch of highway, perking up a bit when the GPS declared that indeed, my destination was ahead on the left, through the iron gates of the MC's compound. I drove up into the lot and parked, and went to the front door, hauling it open and going inside.

"About time you figured it out," Dragon said around the cigarette in his mouth. He sat alone, in the barroom, a bottle of tequila on the table with a glass. An ashtray perched next to it. He folded the paper he'd been squinting at and set it aside. He pulled another of the mysterious envelopes from the inside pocket of his cut and held it up. I watched the envelope rise and fall as he set it on the table and slid it across to rest in front of the empty seat in front of him.

I went to it, and pulled out the chair, taking the seat. My ass wasn't quite covered by the short, plaid skirt I had on. I kept my knees together, my knee-high Doc Marten's flat on the cement floor. I wore a black girl's tee shirt over the skirt, a retro sort of punk look that was more to beat the August heat and humidity.

We stared at each other for a long time and he huffed a bit of a laugh, "Ha, well open it!"

I slid the envelope off the table and cracked the seal, withdrawing the card. The Hanged Man. I swallowed hard. The Hanged Man was one of the most important cards in the major arcana. Where The Fool signified the beginning of a journey, The Hanged Man represented feeling overwhelmed by circumstances. I couldn't argue the sentiment. I knew, by the silver sharpie in the corner, that it was meant to be taken as being in the upright position which meant the need for a time-out. I swallowed hard and my eyes flicked to Dragon's.

"A time-out... am I in some sort of trouble?"

He chuckled and shook his head, "That ain't all it means, is it?"

"No, it also means a change of perspective is warranted."

He arched his eyebrows and said, "Ahhh, does it now?"

"Is that why I'm here? For a change of perspective?"

He smiled at me and it was probably the kindest I had ever seen him. It caught me off guard. "You sure it's about you?" he asked me and I was getting a little tired of each of us answering our questions with more questions.

"No."

"You know, I've lost count of how many late nights it's been just me and Data, alone in this room together."

"Yeah?"

He cocked his head and considered me. "Yeah, and in all that time, he not once mentioned you..."

"I don't know what that means..."

"Means out of all things, he kept you a secret. I didn't know why until you showed up. Now I'm thinkin' that I understand it a little better."

"Care to enlighten me, then?"

"I have a feeling," he ashed his cigarette in the tray and put it back in his mouth, "that it was because he knew, wherever you were, that you might not appreciate it much him talking about you."

I thought it over, running it through my mind, over and over, finally leveling him with a look and asking, "Is this the part where you tell me that I don't have to be so closed off and secretive? That this is a safe place, and I can just be me here, without fear of reprisal?"

He chuckled and said, "You don't seem to fully understand what this brotherhood is about, now do you?"

"I guess I don't," I said softly.

He drew in a long breath and let it out slow, scanning my face as if fishing for just where to begin.

"This here is a *family*, honey. Not like your daddy, either. This is what all those families out there in the citizen world pretend they are but aren't. We don't hurt each other. We don't fuck each other over for love or money. One of us says we're gonna do something, we do it. You belong to Data." He raised a hand and waved me off before I could protest.

"Now, now! You do. Not like any piece of citizen property, like a cage or a house. That's just *stuff*. You're property in the MC sense of the word, which means that any man here would defend you to the last, just as if he were Data himself, *for* Data, simply because you belong to Data. Now I want you to sit there and think about that before," and he reached into the other side of his cut, "I give you this."

He held up another envelope, my eyes following it as he set it down with its pretty rose wax seal on the table in front of him. He kept his two blunt fingertips on it for an extended few seconds before he went for his cigarette and ashed it again.

"Where is this all supposed to lead me?" I asked.

"Well, Sweetheart, I do believe that's up to you…"

The choice was indeed mine. Be open to the possibilities here, or walk away. I could do either… but Kyle had gone to all of this trouble for a reason. He had never done *anything* in all the time I had known him – even when we were kids – that wasn't deliberately thought out.

. . .

HE WAS TRYING to show me something using a language as old as time that he knew I would listen to. Dragon searched my face and nodded after several moments of silence between us, and slid the card across the table.

I picked up the envelope, feeling the weight of what lay inside and knowing that this one would be different. I cracked the seal and withdrew the universal card for change… Death.

Not of the physical self, but of situations. It signified endings and new beginnings. When death occurred it was typically a time for reflection and a time to embrace the change it brought. I turned it over, and on the back was another address.

"As much as that means change, I want you to know – whatever form that takes, we're here."

I raised my eyes from the card in my fingers and nodded slowly.

"Thanks, I think…"

"Don't mention it. Go on, now. You're keeping them waiting."

I went back out and with shaking fingers, plugged in the next address. Back to town… great. I thought about it as I drove and wondered just what Kyle was playing at. I ordered my phone to call him and it went to voicemail. The outgoing message made me smile.

"Ah, ah, ah, baby… That's cheating."

"Smartass," I said after the beep, but I didn't try again.

To be honest, this scavenger hunt was actually kind of fun, for all the fractured ache I was feeling. I didn't know where this was going to lead, or if I would like it, but he was taking me somewhere and I trusted him.

The next destination was Soul Fuel, which, at this hour should have been closed, and was, but the old ladies from the club were all inside and comfortable, laughing and chatting over coffee and wine…

without a single one of their kids in sight. *Weird but okay, let's do this, Mali.*

I got out of the SUV and chirped the alarm as Everett came to the door. She unlocked it for me and immediately handed me another envelope. I opened it and slipped Temperance out of it.

The Temperance card typically represented the needs in life that arise when going through a monumental change. At least, I believed that was the case here. Kyle was trying to tell me to incorporate these new things into my life as I was going through this new growth. Of course, for me, this time of growth had been exceedingly painful, so I had been doing what I always did when I was hurt. I hid and licked my wounds.

He was asking me to do something here, he was asking me to give these women a try. One of the other things that Temperance stood for? Patience, moderation… obviously, and balance. Temperance was about *control* and I took this as a none-too-gentle reminder that mine had been slipping. Of course, I knew that. It was the main reason I felt like I was going crazy.

"Come on in, I'll make you some coffee," Everett said when I finally pulled myself out of my thoughts long enough to look up from the card.

"Thanks. Coffee is the blood, is the life…"

She laughed and said, "Don't I know it?"

I went over and took a free chair and sank into it. All of them were smiling, but it was Shelly who broke the brittle tension in the air by asking, "What up, girlfriend?"

"Uh, I got a job at the guys' tattoo shop and now my boyfriend has me going around on some whacked-out scavenger hunt… All right, after spending the last seventeen years on the run from some crazy Irish asshole crime boss figure for killing his son before the douceweasel popped my Pops…" I swallowed hard. No one said a word, I mean, you could hear a pin drop, but they were all being politely attentive, so I tried, which was what Kyle was asking me to do.

As much as I hated admitting to a weakness out loud, I steeled myself and said the truth, "I don't think I'm dealing or adjusting very well, or whatever."

"All of us have our stories, chickadee, yours ain't nothing new in this circle," Shelly said rolling her eyes.

The steam from the espresso machine went off and I jumped, nearly hitting the roof, but I wasn't the only one. Dani shot me a shy smile and shrugged her shoulders. Maybe it wasn't so far off, what Shelly was saying.

"Who wants to go first?" Doll, er, Hayden, asked.

"I will," Ashton murmured and I blinked. Where had she come from?

She smoothed the skirt of her cute little Havana dress under her and took a seat. Everett came back over and handed me a saucer with a cup on it that might as well have been a bowl. I wasn't really comfortable with the sharing is caring group therapy vibe that was going on, but as long as they were the ones sharing and I was the one caring, I could deal.

Holy shit, did they share... Ashton's ex was a piece of work. Shelly had been through hell and back because of a rape. Mandy had grown up in an ultra-religious abusive household, and Everett, well, *for as tough as she seemed to be, she divulged she didn't really feel like she was* due to her circumstances. I mean, she'd had a normal childhood save for her parents dying young, her mom while she was being born and her dad right as she got out of high school.

Maren's mom was a nut-job, as in *certified institutionalized*, and she was raising her brother. Bailey and Hayden were both born rich girls, and the way you heard them speak, that was its own special kind of hell despite the money. Hayden fully admitted she had it easy, but Bailey's own brother had tried to have her raped into compliance.

"Wouldn't mind giving him a Falcon Dick Punch," I muttered.

Hayley was normal comparatively, just working poor like me. I could relate and appreciate, but then she got into Duracell, who I guess was a brother who had died recently. She belonged to both him and Blue and they had a baby on the way that was more than likely Duracell's. The grief was palpable and I did everything to ground and center myself so I didn't burst into tears just from what was coming off of her.

Melody, too, was working poor but had everything but the kitchen sink happen to her. Mostly back in Arizona where she'd come from. Douchebag ex, fucked up family, pretty much the whole nine yards.

Throughout it all, Dani was silent, watching me and I got a real uneasy feeling that whatever her story was, I wasn't going to like it and that I was about to eat feeling sorry for myself.

I was right. Her story was almost as bad, if not worse, than Faith's back in Florida. Like, damn. I had nothing to really whine about. More perspective... these women were just as damaged if not more broken than I had ever come close to being. I stared into the bottom of my coffee cup and swallowed past the lump in my throat.

"You don't have to say anything," Everett said and I gave her a scathing look that said, *really bitch? Y'all are gonna spill and not expect a fuckin' thing out of me?* There was nervous laughter and Shelly spoke up.

"She means it. Just because we showed you ours, doesn't mean we expect you to show us yours."

"There are a lot of bad people in the world, Amalia. We aren't any of them," Ashton murmured.

I nodded slowly. I was starting to get the idea, and now I was starting to feel bad. I didn't trust anyone as a general rule. The last solid chunk of my life, I didn't get close to anyone, either. I could do those things now, but old habits die hard...

"Oh, you crafty bastard," I whispered. *Habits... 19 days...* Kyle had said it takes 19 days to form new habits and I'd been at the shop for 19 days. I guess he was trying to open me up to the potential of some new habits.

Shelly grinned over the rim of her teacup and shared a glance with some of the other women. All of them glanced at one another and my unease grew. Dani spoke up.

"Sometimes, you have to go backward, to move forward," she said, and produced a white envelope from the seat beside herself. A trickle of dread went down my spine as she reached across the space between us with it. I handed my cup and saucer to a pair of hands nearby, waiting to take it. My entire focus on that red rose seal, dusted in gold.

I plucked the envelope from her fingers and cracked the seal. I had a feeling. I knew, I just knew... I closed my eyes as The Tower slipped free.

I turned it over and on the back?

Go back to the beginning...

Shit. He was right. All had fallen down. It was rubble at my feet and I had to start all over again. What was left when the tower or your house collapsed? The foundation.

Where did Kyle and I first meet? *The school.* Whose house did we go to first? *His.* I rolled my lips and sighed.

"And I'm off..." I said and dragged myself to my feet. "Thanks for the coffee and the reality check."

"Anytime, Sister." Shelly winked as she said it and I smiled even if it was a bit wan. Everett let me out of the shop, and I realized that the guys all had to be at home with the kids so that they could be. That was some more food for thought as I got back behind the wheel of the 4Runner.

I went back to Kyle's house, and taped to the garage door? Another fucking envelope. I got out of the SUV and went to it, snatching it off and tearing it open.

The Hierophant.

The card represented change and expansion, a balance between old and new. I looked up at the familiar old house with its new paint and new windows. This place, here, was surely that. I pulled The Tower out of the bag at my hip and read the message again.

Go back to the beginning...

Maybe he didn't mean this place, maybe he meant another. The fact that there was a bicycle leaning against the garage door referenced that enough. I shut off the 4Runner, and locked it, chirping the alarm. I pulled the bike away from the garage door, went up the driveway with it to the street, and swung a leg over.

There was only one way to find out if the old adage, *it's like riding a bike*, were true. I hadn't been on one in probably twenty years, but he was right, there was no other way I would remember to get there.

I took off and pedaled and had the hang of it in no time. I guess it *was* true. What was also true? I was *really* out of fucking shape. The short ride between our houses had me winded in no time. My heart was pounding with the unfamiliar cardio, and a light dew of sweat broke out over my skin.

I pulled up in front of the empty lot where my old house used to be and felt a desolation creep in. It was empty, razed to the foundation; the only thing left was the old, rusting mailbox at the curb. I opened it, not expecting to find anything but surprise! There was a white envelope waiting for me.

"It's like the game that never ends," I muttered and broke the seal, tipping the card inside to the street light so I could see it.

The Wheel of Fortune – and the game show had nothing to do with it... The 10th card of the major arcana meant a lot of things. In this incarnation, I took it to mean a change in fortunes and he wasn't wrong. My dad and I, moving to this house, had changed my fortunes. I had met Kyle... I had met Kyle and that had made all the difference in my life.

I turned it over and on the back, it said, *still the wrong beginning. Try our beginning. Our real one. Just you. Just me and our...*

Tree. "Just you, just me, and our tree..."; it was a rhyme we'd made up and laughed like dorks over and was code for basically "Fuck everyone else and the world. I just want to spend time with my favorite person."

I turned the bicycle around and rode hard and fast, my heart pounding, through our neighborhood, two streets down, four houses over... I stopped pedaling and let the bike coast.

The old house was gone, but our tree rose into the night, twinkling with light. I got off the bike and walked it by my side through the field. As I got closer, I realized what the lights were.

Lanterns – dozens of old farm lanterns hung from the tree branches, illuminating the underside of the canopy. I dropped the bike and walked past a plaid blanket on the ground, a picnic basket next to it. White fluttered against the trunk, an envelope, and I needed to see, I had to know...

I looked around, but I didn't see Kyle. Still, I felt him. I knew he was watching, and I had to know what he thought of just him, and me, and our tree, so I plucked the envelope from the ribbon holding it, dangling from the trunk.

When I pulled the ribbon away, the seal broke and I slipped the card from the stellar, bright white paper.

The World.

I felt my eyes tear up, not only at the blatant implication of the card, that he thought the world of him and me... but also about the deeper meaning behind it.

The last card in the major arcana, the last stop: The World stood for the triumphant conclusion and the path to inner peace. I looked up at our tree, at the gentle twinkling little lights and heard the grass rustle behind me. I whirled, and just like magic, there he was...

My world.

33

D_{ata...}

From the treeline, I saw her ride up and watched her stop; the awe at what I'd done to our tree was naked on her face. She approached cautiously, and I couldn't say I blamed her. She looked for me, but Trigger had helped me with where to hide and if ever there were an expert at hiding, it was the trained military sniper of our outfit.

She dropped the bike in the grass and went for the card, and when she had it open, I made my move, slipping out of the tree line and making my way around. She whirled when I made some intentional noise, the tall grass rustling against my pant leg.

Her face was a study in both beauty and raw emotion. Her eyes filling with memory and hope. I smiled and held open my arms and she rushed to me, tucking herself tight into my body. She held me tight and I put my arms around her and sighed.

"You *nut*," she declared. "I love you so hard!"

"I love you, too, baby."

I took a step back and sank down onto the blanket, tugging her down next to me. She sat and stared up into the lights in our tree and said softly, "I didn't think it would still be here, you know?"

It almost wasn't. The property had sold, the house had been torn down, and the tree had a fluttering ribbon around it. I'd google-searched some shit and found out it had been marked to be cut down. I couldn't let that happen, only this time, I didn't use my techno-mojo. I'd done it the old-fashioned way. I'd bought this place. She didn't need to know that, though.

She looked over at me and her look softened, all trace of sadness gone, and I felt the weight of worry lift off of my heart.

"It's beautiful," she murmured and I shook my head.

"*You're* beautiful."

I leaned in and did what I should have all of those times we'd been out here as teens. I kissed her. Softly, gently, tasting and asking her. Asking for permission, for her to stay with me, to make a life with me here.

She pushed me back onto the blanket and threw a leg over my hips, grinding her body against mine, her mouth growing insistent. The kiss grew wild, emphatic, and I smoothed my hands along her thighs even as her hands drifted from my chest, down my body.

She sat up and fumbled at my belt and I laughed, digging into a pocket and pulling out a condom.

"You know me so *well!*" she exclaimed in a low, sultry purr.

She had me free, stroking me up and down. It had me gasping for breath and I tore open the condom with my teeth, fumbling it between my fingers just like an awkward teen with my eagerness. I rolled it on myself and Mali rose up on her knees, moved her panties aside, and sank down onto me.

She wasn't quite ready, so we had to work at it, fight for every inch, but it was a good fight and, like anything we'd faced in this life, we won. She rocked her hips with me all the way in and I gasped.

"Take your pleasure, baby. I wanna watch you."

She was an angel, haloed in the light from the flickering stars and lamp lights. She rocked slow and steady, taking her time, making love to me and I caressed her hips over her sexy-as-hell little punk girl school skirt.

Her nipples pebbled under her thin, faded black tee, and I could barely glimpse the glimmer of the piercings through the fabric. Not something you would even see unless you were looking for it.

"*Oh yeah,*" I moaned as she raised up and her hot, wet cunt stroked me, grasping with even and controlled muscle movements on her part.

She threw back her head, her long hair loose and wild, flowing down her back. She'd dyed the ends black last week, so it was back to normal, and as much as I'd enjoyed the colors, I enjoyed her being wholly her and natural more.

A bright light flicked on, blinding us, and Mali raised her hand to shield her eyes, exclaiming, *"Shit!"*

"What're y'all doin' out here tonight, huh?"

Fucking cops…

"Enjoying the evening, officer," I said, keeping my hands up, palms flat so he could see them. He moved the light out of my eyes and back into Mali's. She put her hands up and bowed her head.

"Stand up," he ordered her and she sighed out "I can't, he's inside of me."

"I'm just going to put myself away," I said, and the cop's light shot to my face, then my hands which I was, painfully slowly, moving towards Mali's skirt.

"Stop right there! I don't know if you have a weapon. Now I'm going to ask you a few questions."

"Okay." Mali and I both froze.

"Do you know whose property you're on?" he demanded.

"Yes," I answered evenly.

"Oh, yeah?" he said, like he didn't believe me, "Whose is that, now?"

"Mine," I said evenly. "If you come around to our other side, my wallet and the deed to this property are in the picnic basket, along the side. "

Mali's eyes fixed on mine and she asked levelly, "Yours?"

"They were going to cut down our tree, I couldn't let that happen, so I bought it," I said with a shrug. Right now, I was more interested in getting this cop to put away the gun he had pointed at us.

He flipped open the basket, and the gun still trained on us, which we sure as hell weren't moving, he shone his light down inside.

Wine, cheese, crackers, some fruit, and the wallet and deed should be in there. He came up with the wallet and opened up, squinting. Then he unfolded the paperwork. He looked from it to us, and demanded, "What're you doing out here, exactly?"

"Romantic picnic?" Mali said, and I'd definitely grown soft.

"Sounds like you're asking, not telling me."

"She didn't know what the plan was. I did a scavenger hunt… can I put myself away, now?"

"I don't know if you have a weapon."

"Oh for fuck's sake," Mali said, and lifted her tiny scrap of skirt. We were pretty much hidden by our bodies being joined but the cop could clearly see there was no gun. She dropped the skirt and he nodded.

"All right now, you have to understand it's dangerous for me –"

"We get it", she snapped and lifted herself up onto her knees. I tucked my hands beneath her skirt and got everything buttoned up. She waited and I patted her thigh.

"I'm standing up." She did so and I followed her.

The cop asked a bunch of questions and blustered a minute about indecent exposure. I rolled my eyes and asked, "At one-thirty in the morning on a Tuesday morning? Would you have even known we were here if it hadn't been for the lights?"

"Look, we weren't doing anything wrong and we're on *his* property." Mali added when the silence stretched on too long.

"Right, um…"

"Just call in the all-clear, and we'll clear out." I said.

He cleared his throat, blushing hotly and asked, "Anything I can do to help? Uh, any place I can call a cab and have them take you?"

Mali looked me right in the eye and said, "No, officer, we're fine. We're *home…*"

I smiled, and peace settled over me and in my heart. She was right. We were home, and I was never letting her out of my sight again.

The End

ALSO BY A.J. DOWNEY

Indigo Knights

1. Her Thin Blue Lifeline

2. His Cold Blue Command

3. A Low Blue Flame

4. His Wild Blue Rose

5. Her Pained Blue Silence

6. A Cold Blue Call

7. Her Reluctant Blue Cavalier

8. Forged Under Fire

9. Under A Blue Moon

10. Sound of Blue Thunder

Sacred Hearts MC Pacific Northwest

1. Over the High Side

2. Wind Therapy

3. Apex of the Curve

4. Low Sided

5. Eating Asphalt

6. Hammer Down

7. Only Fool Riding

The Voodoo Bastards MC

1. Bourbon & Blood

2. Whiskey Shivers

3. Moonshine Lullabies

4. Cognac Secrets

5. Tequila Damnation

Iron Wraiths MC

1. Original Syn

2. Love & Fear

3. The Hangman's Rope

Royal Bastard MC: St. Augustine Chapter

1. Iron Hearts

Paranormal Romance (with Ryan Kells)

1. I Am The Alpha

2. Omega's Run

3. Hunter's End

Indigo City Darker (with Jared KingPacal Lain)

1. Triple Threat

2. Double Shot

Standalones

Synchronicity

ABOUT A.J. DOWNEY

A.J. Downey is a Pacific Northwest girl living in an East Tennessee world who finds inspiration from her surroundings, through the people she meets, and likely as a byproduct of way too much caffeine. She specializes in real and relatable romance stories featuring that real-life kind of love that everyone craves.

Stalker Information:

Website
www.ajdowney.com